THE UNIQUE MAGAZINE
Spring 1992

ISSN 0898-5073
Art by Jill Bauman

Weird Tales® is published 4 times a year by Terminus Publishing Co., Inc., PO Box 13418, Philadelphia PA 19101-3418 (4426 Larchwood Ave., Philadelphia PA 19104-3916). 2nd Class Postage paid at Philadelphia PA & additional mailing offices. Single copies, $4.95. Subscriptions: 4 issues (one year) $16.00 in U.S.A. & possessions; $20.00 in Canada & Mexico, $22.00 elsewhere, in U.S. funds. Publisher is not responsible for loss of manuscripts, although publisher will take reasonable care of them. Postmaster: send address changes to *Weird Tales*®, PO Box 13418, Philadelphia PA 19101-3418. Copyright © 1992 by Terminus Publishing Co., Inc.; all rights reserved; reproduction prohibited without prior permission. Typeset, printed, & bound in the United States of America. *Weird Tales*® is a registered trademark owned by Weird Tales, Limited.

THE EYRIE

John Brunner — our featured author this issue — is, in the words of someone we mentioned the selection to, "not a writer typically associated with *Weird Tales*®," even though he did have a fine novelet in issue #297. But he is better known for his science fiction. *Stand On Zanzibar* and *The Whole Man* are unchallenged classics in the canon of science fiction, and he continues to write very distinguished SF, in recognition of which he was Guest of Honor at the World Science Fiction Convention in The Hague, Netherlands, in 1990.

We raise two points here: first, *Weird Tales*® must continue to expand and grow. So, writers are "typically associated with" **our** *Weird Tales*® only if we make them so. Jonathan Carroll wasn't characterized as a typical *Weird Tales*® author until we started publishing him. Some of our future Feature Authors have appeared in the magazine before and some have not. We are planning forthcoming issues around F. Paul Wilson, Nina Kiriki Hoffman, Ian Watson, Joe Lansdale, and several others.

A Brunner issue is entirely appropriate. We looked in the inventory drawer and saw that we had already acquired enough of John's work to do an issue. So we did.

Second point: Sometimes we deliberately feature an author or artist this way to emphasize works which might other-

wise be overlooked. We chose Vincent Di Fate to illustrate issue #295 precisely because he has always been seen as a science-fiction artist and because he gets so many spaceship-&-planet cover assignments. This was a chance to show another side of his work. Similarly, John Brunner has been writing excellent fantasy for many years. This issue is a way to bring that to your attention.

And, we might add, our selection of yet another non-American Feature Author may be taken as an editorial comment on the British- *versus* American-English debate that has been going on among our correspondents in this department.

We don't want to close *Weird Tales*® off to any possibilities.

Farewell to Dan Polster, who has now officially resigned as an assistant editor due to the pressures of both pre-medical studies and involvement with no less than three performing arts groups. Dan will be missed, most especially by would-be contributors to *Weird Tales*®. His *rejections* were so helpful and courteous that they drew a higher proportion of thank-you notes than anyone else's, ever.

Late-Night with Betamax, or How much realism does fantasy need? An excellent, albeit largely negative, example came to our attention the other night. We were up late, watching the 1958 Hammer Films version of *The Mummy*. (And working constructively at the same time, mind you: signing the autograph pages for an upcoming deluxe reprint of *The Year's Best Horror* from Underwood-Miller.)

You may know this film. It is more of a remake of Universal's Kharis-the-Mummy series of the 1940s than the 1932 Boris Karloff classic. Christopher Lee plays the lurching, genuinely menacing title character, a remarkable feat considering that he spends virtually the entire film wrapped in moldering bandages and heavy makeup, which make any range of facial expression difficult. Peter Cushing is the archaeologist who defiled one tomb too many. It's great fun, with all the usual hokum rendered reasonably palatable — even the hero's lady love who *just happens* to be a — er — dead ringer for the Mummy's long-lost Princess, even though the lady is English and the Princess was an Egyptian of 4000 years ago.

We were a bit less able to accept what we might call the standard Mummy Movie Fallacy, that in contemporary — or in this case, late 19th century Egypt — the population takes the ancient, pagan religion of the pharaohs — Set, Anubis, Osiris, etc. — *seriously,* fears (or invokes) the wrath of the Old Gods, and all the rest. Never mind that after the pharaonic religion passed away, Egypt was a Christian country for several centuries and has been a largely Muslim country since the Arab conquest in the 7th century A.D. While we could imagine that the Old Gods might still be revered by some insignificant element shunned by the Muslim majority of Egyptian society, no Mummy-movie scripter has ever bothered with such details. It's part of the ritual in these things that just before the arrogant Western (usually English) archaeologists break open the tomb, some fez-wearing or turbanned

Publisher:
George H. Scithers

Editor:
Darrell Schweitzer

Managing Editor:
Carol Adams

Assistant Editors:
Leslie Smith, Dainis Bisenieks, Diane Weinstein, Michael W. Betancourt, Don Keller, & Dan Polster

Circulation Manager:
Richard Kabakjian

Computer Consultant:
David J. Williams III

Of Counsel:
Yale F. Edeiken

Typesetter:
Campus Copy Center

Printer & Soft-Cover Binder:
Malloy Lithographing, Inc.

Hard-Cover Binder
Hoster Bindery, Inc.

Mailing:
Unit Packaging Corporation

Manuscript Submissions:
Yes; we read unsolicited submissions — **but only if** they are in standard manuscript format. To survive, all editors insist on a few Rules: each submission must be in proper format and must include a return envelope addressed to you with enough postage affixed to bring the manuscript back to you. If you want us to discard the manuscript if not bought, tell us so, but include a business-letter-size envelope with postage affixed, addressed to you, so we can send you our comments. No loose stamps, please!

Proper manuscript format is discussed in many reference works. Some of us have even written one: *On Writing Science Fiction: the Editors Strike Back!* by Scithers, Schweitzer, & Ford; $19.50 in hardcovers, from Owlswick Press, P.O. Box 8243, Philadelphia PA 19101-8243. Another excellent work from the same publisher is Barry B. Longyear's *Science-Fiction Writer's Workshop:* $9.50 in trade paperback. These prices include shipping and handling; in Pennsylvania, please include 6% sales tax.

We are not responsible for manuscripts in our hands or in transit. You **must** keep a copy of every manuscript you send out. You **must** put your name and address on the first page of every manuscript. Please: no binders, folders, or padded envelopes; and especially: no registered or certified mail for which we would have to stand in line at the post office!

native will attempt to deliver One Last Warning . . . It's as if the movie industry thinks Egypt is an imaginary country.

The Hammer Films rendition of *The Mummy* was made by a British company with British actors — presumably for a British audience. What fascinated us was that the movie couldn't make *England* convincing. Costumes were all wrong for 1898. Not a bowler hat or starched collar in sight. And the accents . . . well, why *did* the inspector from Scotland Yard sound so curiously American? Why were most of the peasants sort of half-Irish? In an era when even modest households had a servant or two, why did the mansions of the wealthy characters lack so much as a butler? The Sinister Foreign Gent *answered his own door?* Surely that would have given the game away!

But this is not a column of Old Movie Criticism. We have a serious point: how do you make the fantastic part of a story convincing? The answer is simple yet difficult. As Lovecraft explained in some detail, the horror writer must use many of the techniques of *realism*. One should construct a story almost as if it were a hoax, with every prosaic detail firmly in place, so that when the fantastic intrusion occurs, it seems a possible part of that setting. (H.G. Wells said much the same thing about science fiction.) If the writer can't get the realistic parts of the story right, this distances the reader from the story. Every mistake reminds the reader again and again that "this is made up; it's only fiction," and by the time the fantastic elements arrive — the walking dead or whatever — the reader is *still* thinking, "this is made up; it's only fiction," and the fantasy impact is lost.

Sure, film is a different medium from print. In *The Mummy*, good acting, convincing makeup, atmospheric direction, and vigorous action all helped to gloss over these faults — but they were still there, and we noticed. Getting it

right is a win-win situation. People who don't know the difference will, indeed, not know the difference. Those who *do* know will appreciate the effort and be all that more gripped by the clammy, four-thousand-year-old hand of . . . well, by the story.

Hammer films often contained spectacular blunders in factual geography. Our own favorite comes from *The Horror of Dracula* (1958), which remains, undeniably, the finest vampire film ever, but . . . did you notice? Toward the end the Count kidnaps Mina *in England*, drags her to his coach, gallops away, crashes through one international frontier, and reaches Castle Dracula (in Transylvania) *in a single night*. Never mind the English Channel or the width of France, Germany, and Austria-Hungary. Maybe vampires can travel through hyperspace. But how, we have always wondered, was Dr. Van Helsing able to follow? Go figure.

Not everyone agrees, especially not **Pete Miller** of Redmond WA:

. . . another dogma you appear to be laboring under is the old one about developing "believable characters" in stories. This . . . no longer means much. As we approach the turn of the century an entirely new era in horror literature is slowly emerging. Today's readers are far more sophisticated than most editors realize. They are quite capable of using their own imaginations to "fill in the blanks" of stories they read, and no longer have the time (or patience) to spend yawning through endless pages of character development. It simply is no longer necessary to waste time, and words, on this aspect of writing.

Take, for example, the work of our greatest writers in the genre, Edgar Allan Poe and H.P. Lovecraft. Neither one of them ever developed a "believable character" in his best work, yet they are still fascinating readers of all ages while the work of our current "giants" (King and Koontz) is forgotten shortly after it is read. How do you explain that?

Mr. Miller utters dire warnings of a *"New World Order"* of literature and warns that *whoever refuses to adapt to this will simply be left behind . . .* but he does conclude with cordial best wishes, so he presumably means well.

Somehow, we find it hard to take this letter seriously. We see no need to explain why the work of King and Koontz is *"forgotten shortly after it is read,"* because there's no evidence this is actually so. All of King's novels are in print. *Carrie* has been with us for seventeen years now and shows no sign of fading from view. Dean Koontz isn't doing all that badly either. In thirty years, the verdict may be in, but it seems a trifle premature to consign these two to the dustbin of literary history.

Let's make sure this coming *"New World Order"* of super-evolved horror fiction isn't just a lack of craft. *Stories are about people.* Stories must have real people in them to evoke real emotional responses in the reader. Otherwise the story can never be more than an abstract construct, on the order of most "experimental" fiction. The experimental story, that most rigid of literary fossils, has evolved not a bit during this century. It's usually an attempt to leave the regular parts of a story out — characterization, plot, logic, coherence — and while this may impress a few (usually) young and pretentious writers, the readers shrug and turn their attention elsewhere. Mainstream literature has gone through this in phases since 1910 or so. Science fiction had a spate of it in the '60s with the "New Wave." We suspect that the kind of avant-garde horror fiction Mr. Miller imagines lurking just beyond the horizon is just more of the same.

There *are* good characterizations in Lovecraft and Poe, by the way, but — we hasten to point out — only an amateur writer would confuse characterization with long descriptions and biographies of each character. In a well-constructed story, every passage serves several purposes, one of which, by showing through action, is characterization. But you can never say, "Here, from the bottom of page 6 to the top of page 8, that's where the characterization is." Characterization should be unobtrusively present in every line, like a flavor. And it's not obsolete.

Frequent correspondent **Frank D. McSherry** writes from McAlester OK:

Just a word to say how much I liked the special William F. Nolan issue of Weird Tales®. His novelette, "Broxa," was a nice combination of the hard-boiled detective and the supernatural story with the Nolan specialty — the eerie shudder that stays with the reader even after he's finished the tale. When you've finished a Nolan story, with his best work, you get that same chilling effect every time you think of the story again — somewhat like suddenly realizing there's a big black spider the size of your hand crawling up between your shoulder blades . . .

The interview brought back my own days of encountering weird fiction for the first time, and gave some useful hints on how to write it — and any other kind of work as well. The shorter tale, "The Visions," had the same shivery, unnerving effect. Nolan's stories are always stories, with a point to them, not exercises in fancy writing, unlike some I could mention.

Reader John Bracey's letter makes a good point about including realistic dialog in stories of today, with realistic characters. Profanity does indeed have a point. Men swear for the same reason women cry; it relieves tension; it releases emotional steam. Our culture teaches men not to cry and women to cry instead of swearing. In both cases it's a safety valve, for the individual and for society.

Shut off that safety valve and in a while you're running the risk of an explosion.

About once a year you'll read in the papers of a nice boy who starts shooting people dead for no reason; puzzling his neighbors who say they can't understand why he did it: he never swore, never told dirty jokes. Why did he do it? In part because he didn't swear or tell dirty jokes; that's why.

I'm all for an honest depiction of today's people in stories, using the language they use.

R. Thompson writes:

Here's just a little note to say that I believe issue #302 may have been your best all-around issue to date (except for that reprinted cover, which I had already seen in book form). Other issues may have had stories singularly more popular, but not an entire magazine of top-rate stories (as did #302). In fact, of the entire contents (fiction, verse, & features) of issue #302, I found only two (short) pieces that did not interest me: William F. Nolan's ode to "The Horror Writer," and Robert Bloch's short piece, "The Creative Urge." Other than that, every story, verse, and feature was interesting and exciting. I would like to particularly mention Jason Van Hollander's outstanding "The Hell Book" (I would not be surprised if it someday became a classic in the field, along with Lumley's "Fruiting Bodies," which you also printed in an earlier issue) and William F. Nolan's "The Visions," which was short, sweet, and neat. And, as always,

Robert E. Howard's verse, "Zukala's Love Song," was Epic. Also, your artists in this issue were fantastic. All in all, this was an issue to be treasured.

Lee Prosser keeps it short:

Your special Nolan issue was a treat. This author surely deserves to be singled out by Weird Tales®. *Nolan's material was excellent and extremely well-crafted. He's a real master of characterization. Reading him is like savoring a fine bottle of vintage wine. I hope to see more Nolan stories in future issues of* Weird Tales®. *He's a winner.*

Here's **Tom Draheim,** of Andover MA:

I was a bit leery of Weird Tales® *#302 from the outset. The cover painting looked like the gremlin version of* Field & Stream — *it was too cute. And the William F. Nolan special issue business . . . I had read a couple of good stories by him in anthologies, but wasn't he more of a writer for the slicks, and (heaven forbid) sci-fi to boot? The names Bloch and Lumley on the cover were more reassuring.*

But my fears were unnecessary. I enjoyed the two long stories by Nolan and Lumley, both fast-paced, good reads from a nice blend of sub-genres.

"Broxa" was my favorite story, but I think Nolan overstates his case when he talks about taking "a new route with this novella." I read the story before the interview, and the story reminded me of some Mike Shayne stories from the late

---

THE SHAPE OF THRILLS TO COME!

In Weird Tales® 305 we feature F. Paul Wilson as our star attraction, along with Bob Eggleton as featured artist. Fiction by Avram Davidson.

Appearing soon: stories by Ian Watson, Steve Rasnic Tem, Tanith Lee, Nina Kiriki Hoffman, and Ramsey Campbell along with more poetry by Ray Bradbury.

Subscribe now, before you miss all the fun!

'70s and early '80s. Shayne would often get involved with the supernatural or the occult. That was one of the reasons I read the magazine, and also because I was submitting stories to Charles Fritch, the editor. Then I read in the interview that Nolan and Fritch were business partners and I'm wondering if Nolan didn't write some of those Shayne stories. Do you know? Anyway, I liked the interview with the nuts and bolts material about his writing methods and background.

Nolan's short story, "The Visions," was a little predictable and seemed to be included in the magazine to flesh out the special concept — it's just my opinion — and is the main thing I don't like about the whole concept.

Bloch's piece was too "lite." Must you have these fluffy, clever stories every issue? Give us more in the Van Hollander vein. Schweitzer's collaborations with him have been very good, and he's very good on his own. And I liked his art very much, too. I would like to see a cover of his on Weird Tales®. Is that possible?

Issue #303, of course, does have a Van Hollander cover of sorts, a collaboration with Allen Koszowski, and also with the mysterious artist Pickman, who was carried off by ghouls in Boston in the 1920s. As for "fluffy, clever stories," well, every once in a while, yes. We don't intend to fill the magazine with them, but we can't let every story be a horror story either, or the overall effect will pall, because readers would know how every story will end. We think horror is more effective when unexpected. And there is another Schweitzer and Van Hollander collaboration coming up in Weird Tales® 307, a bit of grotesquerie about the 16th century Netherlands that seems to have stepped right out of a Brueghel painting.

Ryan Lambrecht seems to ask too much of us:

Have you seen the Lovecraft issue (#106) of Fangoria? I think something should be done about this. They just use Lovecraft's name for money. They care nothing about the fact that HPL would have hated anything that went to the screen with his name on it. As editor, you have a little power. I propose that you write them a letter on behalf of some of your readers or say in Weird Tales® something to the effect that true HPL fans will not take even a first look at any of these falsely advertised movies. I know I made a mistake by buying Fangoria #106 because it was a Lovecraft issue. Thanks for listening.

We bought that issue too, and can't fault the editors of Fangoria for their detailed and interesting reportage of six upcoming Lovecraft movies, only one of which (The Resurrected, based on The Case of Charles Dexter Ward), we must admit, sounds at all promising. But if the "them" to whom you want us to write are the movie producers, well, we can only be impressed by such naïve faith in our Editorial Powers. What makes you think that Hollywood cares what readers think? Actually, the most depressing thing about the whole business was that many of the directors and the like interviewed in Fangoria seem to have "discovered" Lovecraft from other movies. There's no indication they've read any of his published works. Don't expect these upcoming Lovecraft movies to be any more faithful than were Roger Corman's adaptations of Poe.

The Most Popular Story was a close race this time. William F. Nolan's "Broxa" just nudged Ronald Anthony Cross's "The Magician" out of first place. Third place was another close contest, this one between Nolan's "The Visions" and Jason Van Hollander's "The Hell Book." Nolan took it by one vote. Ω

THE DEN

by Gahan Wilson

Whatever form it takes — and its shapes are legion — I think it's safe to say that the vampire is the most terrifying of all our basic monsters.

Its dark combination of death, sex, and magic lures and appalls us with a neat equilibrium which locks us in a perpetual hover. Like all the other Lucy Westenras before and after us, we are frozen between attack and flight just within the vampire's reach, staring helplessly at the mocking power in its eyes, smelling the foul reek of its breath, totally unable to tell whether our anticipation of its certain bite is a loathing or a longing.

There are, therefore, endless writings on the subject. Some of them are "fact," and some are "fiction," and the best of them float ambiguously in that glorious and mysterious region where both categories overlap.

Lately there has been a near deluge of books of the first description, which is to say volumes purporting to report on actual vampires: ones that might rap on your window tonight, or engage you in an increasingly scary conversation at a cafe, or even that particularly awful one

which is forming itself from mist behind your back this very moment as you sit there reading your *Weird Tales.*

Most of these "factual" books are dismal rehashes whose main accomplishment is to make bores out of such gaudy types as Sergeant Bertrand, the necrophile of Père Lachaise, and Peter Kuerten, the monster of Düsseldorf. Others manage to convert the sensationally gory scholarship they've pirated from old, reliable Montague Summers's baroque vampire tomes into something reading like culls from a particularly tedious high-school textbook. By the way, for those of you unfortunate enough not to be familiar with the "Reverend" Summers's heavily footnoted grue, The Aquarian Press brought out a reprint of Summers's *The Vampire in Europe* in 1980; and it's still floating around; but a few interesting ones have washed up with the rest.

The best of these, and the solidest, is Paul Barber's *Vampires, Burial, and Death* (Yale University Press). It is a wonderful mine of information regarding vampires, the awesomely ancient

11

beliefs concerning them, and the sociological and physical realities which nurtured and directed those beliefs. Perhaps the most fascinating and revealing aspect of the book is Barber's detailed examination of the folk tales and churchly writings which formed the basis for European orientations towards vampirism, and his meticulous comparison with them to horrendous and mercilessly-detailed descriptions (I warn you: this book is strong stuff, even for *Weird Tales* readers!) of the latest scientific word on the unbelievably Godawful things which that seemingly nice body you're presently sitting in can get up to once you die. This section adds up to being one of the most revealing commentaries on Dom Calmet and those other oft-quoted authorities of the dim, distant past which I have ever read.

Of the two other books I would recommend in this general category, but rather less strongly, the first is **American Vampires** by Norine Dresser (W.W. Norton & Company) which is a jolly, determinedly pop account of how our fellow citizens are coping with the subject. It ranges from "Dark Shadows" Trekkies, to groups of yuppies attempting to figure out how to hold quiet little blood-sipping parties without contracting AIDS, to perhaps a few too many reproductions of cute greeting cards and bad poetry written by members of vampire fan associations; but it does illuminate; and it manages to convey something of the size and complexity (and more than a little of the innocence) of our national approach to this phenomenon.

For the Brits' take on the undead we have Rosemary Ellen Guiley's **Vampires Among Us** (Pocket Books). Far, far too much of this book is taken up with the sort of tiresome rehashes I complained of before, but — rather sloppily scattered through its pages — there are some genuinely haunting accounts here of eccentric, oddly-touching people who have allowed themselves to become so fascinated with vampires that they have dedicated themselves to living (I know it is a questionable use of the word) as much like their weird idols as they possibly can. The results as described are a truly peculiar mix of the ludicrous and the pathetic which somehow, sometimes, appears to result in a game, if very odd, sort of high style. I have no idea how sound Guiley's reporting is, but if you're willing to plow (or, better yet, skip) through a lot of very silly stuffing, there are some really marvelous little pockets of strangeness in this book which I, personally, found worth the effort.

So much for the "fact," now on to the "fiction."

The Ultimate Dracula (Dell) is one of a three-volume set (the others are *The Ultimate Frankenstein* and *The Ultimate Werewolf*) put together by Byron Preiss to celebrate the anniversaries of the famous black-and-white films featuring the doings of Dracula, Frankenstein, and Lon Chaney, Jr.

The notion is, unabashedly, a highly commercial one; and *The Ultimate Dracula* cannily leads off with a story by one of the greatest commercial successes operating in the vampire business today, namely Anne Rice. It is a story called "The Master of Rampling Gate," the cover notes that this is the first publication of the "complete" story, and I must remember to track down an incomplete version in order to discover what base was missed the first time around.

The story operates in a very oddly bent time warp as the narrator's style is accurately that of a best-selling author of the '20s or early '30s, and from that point of view it does its best to very seriously write the sort of Gothic romantic thriller that was popular from the late 1700s to the middle 1800s. The hybrid which results is something like, but not quite, a Harlequin Romance. Every element of the thing is as comfortably worn and familiar as an old shoe; it is all extremely distant emotionally in spite of being a love tale, and these qualities — which are not absent from her longer works — obviously make it marvelous escape reading for a large number of people. I figure it's a free country, and people should enjoy themselves so long as they don't scare the horses. As for myself, when in the Gothic mood, I much prefer to reach for a mouldy volume of Mrs. Radcliffe or "Monk" Lewis and dive into one of the wild and woolly originals.

All the other stories in the collection outside of Rice's have clearly been written under the instruction that they must not only restrict themselves to the relatively broad category of vampires, but further confine themselves to Count Dracula and/or Vlad Tepes, the flesh-and-bloody, fifteenth-century tyrant and torturer who gave Bram Stoker considerable inspiration in the creation of his immortal bloodsucker.

These strictures — plus what must have been the editor's failure to let the authors know when they were stepping on each other's toes — have led to a really enormous amount of duplication, not only in characters, locales, and plots, but in witty asides and hoped-for surprises. One can take only so many variations on " I never drink . . . (this that or the other besides wine)" gags without getting just a little peevish, and you really *do* get near to the point where you wonder if someone actually *is* going to exclaim: "You mean that mustachioed stranger was *Vlad the Impaler!?!*"

However, such is the ingenuity and ability of some of the authors that a number of the stories in the book survive these challenges quite handily, and a precious few of them are very good indeed. Because of the dedicatory nature of the book, quite a number of them take place in Hollywood (I'd have gone for it, myself, I freely admit), and of them Dick Lochte's "Vampire Dreams" has a nice, continuing bitterness concerning "the business," and Kevin Anderson's "Much at Stake" does the good, bold thing by not only starring none other than Bela Lugosi himself, but by giving dear old Dwight Frye (he of the "Heeee-heee-heeeeee!") a good supporting role.

The best of the tales in this division is, I think, Tim Sullivan's *"Los Niños de la Noche,"* which is a clever and highly sympathetic telling of what might have happened during the filming of the legendary Spanish version of "Dracula" which was shot at night by an all-Hispanic cast and crew who used the sets and equipment that Browning and Lugosi and the rest employed during the day. The characters are interestingly alive and nicely relevant both to the antique time of the filming and to this present era; the sense of atmosphere is first rate; the story is full of nicely spooky twists; and the end is a highly satisfactory, unique, and scary method of finishing off this kind of exercise. By the way, Sullivan's narrator states that the film is lost but — excellent news! — it has been found, can be tracked down if you know the right people; and it's fascinating to see this highly successful Latin rendering of the precious classic. My favorite part of it is the handling of the conversation in the coach by the terrified travelers as they enter the looming Carpathians.

Some other stories worth mentioning are "The Tenth Scholar" by Steve Rasnic and Melanie Tem, a nice mood piece on how an old-country Dracula might carry on the good bad fight in the Big Apple; a nicely hopeless "Selection Process" by Ed Gorman, and "Dracula 1944" by Edward Hoch, a clever job of turning what might have been a cliché into a stinger. There is also a neat little sketch on the connection between vampirism and the aging of our bodies by our very own John Gregory Betancourt.

The mood of far too many of the stories reminds me of those basically anti-horror, anti-fantasy things that were the pride and joy of that venerated (but not by me) pulp: *Unknown Worlds,* which was, essentially, a bunch of old-timey science fictioneers attempting to scoff away the awful thought that the darker side of existence might be just a little bit more than an intellectual problem.

Fortunately this is more than compensated for by one single story, Dan Simmons's "All Dracula's Children," which is a nearly intolerably clear and accurate account of the vile fate which overtook — and is, God help us! *still* overtaking — numberless thousands of Romanian children due to the absurd vanity and apparently limitless stupidity of the disgusting Ceausescu.

It was momentarily encouraging when that miserable dictator was shot dead with little more ceremony than is usually given a rabid dog, but the lack of lasting satisfaction which that execution has generally provided demonstrates, perhaps, a unique new argument against capital punishment: why should we give such a one the peace of death?

Simmons very cleverly connects the real horror story — which he tells *most* eloquently — with a dark, Draculian plot, but the irony is that I found myself more than half-wishing his fantasy was true since then, at least, there would be some meaning to the continuing obscenity.

The second anthology of "fiction" is *A Whisper of Blood,* edited by Ellen Datlow (Morrow), which is — not at all unexpectedly — a superb anthology. Datlow is, book by book, magazine by magazine, showing herself to be one of those rare editors who, like Anthony Boucher, say, or Judith Merril, now and then enter this field and quietly change it from top to bottom for the better.

The extraordinary variety of the stories is a clear indication that if this sort of project is approached correctly, a limitation of theme may not turn out to be a confinement at all, but only a stimulating challenge. The book is not nervous about including several more or less traditional vampires, but the authors give them highly untraditional twists.

"Infidel" by Thomas Tessier, for example, is very like an M.R. James tale, with its protagonist wandering ever deeper into the deepest depths of the underground Vatican library, but the vampire encountered turns out to be a gnawing idea. The fiendish technique of devouring the victim by means of repeated attacks will hardly be unfamiliar to aficionados, but it's *what* is eaten in Karl Wagner's "The Slug" that gives this story its special awfulness.

The idea that our dreams may be alien, dangerous things is looked into and played with very differently in two excellent offerings, the first being "Mrs. Rinaldi's Angel" by Thomas Ligotti, wherein the large, pale, reclusive Mrs. Rinaldi propounds a theory of dreams you may wish you'd never heard, and "The Moose Church" by Jonathan Carroll, which gives more than fair warning that knowledge of profound mysteries is not won without profound cost.

Two authors who are particularly associated with vampiric activities present works on the subject which diverge widely from their accounts of the doings of the dangerous immortals they've created and made famous: Chelsea Quinn Yarbro abandons le Comte de Saint-Germain in "Do I Dare to Eat a Peach?" in order to make disturbing exploration into the venerable but seldom admitted connection between vampires and international politics; and in "Now I Lay Me Down to Sleep," Suzy McKee Charnas creates a gentle predator in the person of Rose whose haunting of Apartment 14C on Central Park West is handled very differently from the way it would have been by the same author's sinister Professor Weyland.

The appalling dangers of the absence of self-insight when one wanders on the edge of the abyss is chillingly portrayed in "True Love" by K.W. Jeter, and the benefits of its presence are demonstrated in "The Pool People" by Melissa Mia Hall. Both stories conjure up visual imagery which struck me as being remarkably chilling and malign.

I won't give into the urge to list all the stories ("M is for the Many Things" by Elizabeth Massie and "Teratisms" by Kathe Koja are grand expositions about the institution of the family as a vampire, for instance), will resist the temptation to quote from the afterwords (David J. Schow's is a particularly astute entry), and content myself by finishing this survey of *A Whisper of Blood* with a brief description of two final favorites: do be sure to read "Home by the Sea" by Pat Cadigan as it does a superb job of extrapolating what it might be like if one of the most profoundly vampiric conditions humankind can suffer, *ennui,* visited us in the flesh, and make certain you won't be interrupted once you start out on "The Ragthorn" by Robert Holdstock and Garry Kilworth, as the authors have clearly had a marvelous time sending their hero deeper and deeper into an ever-building, ever-darkening doom as he pursues immortality with the tricksy help of the wedge-shaped characters of Sumeria; a lost fragment of Homer's *Iliad*; a heretofore unknown passage from Caesar; the same from Chaucer, and, as if all that weren't enough to lead him thoroughly astray, a tasty little bit from *Hamlet* which all the scholars somehow missed.

To end this review, allow me to tout two vampire novels which I think are highly deserving of a much larger readership than they got. The first has already been favorably mentioned in *Weird Tales* already, but it didn't seem to help, so I'll try again: do get hold of Barbara Hambly's **Those Who Haunt the Night** (Del Rey paperback) if you'd like to read a rousing melodrama about the infestation of London by a pack of very beautifully realized vampires, and (this I admit will be an almost impossible volume to track down, but maybe it'll inspire a publisher to look it over) **Dracula's Children** by Richard Lortz (The Permanent Press, NY, 1981) which is an even more contemporary account than when it was written about what might happen if the forgotten children of New York decide to give the City back just a little of what it richly deserves.

Thank you for your attention.　Ω

DREAM BOAT

Johnny, Johnny
Willow wisp
hair of gold
the girls to kiss

Love them all
and make them cry
leave them broken
there to die

Johnny, Johnny
what a cad!
not an ordinary lad

— Fred Olen Ray

WHO LIES BENEATH A SPELL

by John Brunner

"Of all the skills you boast, only your mastery of the art of love cannot be magical," pronounced Jarveena with the authority of wide experience. Utter darkness overlay the couch she shared tonight with Enas Yorl. Yielding her body to him during her annual visit to Sanctuary was part of the price she had to pay for erasure of the scars that seamed her skin. But it was by far the pleasantest.

"No!" she went on. "It has to be the fruit of many — should I say conjugations, or conjunctions?"

Relaxed for once, the wizard chuckled. "So it is," he replied. "There was a time, though, when I thought it might be gained by abstract study . . . Odd! I feel inclined to open my heart to you. Perhaps it's because tomorrow, after working so much magic on your scars, I may not have one."

Jarveena rose to one elbow, staring. There was one exception to the darkness: the twin red sparks that the magician wore instead of eyes. No doubt he could see her when she could not otherwise see him. Well, that was the way of things within his palace, and she had long learned not to rail against what she could not mend.

"Literally?" she demanded.

"Why not? What makes you think all living things have hearts? From experience I can assure you that's not so. Indeed, the day may well arrive when the curse that shifts my shape compels me to forgo the delights of your company, since I shall find myself lacking organs even more relevant to conjugation or conjunction — that is, with human beings. No doubt I shall have others in their place. But not a partner of the necessary kind. At least, I hope not. Fortunately they will be transient, like all my forms."

By ordinary the changes he referred to were a source of extra gratification: an unfamiliar but exciting roughness, an arousing odour, the presence of an extra limb to multiply his stimulation of her . . . But that was in the dark. Imagining what she might have seen by lamplight, Jarveena failed to repress an involuntary shudder. However, Enas Yorl seemed not to notice. He continued in a musing tone, as though describing events that had happened to a different person. And in a sense, no doubt, that was the case.

"It all befell a very long time ago, after this wise . . ."

A studious, intelligent, but somewhat gauche young man dwelt in a northern country town. The more fool he, he fell in love with a slim, pretty girl named Lita, whom he used to see on market day. She and her mother would come to town in a wagon, from the back of which they sold the produce of her father's farm, and got good prices for it. This was due less to its quality than to the custom Lita attracted, with her bright eyes, her curly chestnut hair, her ready tongue. Youths clustered round her as do bees to syrup; but she would not favour them with so much as a nod, let alone a smile, unless they made a purchase, whether they had need of it or not. The effect may be imagined: theirs was always the wagon that emptied first, to the resentment of the other market-folk, and — aware of the contribution her daughter had made — her mother would then grudgingly consent to while away an hour at a nearby tavern before returning home. There Lita could be prevailed upon to sing and dance, relishing the attention of her numerous admirers.

Among them was, invariably, Enas Yorl, who ever since entering puberty had been susceptible to female charms — indeed, he dreamed and daydreamed of little else. However, as I mentioned, he was gauche, and somewhat poor beside. He never had a trinket to bestow on her, nor curios to show or fine attire to catch her eye. On the other hand, by local standards he was well-informed, and sometimes told a tale that took her fancy, whereupon he was rewarded with a moment's chat before some more personable fellow began a song or played a pipe or offered to teach Lita a new jig. Thereat, on the instant, Enas was forgotten.

When news came that Lita was betrothed — not to one of the good-looking boys who courted her, but to a farmer nearly twice her age, in order to unite their families' lands — Enas was thunderstruck. He was not the only one; the rest, though, seemed insincere in their protestations of regret, and turned back contentedly enough to less alluring wenches. He, by contrast, determined on a grand gesture. He would leave home and seek his fortune far away. Later, of course, though he did not admit the fact to anyone, it was his intention to return in triumph and make Lita sorry she had disregarded him.

Accordingly, a few days afterward, he set off for Ilsig. In those days it was the capital of an independent kingdom, and Ranke had barely been heard of. [Yes, I said I was talking of a long time ago!] Ilsig then was not what we would think of as a major city; it was not even as large as Sanctuary has become. But to a country boy, naturally, it seemed like a vast and dazzling metropolis.

And, on the morning of his very first day there, he witnessed something that changed the course of his life.

He had had only vague plans about what he would do at Ilsig. Since he could read and write, however, a rare accomplishment, he had thought of setting up as a scribe. The better ones, he understood, gained an excellent livelihood if they enjoyed the patronage of wealthy traders. From the landlord of the scruffy inn where he had passed the night, he asked the way to the street where they congregated, learned that it lay not far from the main temple, and was heading in that direction when he was caught up in a dense, excited throng. Ahead, too,

he heard cheering and a sound of music.

He demanded what was going on, and was informed, "Today the wizard Sigil is to wed his bride Euleen! There's a procession with the King's guards and his band of music. And she's a beauty, too! Just look!"

He did. Oh, yes! She was!

The custom then at Ilsig was not to veil a bride, but to display her charms to public view in order to excite men's envy. Clad in more jewellery than fabric, face radiant under a halo of hair bright as spun gold, Euleen reclined in a palankeen of ivory and ebony, acknowledging the plaudits of the crowd with languid waves of a feather fan. Ahead marched the royal musicians blowing horns and beating drums, while her groom-to-be followed astride a palfrey. Enas Yorl paid heed to neither horse nor rider. One glimpse of that celestial vision, and all thought of Lita in her homespun gown was driven from his head . . . save insofar as he added a gloss to his ambition. Not only would he go home rich; he'd do it with a wife as stunning as Euleen — if such a marvel could be found — and disjoint the noses of his former rivals, too.

Thrusting his way through the crowd, he managed to stay in sight of the palankeen clear to the temple steps. He would have entered for the wedding ceremony, but the way was barred to all save invitees by men-at-arms with pikes and swords. His original mission forgotten, he lingered in the vicinity until noon, when the ritual ended, and was rewarded with another sight of Euleen, walking now hand in hand with Sigil.

"Isn't she gorgeous?" he breathed, and a bystander agreed with him.

"Her nature, though, cannot be too attractive," he added with a headshake. "What woman, were she sensible or decent, would waste herself on that old stick?"

"What?" Blinking, Enas glanced for the first time at the lucky husband —

19

and was horrified. Passing no more than ten paces away, Sigil was plainly seen. He had been tall, but now he was stooped, and needed the support of a staff. His velvet robe was magnificently embroidered, but it hung loose about his scrawny frame; his brow was circled by a coronet of pearls, but his head was bald; while as for his face . . . Sunken cheeks! Bags under his eyes! Wrinkles that intermeshed with wrinkles! How could so beauteous a woman bear to embrace this ancient wreck? Why, even Enas Yorl was handsomer!

He spoke aloud, and his acquaintance snorted.

"She cares, they say, exclusively for luxury. He's given her a dozen slaves, a vast apartment in his palace, a pleasure-barge to sail the bay —"

"But that's not enough," chimed in a woman at his side, belike his wife. "There's one more thing a girl her age desires, if she be halfway normal, and if she's to have *that* from Master Sigil it will need to be by magic!"

"Mayhap she'll take a lover," the husband countered.

"At her peril, then! Did you not hear what happened to that man who fancied he was Sigil's rival for her hand? You may see him any day beside the harbour, exhibiting his sores for alms and pity! And now they're wed she'd fare no better if she were fool enough to yield! Not that she could. She's bewitched, in my opinion. Ah, she must be!"

Enas nodded grimly. Lita, he was sure, would never have wed a man a tenth as ugly as this wizard, regardless of how rich he was. So the woman must be right. It followed that, no matter how unprepossessing he might be, command of magic might win a man a wife far lovelier than Lita . . .

Feeling giddy, he wandered off without another word.

That evening he did something he had never done before, the opportunity not having been available at home. He hired a girl. She was presentable enough, and friendly with it; she was country-bred, as he was, and chattered informatively about the difference between small towns and the big city; but he could not respond to her until he filled his head with visions of Euleen. Afterwards he felt disgusted with himself and paid her off, although she said she would willingly have stayed all night.

Of course, that might have been more because it was raining than on account of any special liking for him.

He slept little. About cockcrow he reached a decision. In the morning he presented himself at the gate of Sigil's palace, humbly begging to be taken on as an apprentice.

To his surprise, the wizard gave him audience, in a strange high hall hung about with tapestries whose subjects moved in disconcerting manner, changing their arrangement when unobserved. There was no doubt of this man's power; before Enas had more than uttered his name his words were being brushed aside.

"You're here because you envy me my bride," said Sigil, and gave a cracked laugh. "Well, envy is as good a driving force as any, and more potent than some. I detect that you have no designs on Euleen herself, being aware that she is bound to me by many strong spells as well as her fondness for the good things in life. That is most sensible of you. And you're correct on another point, as well: without the aid of magic, you stand no slightest chance of winning as fair a wife. Even with it the possibility is slim, inasmuch as girls like Euleen aren't born every day, but without it . . . !"

He cackled again, and sipped a beaker of wine.

"Now you're older than most of my apprentices; generally they come to me at twelve, and I take you for seventeen at least. However, I usually have to waste the first three years on teaching them to read and write, whereas you know how already. I'll give you a trial until the next full moon. There'll be no pay, but you'll be lodged and fed. Agreed?"

"Agreed!" said Enas fervently, and bowed.

He applied himself industriously under the tuition of the wizard's major-domo, not a fully-qualified magician but proficient in minor branches of the art, such that the wine on Sigil's table was invariably sweet, his fish and meat untainted even in the height of summer, his beds — this mightily impressed the new apprentice — free of fleas. But, naturally, he was not at once accorded access to his master's secret lore. Instead, he had to learn about the circuits of the stars and planets, to calculate in arcane calendars, to memorise the rhythm of the tides (a matter of extreme significance at any seaport), and to understand the virtues of plants and herbs.

He proved competent at all such tasks; his memory was quick, and he was good at guessing, too, so that when the major-domo — or, with increasing frequency, Sigil himself — presented him with a jewel bearing a corrupt inscription, or a sheet of tattered parchment whence long years had bleached part of the ink, he was often able to suggest if not the authentic text then an effective substitute. Magic, apparently, was by no means so exact a subject as he had imagined.

Covertly at first, then more boldly when no reproach was forthcoming from his master, he began to enact small rituals in private. Mostly they worked, though there was one embarrassing occasion when he had to admit responsibility for filling the palace with the stench of camels, and another worse than embarrassing when a work of his own interfered with one that Sigil was carrying on nearby, and almost cost the latter his profitable contract to storm-protect the city's fleet of fishing-smacks.

However, like a storm the episode passed into history.

Eventually, after about two years, Sigil began to allot him minor errands: to ensure the fertility of a new-bought mare, to protect a miser's hoard against theft, to locate a missing child (drowned tragically, as it happened, in a well). Those who had hoped for the attendance of the master magician were doubtful at first, but when they saw the results were just as good and the price no more than half, they started to offer him odd jobs in his own right. Enas Yorl duly reported the fact to the major-domo, who in turn informed Sigil. Tolerant, the latter said, "Oh, let him earn a little silver for himself! Just remind him that if he takes his pay in gold it will be in my coffers by next dawn, no matter where in Ilsig he may hide it!"

Enas did not put the assertion to the test. By this time he had vast respect for Sigil's power.

Now, at nineteen, with silver in one pocket, in the other a powder he'd contrived according to a recipe deemed worthless by his co-apprentices, he risked renewing his acquaintance with the female sex. Either the powder was efficacious after all. or he had gained so much in confidence he had no need of it, though for a while he continued using it to be on the safe side; he knew that confidence for vulnerable. At all events, he took to dropping in at taverns for a stoup of wine, chaffing the serving-wenches and performing simple tricks for the amusement of the company, and soon became a welcome visitor. More than one girl agreed to let him walk her home by way of an unlit alley or a bower by the waterside. More than one? Enough, within a month or three, for him to think he was at last a man to hold his own with men; indeed, to have a high opinion of himself. His diffidence lent him gentleness, considerateness, gratitude — all qualities most rare in Ilsig men, greatly appreciated by the girls, who sometimes told their chums about him and said they too should try him out. Life here, compared with what he'd known at home, was free and easy.

And he had more sense than to admit to any of his partners that after his performance for their sakes he only obtained a climax for himself the same way as before: by envisaging Euleen . . .

Whom he had scarcely seen again. She spent her days in her private suite, attended by slaves whom Sigil had enchanted to obey her every whim. Occasionally in fine weather she bathed in the garden under a flowering tree, but none of course except the slaves and Sigil might come near. Now and then, though seldom, she went forth to her barge and sailed the bay accompanied by bards and harpists, jugglers and clowns; then strains of sweet melody could be heard drifting across the water. But what else she did for amusement Enas Yorl could scarcely guess, especially when it was cold or wet. One clue might lie in the fact that every time an argosy from distant shores arrived in port, the major-domo trudged down with an escort of porters and armed guards, and haggled against even the king's own agents for the choicest rarest goods: jars of wildfowl preserved in honey, bolts of silk like spun rainbows, aromatic incense, candies and sweetmeats by the box and keg.

An awful suspicion entered the mind of Enas Yorl.

And was confirmed.

Despite the size of his home, Sigil rarely entertained; however, it was a condition of his agreement with the king that once a year he should provide a banquet for members of the royal household. It was always talked about for weeks before and days afterward — not least because it was among the very few occasions when her husband still exhibited Euleen in garb like what she had worn on the way to her wedding. Food grew cold, wine stood untasted, so it was said, while greedy eyes feasted on that unattainable loveliness, and Sigil preened himself.

Enas Yorl did not dream of sharing that good fortune. But he had not yet so much as caught sight of, let alone enjoyed, a woman who came near to matching Euleen.

However, on the eve of the banquet next after he completed three years as apprentice, Sigil summoned him. In his usual curt manner he said, "You're doing well, young man."

Enas Yorl bowed, in a more courtly fashion than at their first encounter. He was also far more smartly dressed — indeed, he had become a trifle foppish.

"You may cease to call yourself apprentice. You may say passed enchanter. In two more years, if you continue as you go, you'll be a thaumaturge; in another, I shall name you adept, whereafter you may choose to leave and work alone . . . or else become my partner and my heir!"

So taken aback that he stammered, Enas Yorl forced out, "Master, I'm not worthy — !"

"Are you trying to tell me that I'm wrong?" roared Sigil.

"Of course not! I only — "

"Then save your breath! Here's a stater for you. Repair to Hey the tailor and buy a decent robe. What you have on may pass at inns and taverns, but tomorrow night we dine in royal company!"

All boy again, Enas seized the gold coin and fled.

The whole of that night and the day after, he could neither sleep nor eat, so excited was he at the prospect of seeing Euleen. He had though himself a man by now. He had been wrong. He was still at heart that same shy silly youth who in a single day had lost his head over the bride of an elderly stranger and found the one career that he was suited for.

When Euleen came forth, seeming sullen, to greet the king and queen, Enas

Yorl looked at her eagerly.

And stood shocked into silence while everybody else exclaimed and gaped.

She had grown *fat!* In three short years, as though she were a piglet being readied for the table! Her jewelled harness strained to meet around her belly; her bracelets bit deep into her arms; her necklace barely closed around her throat; as for her face, plump cheeks met rolls below her eyes.

And from those eyes seemed to look out a soul in torment pleading for she did not know what kind of help . . .

During the meal, when he was seated with junior officers of the royal guard, Enas Yorl ate little and drank much, though keeping up polite appearances. They, clearly, could not have seen Euleen before, inasmuch as they talked about her beauty nearly as often as their exploits out hunting or on border patrol. When the host and hostess had with-drawn to entertain the king and queen in private chambers, Enas recovered sufficiently to perform a few of his old tavern tricks, and at midnight when the visitors departed some of them did so with insincere proposals that he call on them at barracks or even the royal palace.

He made his way to bed, and lay, despite the wine and last night's lack of sleep, staring into space for hours on end. How could he have let himself be obsessed for so long by someone who had sold herself to a hideous old man for the chance to gorge on endless foreign delicacies?

He resolved never to think of her again — or at least no more than he had of Lita after leaving home.

Yet there had been something in those eyes . . .

In the next two years he worked

23

harder than ever, and grew immensely skillful. He rarely returned to his former haunts, though sometimes when one of his old flames was to be married he accepted an invitation to the wedding feast and entertained the guests with petty magic.

This was in part disguise. By now he felt he had little to fear from Sigil's probing of his mind; the old magician was content with his original assessment of his employee, who had always proved scrupulously honest. Nonetheless, he had learned spells to help him hide his inner thoughts, preserving a mask of quotidian concerns. It was as well. His attempt to think no more about Euleen had failed.

Little by little the possibility had wormed into his mind: *Suppose she's being reduced to this mound of wobbling flesh because Sigil is growing old and tired! Given that she's so addicted to the pleasures of the body, and he must gratify them using magic, could his efforts in that regard not explain his recent behavior, even his willingness to name me as his heir if I so choose?* (The prospect made him shudder. Nonetheless, if he were also heir to Euleen . . . !) *If that's so, then she doesn't really want to be fat. He's letting — no — making her be fat, so that she will be less attractive to potential rivals . . .*

There was still a flaw in the argument. He knew it, but because he heard it in the voices of the young officers he skipped over it to the pleasantest possibility: *Suppose I could release her from bondage to this old impotent fool, could I not then also make her slim and beautiful again?*

And . . . mine?

It was a measure of his youth and naïveté that he completely overlooked an obvious corollary. Given power enough to pry Euleen away from Sigil, he would be capable of finding another girl who had no lust for self-indulgent luxury and making her appear still lovelier — even to his own eyes. Certainly he did not lack the necessary capacity for self-deception. It affected him so much that for the next two years, despite the absence of Euleen from further royal banquets on pretence of illness, the majority of his studies were directed to one single end.

In the interim he hedged whenever Sigil inquired whether he had yet made up his mind: did he want to stay on as a partner, with the chance of inheriting the palace, or did he want to move elsewhere? Not that there were many places whither a skilled magician might resort. Perhaps one might consider the upstart city, Ranke; though its folk were accounted brusque and unsophisticated, that might be all to the good for a young man starting out on his own. Alternatively, there were a few other towns of fair repute, not all inland — one in particular, to the east of Ranke, was on the coast though less well sited than was Ilsig, and his experience here in a seaport would stand him in good stead. In none of them, at least, would competition be extreme . . .

Sometimes it was hard to tell whether Sigil was trying to persuade him to stay or drive him out.

Using all his talent for dissimulation, Enas Yorl maintained a veil of ambiguity until one climactic night when Sigil confronted him in the great hall with a compliment — and a challenge.

"Young fellow, it has been six years! I pass you adept as I must! One dare not lie — as by now you know — in his appraisal of a wizard's skills! When you first came to me I sensed at once that you had vast potential. I could have sent you away. But, glorying in my marriage to a girl more beautiful than any seen before in Ilsig, I felt I was the master of the city — of the world! Let any wizard come against me, so I thought, and I will turn him to a toad or turd! Indeed I can! That's why I want an honest answer!"

He leaned forward on his throne; it was of ebony and ivory, like the palankeen Euleen had ridden to her wedding.

"I may be old, but my memory is keen as ever. I recall when first you came here you had no designs upon my wife. Then, though, you were humble as befit your rank and station. Now you're changed! You — whom I no longer plan to make my partner! — think that after scant six years of study you can lure Euleen away from me when you depart! Deny it at your peril! *Well?*"

On hearing his secret dream laid bare, Enas Yorl shook in his shoes. but he summoned all his self-control and made a brazen reply.

"On the day of your wedding I heard one of the townswomen say, 'There's one more thing apart from luxury a girl desires, and she'll not get it from a man as old as that except by magic!'"

Sigil clutched the arms of his throne. His face turned pale as chalk.

"That comes amusingly from you!" he hissed. "Who cannot stiffen for a girl unless he thinks of Euleen!"

"How did you — ?" Enas blurted, and bit his tongue. Too late. Sigil was relaxing with a chortle.

"Why, you silly bumpkin! You never realised — did you? — how ingenious my protection of her is. Not even when at your first royal banquet I had you seated among subalterns of your own age, young and randy, and let you hear their opinion of Euleen after she had stuffed herself with sweetmeats month in, month out, until I had to charm away her toothaches! You *idiot!* Only a magician like yourself could have seen through the glamor that I cast around her — which is so strong it binds her, too! She sees herself as everybody sees her, except you: as lovely as she ever was, as slim, as graceful ... Even I do so when I go in to her! Do you not therefore envy me?"

"No, I do not!" The words burst from Enas Yorl before he could bridle his tongue. "It's not worth possessing a woman save of her own will!"

"Fine words!" Sigil mocked. "From one who mixed a certain powder that saved him having to pay for female favours in good solid coin!"

"Had I not made trial of it, then won to women with no magic aid, I'd not have learned how great the difference is!" Enas Yorl set his shoulders back and stared Sigil defiantly in the face. "You know how long it is since I enjoyed the powder — and how little it was worth in fact!"

A hint of alarm came and went in Sigil's eyes.

"You seem to be claiming that ... " His voice grew thready and failed him.

"That Euleen wants to run away? Indeed I am!"

Recovering his normal poise, Sigil said contemptuously, "You and she have not exchanged two words. If you had, my charms would have dissolved you into slime."

"But you just said yourself" — Enas Yorl was growing reckless, and somehow he didn't care — "I'm a magician! During that banquet I looked at her eyes. Behind them I saw a prisoner struck dumb yet pleading for escape! If that's not so, *why have you kept her from all banquets since?*"

"It's true!"

The words were a dreadful shriek from the far doorway of the hall, the one that led to the private quarters of the palace. They turned to stare. Revealed in glimmering torchlight was Euleen herself: richly gowned, immaculately coiffed — but bloated so that she could barely walk.

"Help me!" she moaned, staggering toward Enas. "I'm going mad! Each passing day I'm more a prisoner! He no longer lets me go aboard my barge! He's kept me from my friends, my family, the royal banquet ... ! All he does is ply me with sweetmeats that I'm sure are drugged — "

"Silence!" Sigil shouted. "Return at once — Ow! What?"

With grim amusement Enas Yorl, who had by reflex hurled a spell to weaken him, reflected that he hadn't known it could elicit such a commonplace response as "Ow!"

But now not just the spell was cast: the die of fate. And as to "die", he might well die within the hour. He summoned all his wits, clinging to the knowledge that Sigil was old and exhausted thanks to the web of spells he'd woven round Euleen. Nonetheless, what he lacked in energy he must no doubt make up in knowledge and experience . . .

What a plight! Now he would never make it back to his home town, with or without a fortune and a gorgeous bride —

"He's sneaking past your guard!" shrieked Euleen. "As he did to me! I thought I was marrying him because he was comely as well as rich! When he stopped bothering to keep up the pretence I realised he'd cozened me with magic! But by then he had me in his power!"

With vast effort Enas forced aside despair, and found new strength in doubled loathing of the wizard.

But what, in this unanticipated contest, could he rely on to defend not himself but Euleen? Scores of remembered spells flashed through his mind, most horribly distracting to him, for only those that needed no sort of apparatus — those he could invoke exclusively by words and gestures — would be of service now . . .

Or — ?

Inspiration struck. He muttered a six-word cantrip . . . and misspoke it. Sigil realised his intention, and called on the figures from the tapestries, who began to emerge, slowly but purposefully, and plod in Enas's direction. They had changed vastly over the past six years, and all for the worse. Some had fangs, or beaks and tentacles; some

dripped yellow burning ichor; not one was half as human as it had been.

Enas tried frantically anew, and this time twisted his tongue around the arcane phrase. All of a sudden, ridiculously, the spirit of the mammoth that had bequeathed its ivory to build the throne returned to it, and made it toss like a small boat on a stormy sea. Thus distracted, Sigil turned his next spell into gibberish, and Enas was able to fling a charm compound of reassurance and relaxation in the general direction of Euleen. It was meant to silence her until the battle was over.

It missed.

It did, though, quiet a few of the tapestry figures, lurching onward in their extraordinary incarnation of tarnished gold, faded green, brownish red, dingy blue. . . . But not all. Some were coming far too close for comfort.

Where, Enas Yorl wondered, did he ever get the notion that magic was exact?

And next to Sigil he was an amateur, a trifler!

Yet, miraculously, here came a distraction! Sensing perhaps that he had been put off his stroke by that last misdirected spell, Euleen was wrapping her fat arms around her husband's scrawny ankles and moaning as she wet his feet with tears. What she was saying could not be made out, but the thought of this once-incredible vision of loveliness being reduced to such pitiful humiliation again redoubled Enas Yorl's fury. At the top of his voice he shouted a spell he had only read and never dared to try, for it was far too powerful. A softer version of it might have been used to create Sigil's strange tapestries, for it was intended to change shape and shapes.

The air within the hall resonated like the welkin ahead of a new-brewed thunderstorm.

And this spell . . . *worked.*

All of a sudden the woman clutching

at Sigil was other than Euleen, and still more beautiful. Moreover, she was composed and confident and rising to her feet commandingly, bestowing smiles to left and right that made the figures from the tapestry come fawning towards her. She stroked their heads and at her touch they changed, retreated, resumed their places in the hangings on the wall, miraculously depicting calm and lovely countryside, a fine spring day, an idyll of repose and happiness.

Abruptly Enas realised: *This is the woman that I dream of winning for myself. I didn't know, but there she is.*

And, having called her into existence, I dare not be distracted by her.

Because if I do, I'm lost.

And so is she — TO HIM!

His rival's power was outdoing his! She was turning to bestow her smile on Sigil! Just so had Lita turned away, in the shabby tavern by his home-town's market square, her lack of interest made evident.

The woman whom I never met yet most desire, to do that to me? NO! She won't!

Boiling with rage, half-blinded by his tears, Enas Yorl stumbled forward, prepared to tear Sigil apart with his bare hands. Perhaps the unexpected shift of emphasis from abstract magic to direct violence was what threw the master mage off-stride, for, as he beckoned Enas Yorl's oneiric mistress to bend and kiss his feet as Euleen had, he allowed himself a gloating smile of victory. He even said, "Before you're ready to match against me, boy, I shall be dead, and you'll be mourning your lost chance to be my heir. Would you not have wanted to inherit — *her?*"

He caressed the woman's locks with a claw-like, malformed hand.

Malformed?

But while they bore the liver-spots of

age, Sigil's hands had always been well-shaped. His face might be furrowed, his throat stringy, his limbs and joints afflicted with rheumatics . . . but his hands — !

That means that some of my last spell struck through to him.

Calm, Enas Yorl reviewed the situation; mustered all the charms and cantrips he recalled that could change shapes —

And uttered them in one hoarse frantic shout.

The effect was instant, and tremendous. The hall was not a hall, but a cave, or a tunnel, or a mineshaft. The air was not air, but water, or quicksand, or urine. The temperature was not cool, but burning or freezing. The walls were not solid, but phantasmal. There were gales and thunder and earthquakes and a flash of scarlet lava between the floor-flags. There was disease and health and open sky and crushing rock and sanity and madness and terror and rest and power and weakness and animals and desert and clouds and plants and help and terror and screaming and waterflow and terror and eruption and terror and ice and terror and terror and terror . . .

Very far away from himself, as though his intermix of spells had managed to transform the location of his mind into something he had never even remotely resembled, like the awareness of a whole planet, Enas Yorl felt as though he was splitting into a million million fragments all of which were both him and someone else, and in the midst of chaos he could still hear the voice of Sigil bragging, "I was too quick for you! I made a shield that turned your spell back on its speaker!"

But . . . *Spell?*

Strictly, it had not been singular. It had been as many as could be crammed into a single breath, some of them sharing the same sound so that they interlocked in space as well as time. It was a contrivance of his own, that he was proud of. If Sigil had in truth been misled by it . . .

There was still hope. Enas Yorl, not knowing where his body was, or even whether he still had a body, waited for surcease. The universe calmed. He was able to see, and the first thing he looked for was the woman of his dreams, the one he had not even realised he'd dreamed of until she became manifest, the one who could have driven all thought of Euleen as completely from his mind as Euleen had Lita.

Wryly he thought: *Never again!*

But no matter where he looked, there was no sign of the woman, nor of Euleen, nor — come to that — of Sigil. Not unless that formless shadow over there was Sigil, sitting on his backside on the rubble-strewn floor . . .

Rubble-strewn?

Fine cold rain was sprinkling his skin. He was naked. The gale that had borne away the roof had also ripped off all his clothes, yet without bruising him. How . . . ?

He was too exhausted to wonder. He fell forward on to wet and gritty ground, and fainted.

When he awoke it was dawn. In his sleep, he found, he had wrapped himself in some of the tapestries — or they had done it of their own accord. Though damp, they had sufficed to keep him from the cold.

And now there were no more walls for them to hang from. The shape-changing spells seemed at last to have expired, though they had done vast damage. Walls had become heaps of random stone, but sprawled inert. The throne lay in fragments that showed no sign of reassembling themselves. And on the tapestries there were no more figures, shifting or otherwise. They were just sheets of coarse cloth.

He should have felt elated. On the contrary; he felt extremely odd. He felt as though something had penetrated his body, and now itched constantly inside his skin. Seeking distraction, he rose shakily to his feet and began to prod and poke among the ruins.

Everything was eerily quiet. No one came to his aid, or even to find out what had happened.

In a short while, brushing aside dirt, he came across Euleen. She lay completely still, with a smile of bliss upon her face — the face he remembered from her wedding day. He moved a few more scraps of debris, enough to satisfy himself that in her last moments of life her body too had been restored to its lost loveliness. Then he could bear it no longer, and turned elsewhere.

Beyond another pile of rubble he found Sigil trying to crawl away. His lips were drawn aside from rotting teeth, eyes wide and staring as though he were afraid to shut them because the visions in his mind were more dreadful than outside reality. Enas contrived to make him sit upright, as though encouraging a clumsy child, but when he reached a squatting posture all the magician did was moan aloud and try to count his fingers. In his eyes there was a dreadful blankness worse even than the imprisoned look of Euleen. And all the time cold rain was sifting down.

Then there was a disturbance. In the frame of what had been the arched main doorway to the hall appeared the major-domo staring around in horrified bewilderment. Rising into view, Enas Yorl called him by name.

The major-domo screamed and turned to flee.

A terrifying thought occurred to Enas Yorl. That final, plural spell . . .

Oh, yes. That must have been the way of it. Sigil had driven part of it aside, but at the cost of all his force. Foolishly he had weakened himself by lying to another wizard about his powers, something he himself had said one dare not do. He had known he was uttering a

falsehood when he boasted that before the younger man was able to outdo him he himself would be long dead. Here was the proof. Now he was doomed to gibber and count fingers for the rest of his life.

But he *had* flung part of the magic back . . .

Very slowly, very sorrowfully, the still-young Enas Yorl looked at his hands, his body, legs and feet, and learned what had become of the lost figures from the tapestries. No wonder the major-domo had fled.

He would have fled from himself, had that been possible.

All that day no one dared approach the ruined palace. Meanwhile, resignedly, he made shift (the phrase evoked a bitter laugh) to gather up as much of Sigil's library as he could load upon a pack-mule. After dark, by stealthy ways, he gained the One Great Road. He walked southeastward until dawn; then, wanting to avoid the king's patrols, he forked due south along a narrow trail which petered out beyond Forgotten Pass, at a humble fishing-port where people sacrificed to Dyareela of the Stormy Sea. It was their conviction that each catch they made, because it kept the folk alive, had to be paid for with a human life.

In consequence there were extremely few of them.

It was befitting he should settle at what was to become Sanctuary, among a people even sillier than himself.

Fighting sleep, Jarveena said, "This is not wholly in accord with what you told me when we met the first time."

"Is it not?" There was vast weariness in the magician's voice. "So be it, then. My powers dwindle, as did Sigil's, with the passing of the years, and sometimes I wish the process were complete already. One power, though, remains to all of us, not solely to us wizards, and that's the power to amend the record of the past. Without it, how could anybody cling to sanity?"

"You know . . ." Jarveena was so drowsy now, she seemed not to have heard his last remark. "I'm glad you confided in me. It makes me like you much more than before."

"You think that was the purpose of the story?" Enas Yorl demanded gruffly. And, when no answer was forthcoming, he sent her back to wake, as always, in guest quarters at the house of Melilot the scribe, while he endured his time upon the cruel rack of change.

AFTERWORD

I do a lot of my best thinking at science-fiction conventions. (And a lot of my best drinking, come to that.) Nowhere else do I find such concentrated input, so much stimulating conversation.

Some stimuli, of course, are more productive than others. Had it not been for encountering Robert Asprin at Boskone in 1978, I'm sure I'd never have created Enas Yorl. (For fuller details of that meeting see the postface to *Thieves' World.*)

This is mainly because I've written relatively little fantasy, with the significant exception of my stories about *The Traveller in Black.* However, I enjoy it as a change of pace, and when I do tackle fantasy I like to hark back to what has always been my favourite variant of the genre, the type of story pioneered by the magazine *Unknown Worlds,* rather than — for instance — the heroic fantasy of Robert E. Howard. To quote David Conway's *Magic: An Occult Primer,* "Even magicians have their off days." So they should, in fiction too, and so should super-heroes. Maybe Conan never caught a cold, but I can't believe he never caught the clap . . .

I suppose that's why, when I invented Enas Yorl, I decided he'd be different from your ordinary wizard. I set out to see if I could make him vulnerably human. Judging by the way in which other contributors have invited him into their stories — which I find very flattering — this must have been a sensible idea.

Considering I met him totally by chance at a convention, I've grown very fond of him. But then, that's how I've made a lot of my best friends.   Ω

MOOT QUESTION

Higgledy-piggledy
Lovecraft in Providence
Thought Elder Evils crawled
Out of the sky

What with defective planes,
Third World nukes, acid rain
Nobody's asking old
HPL why.

— **Ann K. Schwader**

CONCERNING THE FORTHCOMING INEXPENSIVE PAPERBACK TRANSLATION OF THE NECRONOMICON OF ABDUL ALHAZRED

by John Brunner

I:
THE PEABODY LEGACY

My hand shakes, my spirits fail, as I attempt to set forth this record which is at once a catharsis of the terrors that besiege my broken mind, and — more significantly — a warning you will disregard at your peril.

It has been said, "None so blind as those who will not see." That at best is only half a truth. Still blinder are those who desire, without regard for consequences, to see what ought never to be seen!

What follows is an exact account of the circumstances which have led me to a noisome dungeon, under constant observation by alienists, brutally misused by simian thugs in white coats should I so much as refer to the hateful knowledge in my brain. I have committed no crime! On the contrary, I am a benefactor of humanity! But not even the consular representatives of my own country will aid me! Has the stock of once-Great Britain truly fallen so low that its citizens can be unlawfully confined in one of our former colonies without a whisper of diplomatic protest? It seems so, for the official who visited me the day after my arrest was scornful of my tale — though, of course, he may have been an impostor. . . .

I ramble. Small wonder after the fearful experiences I have endured! But let me with all my forces compose this narrative into logical order. One dare not look forward to long supremacy for logic in the world, now the denizens of primal chaos press upon us anew.

Be it known, then, that I bear the honourable name of Jasper Abraham Wharton; that I am fifty years of age; and that my tale for present purposes commences at the small town of Arkham, overlooking Marshwood Vale in the county of Dorset, England. There, in accordance with the bookish nature which I have been pleased to acknowledge since my childhood, I have for many years discharged the duties of a librarian. The stipend of such a post is small; my needs, however, have always been few, particularly since I have never been a victim of those promptings of the flesh which drive the majority of men to marriage, or to even worse predicaments. I have ever appreciated far more highly the pleasures of the mind than those of the body; and, although the setting of a rural community may not *a priori* seem to afford any great variety of intellectual stimuli, it was my good fortune while still in my twenties to become acquainted with the then Lord of the Manor of Dunwich, a parish whose boundaries adjoin those of Arkham. I speak of Sir Adrian Peabody, Baronet, scion of a family long established in the Vale, and last of its direct line inasmuch as its more vital cadet branch had emigrated to the New World.

Sir Adrian was a recluse, not entirely from choice. At all events he was shunned in the vicinity. Gossip has never appealed to me; I could not however escape gathering that there had been some sort of scandal before I was born, the nature of which I did not inquire about. It made no difference to the fact that he befriended me despite the disparity in our ages, he being well advanced in years. Fortified by recollection of vicious rumours circulated long ago, the townsfolk would have it that he was senile. I never found him so. Labouring under the burden of a failing frame, admittedly, and resentful of the cataracts that rendered him three-quarters sightless, he yet retained a mind of great keenness behind the deceptive mask of his slack features. Indeed it is past a doubt that he remained in possession of his essential faculties, else he would not have been permitted by his legal advisors to amend his will, as he did some five or six years after our first meeting, to make me the inheritor of his compendious and recherché private library, amassed over five centuries by his ancestors.

A small legacy accompanied the bequest, which enabled me to finance an extension to my modest dwelling adjacent to the Arkham Public Library — I have always preferred, for personal reasons, to live as close as possible to the place of my employment — and equip it with suitable storage for the eight thousand, two hundred and seven volumes Sir Adrian had left me. There was some outcry locally upon news of this provision being noised abroad, from two quarters: from the native farming folk (one would not do them injustice by terming them "the peasantry"), who had notoriously little love for the baronet and his predecessors; and likewise from newcomers to the area, city-dwellers lately become *nouveaux-riches,* who had tried and failed to cultivate their titled neighbour; who upon it being learned that Dunwich Great Hall would be put up for sale fell to squabbling over the estate and the lordship of the manor like cur-dogs over a bone; and who were

(as I told a reporter from the *Arkham Gazette* on the only occasion of my granting a newspaper interview) solely interested in the library as an investment rather than a repository of knowledge . . . a point which I regret to state was not repeated in print.

The reporter, I recall, demanded with quite insolent persistence whether I had pressurised — dreadful neologism! — Sir Adrian into making the codicil to his will. I denied the charge, but admitted that I had suggested the financial component, Sir Adrian not having been entirely aware of my straitened resources. What else could I have done, once it was plain he had set his heart on my receiving the library? To have sent it piecemeal to auction would have put me on all fours with those greedy strangers above-mentioned!

That clamour, fortunately, died away upon the destruction of Dunwich Great Hall a week or two later, the consequence of suspected arson. The tune of these invaders from the city altered immediately, and they conceded it was a stroke of luck that the books had not lain among the embers. (And incidentally, I may say, then proceeded to prove my point about their limited concern for the collection by never requesting the opportunity to consult a single one of its items!)

For my own part, at the time of the conflagration I wholly concurred in the opinion that the removal of the volumes had been beneficial. It was not until later that I realised how much better it would have been for the world had certain holograph texts, certain rare and curious tomes — not, according to the British Library, the Bodleian, the London Library and other authorities, to be found elsewhere in the United Kingdom — been incinerated in the pyre. . . .

On the other hand, but for my acquaintance with them, all knowledge of their contents might now repose in the deformed cranium of that fiend in —

dare one debase the phrase "human form"? No, never! *Sub-human* is the word! As are the diabolical machines to whose mindless circuits he proposes to commit . . .

But I race ahead of my promised logical order.

II:
THE VISITOR FROM AMERICA

Suffice it to say, then, that for two full decades after the demise of Sir Adrian I led a rewarding albeit solitary existence, much engaged in cataloguing my acquisitions, a task for which (as Sir Adrian had recognised with perceptiveness belying the charge that he was senile) I was ideally suited. I do not say so in any immodest sense, for it is a matter of simple fact that there was scarcely one script or language among that vast array of literature with which I could not claim some passing familiarity. Disdaining the company of my rude schoolfellows, who regarded learning as inferior to barbaric pastimes such as football or stealing apples, from boyhood up I had explored the byways of philology. By ten I could make shift at the decipherment of Umbrian, Dorian, Sanskrit and other commonplace tongues, and I had subsequently investigated — in addition to the Indo-European — the Semitic, the Ural-Altaic, the Sino-Mongolian and (insofar as they have been committed to writing) the African linguistic families, not to mention those of the Pacific and its conterminous zones from Japan to New Zealand as well as countless shamefully inadequate missionary transcriptions of aboriginal Australian dialects. I had appended a footnote or two to the literature, particularly in connection with the vexed matter of Basque radices.

It had, I confess, occurred to me that in the twilight of my days some meed of glory might befall me for having all by myself completed such a monumental undertaking. Vain dream! Obstacle after obstacle impeded me. It certainly was not my wish that the existence of the unique items in what I had now come to regard as my collection should be publicised, for an absolutely quiet life was imperative for success. I have ever been fond of orderliness; the greater world, the metropolis, the hurly and burly of travel, held no charms to tempt me; and while on occasion a fellow-enthusiast in my own speciality who happened to be touring in the area might presume upon my time to request assistance in unravelling some conundrum in bibliophilic lore — and while I never refused such counsel if it lay within my power — those who did visit me were for the most part sufficiently sensitive to my preferences to confine themselves thereafter to Her Majesty's Posts.

Yet, inevitably, there were certain lacunae in the wall of protective indifference which I contrived around me. For all my fervent pleadings, untrustworthy members of the staffs of the great libraries to which I must now and then have recourse, to confirm or refute hypotheses concerning the provenance of a binding-material, the characteristics of a scribe, or the regional frequency of a turn of phrase, abused my confidence and repeated the content of my inquiry to a third party. Time and again I was pestered by requests, bribes and even barely-veiled threats from what I had previously imagined to be respectable academic bodies whose directors had got wind of the Peabody Bequest and demanded that it be ceded to them!

Horrors! To set these priceless tomes at the beck and call of every long-haired, unwashed, half-literate student on his or her way to a degree in some fashionable but nonsensical subject! I not only learned of the existence of such persons as I describe from the newspapers I daily perused at the public library (arriving early for the purpose so that no one should be deprived of their use during opening hours); during university vacations I actually saw some of them on our premises . . . though fortunately I never had to deal with them personally, since I had grown accustomed to concentrating on administrative matters and left encounters with the subscribers to my assistant Mrs Craven, widow of a former schoolteacher in Dunwich. Despite this small mercy my salaried employment seemed daily to grow more onerous as an ever-greater proportion of *hoi polloi* were accorded that superficial veneer of education which nowadays serves as an *Ersatz* for the real thing. In order to escape I devoted every instant I could spare to my correspondence (which was extensive) and my catalogue.

But escape was to be forbidden me.

On a certain morning in the spring of the present year — I recall it must have been a Monday, since I was engaged in making up the weekly account of books overdue for return — Mrs Craven informed me that an American was at my door, a certain Hiram Schultz, claiming to be a doctor of letters and engaged as a lecturer at a university with a peculiar name. I heard it (as one might expect, he had not the courtesy to send in a visiting-card) as "Mixed Atomic," the very epitome of that misguided and futile bias toward the sciences which has been the bane of true scholarship for the past century. "Doctor of Letters"! What a sham!

I demanded the ostensible purpose of his call, and Mrs Craven advised me that he was engaged in analysing the verbal content of incunabula and other rare works by means of computers.

"Computers!" I exploded. My outburst, born of conviction that they are anathema to honest scholars and those who trust in them lack souls, was louder than I intended — so loud, it reached the ears of the stranger. And he, with the insensitivity typical of American so-called academics, interpreted it as due to excitement rather than fury.

At any rate that is the only excuse I can conceive for his ill-mannered intrusion, a second later, into my private office, beaming all over his bovine features and exclaiming, "That's right, sir! The greatest breakthrough in the attribution of —"

He broke off, doubtless on seeing how my expression contradicted his erroneous assumption, and stood abashed. Since he was, however, a very tall young man, his single stride had taken him halfway from the door to my desk. The ratable value of a community like ours being small, naturally the Arkham council has only an exiguous fund from which to provide premises for its public servants. Finding himself adjacent to the chair which Mrs Craven used when discussing administrative matters, he proceeded to sit down, stare me in the eye as though we were old friends, and pour out a garbled, parasyntactical, and barely more than half-comprehensible explanation for his discourtesy.

"Well, sorry to crash in on you like this, Dr Wharton — hey, sorry! It's *Mister* Wharton, isn't it? Just that I thought, reading your bits in like the *Journal of Philology* and the *Annals of Bibliophily* and all like that, no one could be that good without he had at least three pee-aitch-dees, heh-heh!" (I transcribe his barely articulate utterances with such precision simply because every word ate into my memory with the fierceness of acid.) "But you see when I cottoned on to this link between our little thinkshop at Arkham Mass., plus this great deal we have going with all those like old forgotten em-esses we turned up, I don't mean *we* but this crazy chief of mine Dr Abner Marsh, you should meet him, you really should, you'd get on like a house on fire — like Dunwich Hall, heh-heh . . . !"

It might occur to the reader at this point to pose a question I have some reluctance about answering; I must, however, oblige myself to forestall puzzlement, and state candidly that among the reasons I prefer a life of seclusion is that I have been since infancy afflicted with a stammer. Confrontation with even an old acquaintance may trigger it, and when it comes to a boisterous and unwelcome stranger my difficulties are redoubled. Additionally I am perhaps not the most prepossessing of men, and living in a small community with little society I have never taken great pains over my dress or appearance. One may readily deduce from that another reason why my preference is for contact by letter; persons given to making hasty judgments based on superficial impressions could so easily form a wrong impression of me as an individual.

Nonetheless I was on the verge of being able to tell him to leave my office at once and write for an appointment, which after such rudeness I would be disinclined to grant, when something in the midst of his chaotic outpourings caught my attention.

He had spoken, with casual familiarity, of the *Necronomicon* of Abdul Alhazred!

III:
AN APPALLING DISCOVERY

It was like a thunderbolt! I had believed the manuscript copy in Latin, in a crabbed late-medieval chancery hand, which I had discovered — although not perused, its decipherment clearly being a long and quite likely unrewarding task — in Sir Adrian's collection, to be the only one extant. The British Library, the *Bibliothèque Nationale,* and every other authority I had consulted had assured me that nothing was on record concerning that text, apart from veiled unhelpful references in other works of a slightly later period, uniformly suspected of being the products of disordered minds.

So great was my astonishment, it deprived me of speech completely, to the alarm of Mrs Craven, who turned as if to offer assistance even though she knew how I detested any reference to my disability. Scowling at her, I fought my disobedient tongue towards a newly-framed denunciation: not now of this brash intruder, but of those supposedly dedicated to the same cause as myself, those scholars unworthy of the name who must, I presume, have let word of my letters loose along that channel of communication known as "the grapevine" — a graphic image enough, though why such an innocent plant deserves to be tarred with so foul a brush I have never established.

And then, as more facts emerged from Schultz's gabbling, I realised with a still more violent shock that my initial conclusion had been mistaken. It was not the fault of those I had confided in that this disgusting person had broached the secret of my prized volume.

There was another copy in existence!

Worse yet! No mere translation like mine, *but in the original Arabic!*

How often had I planned, given enough time in this vale of tears following completion of the catalogue which was my major task — albeit not yet half accomplished after twenty years — to redact and publish for the first time ever the most select items in my possession: this one whose name Schultz was bandying about, those others by von Junzt and d'Erlette which, judging by their titles, might constitute a valuable accretion to the corpus of accounts of medieval demonolatry . . . !

Trembling with rage and frustration, disappointed beyond measure, I was told how it was that he had heard about my — no, not "my," only "the" — *Necronomicon.* Shorn of its trans-Atlantic jargon and sub-literate verbal frills, his story ran as follows.

The peculiarly-named college where Schultz worked (it transpired he had accepted his post on a temporary basis, in the hope of moving on, once he had accumulated a morsel of renown by publishing a few papers, to some more august centre of learning) was located in the equally oddly-named state of Massachusetts, and indeed in a town which was the namesake of my own birthplace, another Arkham. Eager, by his own admission, not to remain any longer than necessary in such a "one-horse burg," he set about determining what if anything in those fields of study touching on his own other members of the faculty were engaged upon.

He decided almost at once that Professor Abner Marsh, already mentioned, was the likeliest candidate for international fame, so he "thought he might as well take a ride on the guy's coat-tails." He set out to cultivate him. For reasons he did not elucidate this proved a difficult chore, but in the end his efforts were crowned with success.

Marsh, termed "crazy" in an almost affectionate tone — which puzzled me — was apparently a respected though not greatly liked individual, of outstanding intellect but little given to companionship. (I recognised an echo of myself in the description, discounting it however in case it was as I suspected founded on pointless sympathy.) Despite whatever handicaps they were that Schultz was hinting at, he had nonetheless stumbled on an academic treasure trove. During the demolition of an old house — situated, remarkably but not astonishingly, in a nearby town named after the village which had so long been the seat of the Peabody line, another Dunwich — certain books had been found behind a roughly-plastered wall. Mouldy, damaged by time in addition to frequent earlier use, they were

brought to the college by the workman who disinterred them in the hope some reward might be forthcoming. The Dean had been inclined to dismiss them as worthless; Professor Marsh, by contrast, on being asked to evaluate them, realised they were rare and potentially valuable. (I stifled my normal reactions at this point. I have always loathed people who paste financial labels on pure scholarship — but I realise now, only too clearly, how ingrained that attitude must be among Americans!)

The workman was fobbed off with a tip, and Marsh wished to confide in someone how clever he had been. The lot fell to Schultz, and he now recounted to me with equal glee that the main prize was . . . the *Necronomicon*. Having only some fifteen volumes on his hands, Marsh proposed to edit and issue them, and would do so long before I had even finished listing the eight thousand-odd that I was saddled with! My gorge rose; my mouth tasted of bile.

In order to lay a veneer of colourable scholarship over his slapdash work, Marsh wished to investigate the connection between the Dunwich of the Old World and that of the New. Being unable to travel — Schultz intimated that he was in constant need of some sort of medical attention — he invoked the aid of his younger colleague, who consented in exchange for the right to publish computer analyses of the texts. Heaven help us! As though a machine could read and appreciate a book!

Arriving in Dorset, learning of the Peabody Bequest, he had no other thought than to "barge in" and offer — this took my breath away with its sheer gall! — a thousand dollars for the opportunity to "glance over" my collection. Moreover he assured me his college would willingly buy the lot for a to-be-negotiated sum, because "it would provide thesis material for our kids for years!"

That was the absolute limit. Rage lent me fluent speech for once, and in no uncertain terms I told him what I thought of him and his professor. But when I finished he did no more than shrug and rise.

"Too bad," he said. "I did think you might help out with translating. There aren't many as well equipped as you are for the job. Even proof-reading, come to that."

"You're actually going to publish them?" I whispered.

"Sure! Original and English on facing pages. Thanks to the computers you hate so much, we can keep the costs right down. A few years ago we'd have had to charge two hundred bucks a copy, but now we can do it for a fraction of that. We can design any type-face we like, you know, and using a laser printer and an OCR . . ."

He went on talking, but I could no longer hear. I was envisaging defeat: hundreds, maybe thousands of reprints of what had been unique books, cheaply bound in card or even paper covers — no leather, no gilt tooling, no . . .

On the point of leaving, he sensed my lack of attention.

"Mr Wharton!"

I recovered, a little.

"If you change your mind" — he commandeered a pen from my desk, and a sheet of paper, writing rapidly — "this is where I'll be for the next few days. Get in touch, hm?"

I accepted the address with nerveless fingers, and he was gone.

I fought my anger for long minutes before recovering a semblance of normality. I tried to resume my work. I failed. At last I was compelled to abandon the attempt. Telling Mrs Craven that I needed a breath of air, I adjourned homeward — more exactly, slipped by a private route into the library extension of my home. There I at once sought out the *Necronomicon* and clutched it to me, foolishly seeking assurance that it was indeed still here, had not been purloined so that Marsh might boast of owning both the original and the translation. I had not thus far made any attempt to read it, beyond a preliminary inspection to ascertain the general run of its contents. I knew it was ascribed to an otherwise unknown Arab writer, that some pages had been defaced with a poor-quality ink through which the original text might with great effort be deciphered — and of one thing more I was abruptly certain.

I was not going to let Marsh cheat me of my right to edit and issue a translation first!

On reflection, perhaps I had been over-ambitious in my plan to catalogue the entire collection before publishing any of the individual items. More to the point, I could thank Schultz for a useful new idea. Why should I toil day in, day out, behind the scenes of the Arkham library, when — without actually *selling* the book, which I would have regarded as a betrayal of Sir Adrian's trust — I might request financial support from a publisher in order to translate and annotate it?

My course of action became clear at once. I had gathered the distinct impression from Schultz that American so-called "scholarship" was organised like an office job; one put in a certain number of hours per week, and the rest of the time ignored one's proper duty. Given that, once free of my quotidian grind, I could call the rest of every day my own apart from time wasted on eating and sleeping, a dedicated person like myself could not fail to beat Marsh into print, if not with preliminary announcements (his, Schultz had stated, were already *en route* to the appropriate quarters), then at least with the actual text. That would be a blow struck for genuine devotion to learning!

If only he had the translation, and I the original . . . !

But there it was.

My decision made, I acted on it instantly. I instructed Mrs Craven not to bother me except in emergencies, selected those dictionaries I foresaw as being most useful and disposed them handily by my chair, and after locking my house-door and barring my windows to prevent interruption (owing to my problem with unpremeditated conversation I had never installed a telephone, so I was safe from that devilish form of distraction), with tremulous hands I opened the precious volume and applied myself doggedly to the elucidation of its mysteries.

Within at most an hour, as my practised brain gained the measure of the obscure and abbreviated writing, I made the acquaintance of the Elder Gods.

IV:
THE TIME OF TORMENT

No reference to those Beings was to be found in the preface, a passage clearly not belonging to the original work but an addition by the translator — composed, what is more, prior to the inception of his main undertaking. As I mentioned above, I had read portions before but with scant attention. Now I had to concentrate, for on the second page the text grew more turgid as the anonymous writer explained how he had been told of the importance of this book, how he had sought far and wide for a copy from which a version in Latin might be derived, how having achieved his goal he was settling down "early in the morning of St Priscus's Day in the year of Our Lord MCDXXXII" to his long-delayed task, trusting to Divine Providence to guide him where meanings were obscure — and, I may say, doing little to assist his readers to avoid the same problem, for he displayed all those irritating habits common to scribes of his generation, employing cryptic abridgments, running his **i**'s, **u**'s, **m**'s, **n**'s and even **o**'s into shark-tooth jags where sometimes only a bar above a doubled letter offered guidance to the intended word, plus such other tricks of the trade as sometimes deducting a numeral from the larger following it, sometimes presenting the larger first and adding the lesser behind. I pictured him as an old man, or maybe sick; at all events impatient, uncertain whether he would survive to his last page. (I noted that down for possible use in my commentary.)

In his preface he also explained the supposed authorship of the original — stating, with unexpected awareness of bibliographic niceties, that an Islamic invocation had been pasted into the front of his Arabic copy, warning that Alhazred had gone insane, so that the book would have been burned as diabolical had not its author been renowned for his early poems, of great delicacy and beauty, "wherefore it seemed amiss to the Moors that Satan be fancied to have claimed such a sweet singer." This enabled me, after delving into the *Encyclopedia of Moslem History,* to date his lost Arabic MS to a period of half a century between two outbreaks of intolerance and book-burning.

That remark was, by the by, accurate. It was not Satan who claimed the "sweet singer" — whoever or whatever did so . . .

But there would be time later to deal with the trimmings. My eyes raced over the last paragraph of the preface ("Ignoring the unbelievers' invocation to their false Lord and praying for their early gathering into the fold of the True and Triune God, I commit my mind and purpose to the will of heaven, *In Nomine . . .*" and so forth), and as I turned the page I made my first contact with that fearful, that abominable, that loathsomely obsessional history which tells of unspeakable horrors beside which the foulness of modern war, torture, concentration camps and whatever else anyone may care to name pales into insignificance. It was like being shown the interior of a madman's mind.

At first I did not realise what was happening to me. I mistook my almost hypnotic fascination with the subject for simple concentration, born of my determination to complete an English rendering ahead of Marsh. Little by little, though, I came to understand. Feverish, I stared at an obscure word and tried to deny to myself what I knew it must mean; I fought to distract my attention by searching for it in a dictionary where I knew it could not be found, hoping that afterward I might laugh at my own intensity, but in vain. Hour after hour leaked away. It grew dark, and I strove to prevent my hand from switching on the light that would enable me to continue — and failed, and saw those implacable lines stretching on for page after hateful page. . . . My eyes sought to roll upward in their sockets, to fasten on some object other than the book, and were no more successful than had been my hand in avoiding the lamp; at last my very brain felt as though it were curling up inside my skull to hide from the external world, and I lapsed into exhausted slumber across my table.

Even in sleep there was no surcease. Down the haunted corridors of memory they stalked me: sinister Nyarlathotep who had perambulated the temples of Egypt in a rictus of scorn for those bastard reconstructions of ancient deities whose forms surrounded his passage; revolting Cthulhu who bided his time in a sunken city so monstrous it alone was a fit frame for his appalling shape . . .

I woke moaning, and it was only midnight, and the lamp still shone, and I was afraid to go on sleeping. My glance fell on the page where I had broken off my reading, and a half-grasped phrase concerning one 'Astur (or Hastur, or "Xastur" as the scribe had here set down, employing by a *lapsus calami* the harsh aspirate of the Greek letter *chi* as the nearest counterpart to the Arabic sound) lured my terrified mind back to those scenes of fear and desolation where he had reigned . . . I could not stop. I read on, guessing *here* and failing despite my best efforts not to understand *there*. . . .

And when I had, absolutely had, to close my sore eyes again, although dawn was painting the windows red, I happened to glance at the remaining thickness of the book.

I had read barely a tenth of it!

Those nightmares! Within the day they had escaped from the zone of sleep which now I suspected I would never again dare to enter without some drug to blot my consciousness entirely out, and were assembling in the shadowed corners of the room to mock me in my waking state. I turned leaves randomly, noticing by chance that next beyond the folio I held open there was a page partly obliterated by that ink I have already referred to — and deluded myself for an instant with the hope that that might prove a barrier, break the train of thought I was embarked on — and found my hope hollow, for the context and the strong dark strokes of the original writing which showed through the futile overscores indicated what the meaning was, what it must be.

Haggard, worn-out, blear-eyed, head ringing, belly rumbling (in all the time I was riveted to the book I believe I ingested a little water and a spoonful of sugar that I did not taste), I followed the tale to its end. I learned of the tremendous conflict between the forces that reigned before man; I realised that our species had arisen on the planet when it was already the abandoned battle-ground of a struggle between more-than-titanic opponents, whose psychic forces drawn from the stars, and in particular from the evil (or delightful? I was too confused by then to draw a merely human distinction between the two) Hyades — where by a lake called Hali pitiful creatures, vulnerable as men, scuttled to hide from grasping tentacles — shattered the very boundaries of being, confounded the progress of evolution, diverted high intelligence into brute forms as soft as slime, grafted features both batrachian and saurian onto bodies that walked as upright as do we . . .

Some sort of portal, it appeared, had been barricaded between Earth and its sky. Barricaded only; it was still where it had been, and what closed it was capable of being eroded. Certain chinks had been created, by the application of those psychical forces which (as I now learned against my will) are stronger than the forces powering the stars, those that we poor fools of men believe to be the ultimate and seek to mimic with our puny H-bombs. Given that proper ceremonies were enacted (being an Arab, the author had not compared them to keys, but the translator had thought to do so), those chinks might be held open. Whereat what lay beyond would re-emerge.

There was mention also of a still more ancient power, that strove to counteract such work. But I could not imagine anything capable of overcoming Yog-Sothoth, and Shub-Niggurath, and . . .

Bright sunshine gleamed outside. It drove away the dreadful visions haunting me. Resolution hardened in my mind. If an archaic Latin translation could so affect myself, inoculated by long study against ancient superstitions, what might a version rendered directly from Arabic to English (and with the help of machinery, what's more!) not do to an ignorant and untrained mind? At any cost, Schultz and his professor must be prevented from fulfilling their intent. I could foresee horrors: mass insanity, an epidemic of suicide, worst of all a cult arising dedicated to the recall of the Elder Gods! We are, heaven knows, capable of all and any foolishness!

Rising, I caught sight of myself in a mirror. I was haggard and pale almost beyond recognition. With immense effort I forced myself to wash and shave and change my shirt, before returning to the library, if not to my duties there. Fortunately Mrs Craven was alone. At the sight of me she nearly dropped the books she was disposing on that anomaly, the over-size shelf. (I always detested that. It disturbs the tidy order of — but never mind.)

"Mr Wharton, you look ill!" she cried.

I admitted that I wasn't feeling myself, and added, "In fact I think it's time I took some leave."

Setting down the books, approaching with a look of sympathy, she said, "Haven't I told you before, and often? It can't be healthy for you never to take a holiday. Even at Christmas and New Year you never go away anywhere, do you?"

My excuses were obvious at once. I said dishonestly, "I should have listened to you before. Could you manage without me for a week or two?"

"Yes, of course!" — huffily.

"Very well, then. Where's that piece of paper Dr Schultz wrote his address on?"

"You're not thinking of going to America?" she breathed.

"That's exactly what I am thinking of."

"To look at these books he was talking about? Oh, dear! That'll be as bad as staying home! It won't be any sort of rest, will it?"

"It'll be a change," I retorted. (With Mrs Craven I seldom stammered, we having worked together for so long.) "And they say a change is as good as a rest. Where's that bit of paper?"

"Where you left it, on your desk."

So, with determination, I employed the detestable telephone, and caught Schultz in his hotel. After many false starts, avoiding words I knew to be tricky, I conveyed to him my change of mind.

"That's great!" he exclaimed, sounding as though he meant it. "We'll cover your expenses, naturally. How soon can you come over?"

"Well, I suppose I'll have to get a passport, and a visa as well, I believe, but I don't imagine that will take too long."

"Spring vacation doesn't end for another two weeks. If you can come over say a couple of days after the start of the new semester, that'll be fine. And by the way!"

"Yes?"

"I'm sorry about that joke I made, the one about Dunwich Hall. I didn't realise you'd been so close to the old guy. But you and old Marsh will get on swimmingly, I promise."

So he'd been making inquiries about me! Why?

But I controlled my voice with surprising ease. I said only, "Will you arrange for me to receive a formal invitation, including some assurance of reimbursement I can show my bank?"

"I'll get it faxed over right away," he promised.

"Excuse me — what did you say?"

It took a while to make him believe our library had no such facilities. He shrugged off the problem and suggested air express instead. I settled for that, and he rang off, leaving me in a state of total disbelief at what I had committed myself to — and more than a little scared.

But, I consoled myself, it was for a greater good.

V:
A WORLD OF ABOMINATIONS

I had been wrong to assume that a passport and visa could be obtained with promptitude. Bureaucracy delayed their issue for a good five weeks, during which time I was frequently incapable of discharging my regular duties. Luckily the arrival of summer entailed as usual a down-turn in demand for books while people turned to more sybaritic pastimes — among them "sunbathing," a custom dedicated in my view to the sole purpose of making normal human skin resemble the hue of a boiled lobster.

Not that, this year, I saw any of its victims. I spent every moment of spare time poring over more of my books.

Was that delay in issuance of my passport perhaps a blessing in disguise, after all? Certain it is that, had I been able to depart at once, though I would have done my utmost to dissuade Schultz and Marsh from their appalling scheme, I would not so completely have comprehended the menace that looms over us. I would still have been mercifully ignorant of the full range of abominations haunting the world: the creatures that assail the island of Ponape, after which the inhabitants pattern grotesque masks that reflect a mere fraction of their originals' repulsiveness; or those beings, partly human, partly of the race of toads, that live among and interbreed with isolated littoral communities, giving rise every so often to children possessed of powers passing the human, totally repugnant; or what may emerge at certain phases of the year from deep lost canyons underneath the sea, to claim unwitting sacrifice of man or beast. . . .

Compared to some of those I had first encountered, though, these later horrors seemed almost benign. When they came to me in dreams I bade them welcome, hoping they might distract me from Shub-Niggurath and Cthulhu.

Yet those ghastly monsters loomed ever shapeless in the distance, loomed like the aura of a rumoured plague. . . .

Over the yet further agonies inflicted on me once my passport and visa did at last arrive, I shall pass lightly. Let me no more than animadvert upon the aeons that I spent among folk more devoid of hope than even I, trapped in the uncertainty of an anteroom to Hell, awaiting with sad countenance and weary limbs the call that would release them from one captivity to another; the succeeding prison-close confinement that I feared would never end, or if it did would terminate in tragedy; the strange unwholesome food, the dark and bitter drink that were the common lot of all us pitiable souls — surely such torments could only be hatched amid the primal source of evil in whose nature I and I alone in modern times had been vouchsafed a glimpse!

Yet how could these sheep-like apologies for people be so dumbly unaware of the truth? Regardless of which way I looked, I detected symptoms of what I now recognised to be the archaic infection of humankind with non-humanity. That woman moving her neck sinuously, like a serpent; that fat child, broad-mouthed, slack-lipped, engulfing food like any frog or toad; that pot-bellied man shamelessly stripped to a singlet, marked with suggestive tattoos in blue and red that writhed with every movement of his biceps . . . !

In semi-darkness images of corruption danced before my eyes, a parade of seventy times seven deadly sins. I tried to drowse, if not to sleep, but had no surcease. Time stretched elastically, making each hour seem like two.

I wished I could pray, but knowing what I did I had dismissed all notions of a kindly god, and was afraid to make appeal to any other sort.

Or ashamed.

Then, at last, at what should have been five in the afternoon but, so declared our bright-faced jailers, was actually midday, the plane touched down at Logan Airport, Boston, USA.

So altered was my case that when Schultz spotted me amid a seething throng, reunited with my luggage but at a loss which way to turn, I positively welcomed him and even shook his hand.

"You look like death warmed over!" he exclaimed. "You must have had a Hell of a trip! Come on! My car is just across the way!"

I raised no objection, not even when he took my arm, not even when he started to address me as Jasper. I let him guide me to and into his car — small and cramped, unlike those that I (even I!) had seen portrayed by films, if not the television which I do not own — and drive me away to a destination that might as well have been in the middle of a jungle. It had crossed my mind to look up the New World Arkham in a gazetteer, but none of the atlases in the public library included it. Nor Dunwich, come to that. At least I had located Massachusetts, and knew I was already in it.

So, I assumed, the ride would be a short one. I had not bargained for the sheer size of this young country.

My impulse to respond politely to Schultz's garrulity fell foul first of a recurrence of my stammer, then of the overwhelming urgency of my mission, which I wished to complete with all possible dispatch, having already developed an extreme distaste for America. My impediment, however, prevented me from interrupting the tour-guide lecture he delivered as we followed a series of identical concrete roads aswarm and astink with such traffic as I had never seen (and in which I once more detected the force of evil at work). Before he finally broached the subject that had lured me here I had fallen prey to exhaustion, so that instead of impressing on him the need to abandon his and Marsh's project I yawned and yawned, and yawned again, in vast embarrassment.

"Sorry, Jasper!" he cried. "You go ahead and get some shuteye! I guess you must be pretty badly jetlagged!"

Miraculously, as though the images that had been haunting me had proved incapable of crossing the Atlantic, lulled by the susurrus of the engine and the wheels I fell into a dreamless sleep.

From which, all too soon, I was aroused. Yet it was as though I was continuing to sleep, despite my open eyes, my coherent answers to such questions as were put to me, my ability to register what room I'd been assigned to in the guest accommodation of the university whose name I'd first misheard as "Mixed Atomic." I even glimpsed some rather handsome buildings dating at a guess from the late eighteenth century. (My accommodation was not in any of them, alas, but an ugly modern abortion of concrete and glass.)

Moving like a somnambulist, I declined refreshment and the offer of an "evening" meal, and contrived to indicate how much I needed rest. Schultz took his leave with a final promise that penetrated the veil of my fatigue.

"I'll pick you up at seven, okay? We can have breakfast before going to the lab."

Lab? My sluggish mind interpreted: *laboratory.* But what could one of those ghastly places have to do with the study of ancient manuscripts . . . ?

Oh, yes: that was the sort of place where they kept computers.

"There'll be plenty of time to show off what we're doing before you meet old Marsh. He never turns up much before nine. See you in the morning — pleasant dreams!"

I almost screamed at him. How pleasant did he think the dreams could be of someone acquainted with Tsathoggua?

Still, I had slept relaxedly in the

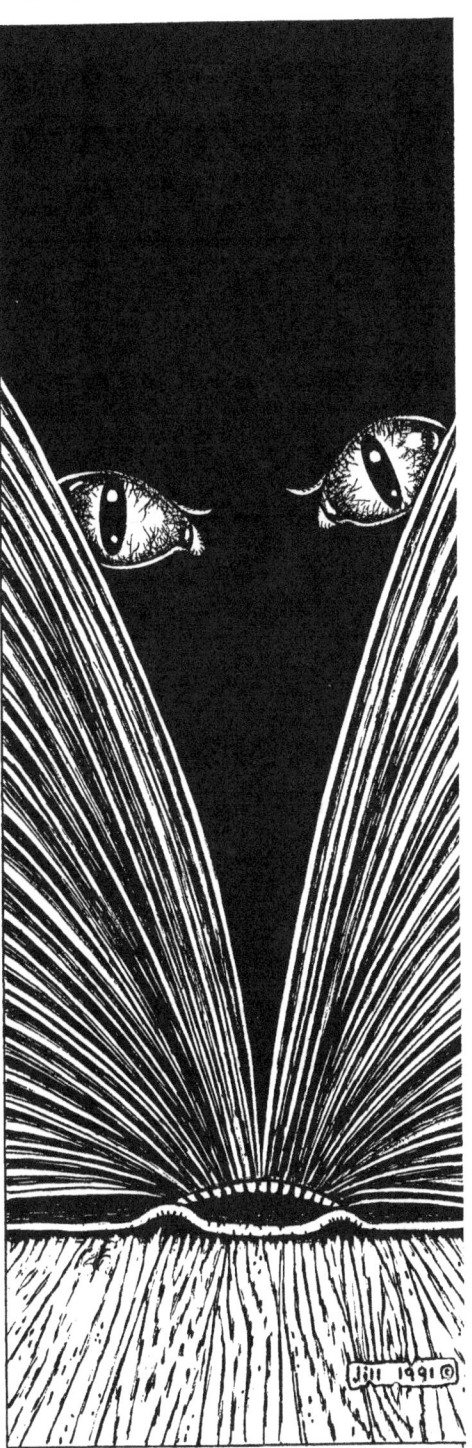

car. . . . Perhaps with an ocean between me and the revolting *Necronomicon* I might look forward to more blessed rest. I tumbled into bed with a degree of hope.

Blasted once more. As though a tentacle of thought had stretched immaterially from a place beyond our universe into my brain, when I awoke at three o'clock their time, a lazy eight by British, it was to hear a soundless sniggering voice:

"Ah, but all you have is a translation. Here they have the Arabic original."

I slept no more, and when Schultz called for me I was as haggard as I'd been the day before.

VI:
MY WORST FEARS CONFIRMED

A few nearly familiar items among what I was offered for breakfast — cereal, offensively sweet and drenched with "milk" that tasted as though it emanated from a factory and not a cow; coffee, dilute and lacking in aroma — restored a fraction of my spirits, though I was completely unable to match Schultz's effusive morning *bonhomie*. I had barely swallowed the last mouthful before he summoned me to his laboratory.

Apprehensive of imminent dyspepsia, I perforce obeyed.

Conceivably, had I not been exposed to awareness of the horrors that underlie the most idyllic scenes on Earth, I might have approved the surroundings in which I found myself, for — unlike my preconceived impression of American towns and universities — there was some sense of history, of continuity, about this Arkham, petty though a memorial boasting of events in 1812 might appear beside the timber frames of Dunwich Great Hall, erected in the fourteenth century. . . . Ah, but I'd seen those shrouded in ash, then sold for kindling-wood — "One with Nineveh and Tyre!"

And indeed the taste of ashes filled my mouth as we entered Schultz's laboratory, where two swarthy young men and an olive-skinned young woman (I guessed them to be Egyptians or Syrians) were busying themselves about luminous screens and humming cabinets. Here was a room from which all sense of the past had been excluded so completely that even the stench of its air made one feel queasy. This place was consecrated to the false gods of tomorrow — those of hope and progress, those of enterprise and understanding. How could anyone aware of Shub-Niggurath and Cthulhu, Yog-Sothoth and Tsathoggua, look on such empty dreams and be convinced? Sooner or later, inevitably, it would be the fate of places like this to be trampled into dust. What hollow aspirations, what sins of self-delusion, did they stand for!

Schultz immediately lapsed into jargon I found incomprehensible. His talk of "flops" and "mips" sounded like puerile gibberish. In vain I searched the screens, that displayed letters as well as numbers, for plain honest English. I found nothing but nonsensical abbreviations and ungrammatical incomplete sentences:

PROCESSING JOB #216 – SEARCH
UNSUCCESSFUL – ALLOT PRIORITY⤶
@p:X *vocab\sort – STALLED DUE UNDEFINED
PARAMETER «limit +» . . . ⤶

As someone spotted the last and, appearing to understand what it implied, pressed a key that started the machine working again, I found my voice and forced out, "But what exactly is it you are *doing*?"

As so often when I at last utter a question after being frustrated by my stammer, the words emerged shrilly, in a near-screech. All those present turned to stare at me — Schultz, discourteous as ever, had not troubled to make in-

troductions — exchanged glances and shrugs, and went back to what passed for their work.

Schultz said after a moment, "Ah, that's right. You don't even have fax at your library, so I guess you don't have computers, either."

His pitying tone made me feel like some kind of naked Kaffir, which I presume was the intention. Before I could bridle at the offence, though, he was talking again.

Slowly and more comprehensibly, thank goodness — though what he told me was the reverse of reassuring.

"These kids here are native-born Arabic speakers. I set them to producing a rough translation —"

My heart sank. I blurted, "*What of ?*"

"You mean I didn't tell you? I'm sure I did, back in Britain!" He stared at me blankly.

"Not . . ." I ventured faintly.

"Sure! The *Necronomicon,* what else? You were the only guy I ran across in the whole country who even seemed to know what I was talking about, so . . . Sorry anyway. But since we seem to have absolutely the only copy in the world — and since it is referred to in a good few other texts — it struck the prof and me as the obvious place to start. And on the basis of the rough draft . . ."

I lost the next couple of sentences, overwhelmed by the realisation that he was still unaware of the existence of my copy in Latin. When I heard clearly again, he was saying:

"Hey, Sayeed! Mind if I suspend the run on Two? Dr Wharton here — excuse me, Jasper! — *Mr* Wharton wants to see how the text is being processed."

"Sure, go ahead," said Sayeed, who was about twenty-five and handsome with a dark pencil moustache. At that age he was plainly the oldest of the three. The girl looked as if she might still be in her teens. What in the world could these *children* bring to the decipherment of so precious a bibliographic treasure?

I forced myself to go on listening.

Pressing keys, Schultz (he had told me to call him Hiram when he started addressing me as Jasper, but I was disinclined to comply) continued in the patient tone of one addressing a dullard.

"First, of course, we catalogued all the words in order of frequency of appearance. See?"

A vocabulary list sprang to the screen, Arabic on the right, on the left known and tentative equivalents. The first few score were so commonplace I asked why they were included.

"Oh, the incidence of use of conjunctions, common verbs and adjectives — that can help determine whether it's the work of a single author or whether it's been added to by other hands. . . . I'll skip this, and show you the list of words that don't appear anywhere else — no, hold that. You should see the anomalous frequencies first. Look how often the word 'horror' shows up, and 'evil,' and 'monster'!"

He turned his head and grinned, displaying massive white teeth.

"No wonder they said the old guy was nuts!"

"But . . . !"

The word emerged late, as a whisper. He had already dismissed that list in favour of another. I shook in my shoes as I saw, in a dozen variant spellings, Cthulhu, Hastur, Shub-Niggurath, Tsathoggua, Yog-Sothoth . . . !

Why are these people not aware of what they've stumbled on? Is it that their machines still insulate them? If so, what will happen when they find themselves reading a text superior to mine?

"These appear to be names," he went on didactically. "None of them are Arabic." (I wanted to correct him: he should have said "is" — but again it was too late.) "What we need to establish now is what language they were borrowed from. That's what Fatima is doing."

Overhearing her name, the girl turned and smiled. She was pretty in a dark-complexioned way, and it horrified me to think that someone so young and innocent had been assigned to delve into such arcane and dreadful matters. In that moment I could have strangled Schultz . . . but most of all I needed to sit down with him and his professor and reason with them, tell them why they absolutely must give up this perilous notion of making a cheap translation freely available to the public!

So I calmed myself as best I could. I even said, "Go on."

"Fascinating, isn't it?" he crowed. "So. . . . Ah, yeah. Fatima is running comparisons of the possible roots of these here names, using a data-base containing first of all the languages known to have donated a word or words to medieval Arabic."

I found my voice at last. I said, "I bet she hasn't made a single match."

Schultz straightened, beaming at me. "I *knew* it was a good idea to bring you over!" he declared. "Here you haven't been in the lab half an hour, and you have that much insight into the problem! You're right! We drew a blank with all the non-Arabic languages of North Africa and the Middle East, barring a few possible resemblances in Coptic."

He paused meaningly. More or less against my will, I said, "Surely those are more likely to be borrowings from the same common source."

"*Pree*-cisely the conclusion we already came to!" he said in delight. Glancing at his watch, he added, "The prof ought to be here soon. I look forward to seeing his face when I tell him what you just said. We need insights like yours to get this show really on the road."

Unscrambling his *argot* as best I could, I hazarded, "Am I to assume that so far you haven't translated the whole work?"

"Hell, no!" — with a rueful shrug. "We have a credible rendering of maybe a quarter, but a lot of that is still pretty tentative. That's why I appealed to you. Want to see how far we've got?"

I drew a deep breath. Did I . . . ? But though my palms were sweating and my heart was pounding, scholarly curiosity overcame my terror and I gave a nod.

Up on the screen came a complexly-annotated version of the first page. For an instant my heart leapt; I thought this was a completely different work, perhaps a forgery — but no. Subconsciously I'd been expecting to see what I had so often read and re-read, the introduction in my own copy. Instead, here was the Islamic invocation the translator had mentioned, in virtually the identical form. A horrifying thought: could these people be in possession of the actual copy he had worked from?

If so . . . !

Here "Satan" was rendered as "Shaitan," but that was the sole difference apart from phrasing. I began to shiver.

Over his shoulder Schultz said, "Be interesting to find some of Alhazred's juvenilia, hm? I've got Gamal looking into that" — with a jerk of his thumb at the so-far nameless third student. "No luck so far, but we live in hope."

My gorge rose. I tasted bile. The resources these — these *charlatans* disposed of, while I was compelled to eke money from my food-budget in order to buy stamped return envelopes for distant libraries!

The display changed again. In utter despair I read familiar meanings in unfamiliar form. My Latin version was, it seemed, at best fair. Its unknown author had missed subtleties and overtones in the original, so vivid even in this cold and passionless context that my skin crawled. When Schultz asked if I had seen enough I waved impatiently: go on, go on!

At last the screen blanked, and standing up, stretching his long arms — they struck me suddenly as ape-like, and

my nape prickled — he said, "That's as far as we've got. How does it grab you?"

I stared at him in disbelief.

"How can it not grab *you*?" I countered, borrowing his crude but graphic phrase. "Have you actually read this?"

"Sure! Lost count of how many times!"

"And you're not affected? You're not worried" — here at last I came to the purpose of my visit, so different from what he was blithely assuming — "about making this available in a cheap paperback?"

"Why should we be?" — dropping his arms again. "It is kind of esoteric, granted, but with the right promotion it might attract a cult following, sell maybe a hundred thousand, cover a good slice of our costs. Provided, of course, it takes off among the New Age people. The Dean wasn't too sold on the deal at first, but since Professor Marsh ran a snow-job past him he's gung-ho for the idea. Speak of the devil — ! Prof! You're early! Eager to meet this bright spark from Britain? I told you he'd turn up trumps, and he's already second-guessed us on at least two points!"

I turned very slowly to see whom he was addressing, and the moment I set eyes on Abner Marsh, I *knew*.

Knew why these people were untouched by the horrifying truths Alhazred had expressed.

Knew why they were so eager to mass-market them.

Knew why they wanted to trap me, the only person in the world who could have given them the lie direct. . . .

For this — this *thing* that lumbered into the laboratory was clad in scales! Stumping along, it slobbered from its loose-lipped mouth. Between crusted eyelids its evil gaze met mine. It offered what was not a human hand disguised in a cotton glove, its other hidden in the pocket of the jacket that it wore. Its voice was less than human, too: instead, a croak!

Yes, in that instant all was clear. I had had access to books these idiots did not — books which would have let them at any rate suspect the reason for this frightful plan to loose the Elder Gods upon the world. They did not know about the masks of Ponape — about the dwellers in the ocean deeps — about the doom upon the Tso-Tso of Tibet — most of all about the unholy liaisons between human and inhuman that had taken place here in this very state of Massachusetts since the arrival of the first settlers from Europe!

Here, plainly recognisable save to those whom it had duped, was just such a hybrid monster as would serve the purpose of the Elder Gods. Under its sway Schultz and his companions were engaged in opening not one path for their return but thousands, soon as a horde of pitiable fools laid hands upon their version of the *Necronomicon*! Most would fail in the enactment of its ceremonies, but here and there a gifted mind, perverted to the paths of evil, must of a certainty succeed . . . !

The doom that came to Sarnath would be as nothing to the horrors so vast a breach in our defensive barricade might let loose on the world!

I had to act! For the sake of humankind, of life on Earth, I had to act!

Casting around for a weapon, I found none — not a stick, not a paperknife, nothing. At least, though, I could smash and strangle with bare hands! I know nothing of computers, but it seemed plausible that if I slammed down all the keys on all the keyboards randomly that might disrupt their evil task. I did so, trusting that I could distract them while I poised to launch myself at the weakly-seeming entity who posed as Marsh. I flailed to right and left, heard cries of anger first, then gratifying terror, knew I had achieved the first part of my plan, and rushed at Marsh. Talon-curved, my

hands approached his throat —

Something hard and heavy struck my nape, just below the occiput. I had not even time to cry aloud before I fell.

VII:
THE TRIUMPH OF EVIL

"None so blind as those who will not see"? It's worse than that! None are so deaf as those who will not listen! They've spun me endless lies concerning Abner Marsh — used words like "ichthyosis" expecting them to baffle me. Me, who read fluently in Ancient Greek at ten? It implies skin growing scaly, like a fish's. I know that!

But when I ask them *why* a human being grows a scaly skin, they cannot answer. I tell them why, and they refuse to listen! The same when I ask why a biped should have eyes with crusted lids, a flattened nose, a wide slack mouth, stump legs and hands deformed so they must hide in gloves!

I know! I can tell them! I have told them, over and over! And such is the power of the hybrid servants of the Elder Gods, their ears are closed alike against my pleading and my reasoned arguments.

I wrote to Mrs Craven, who did not reply. No doubt they destroy my letters. I wrote to others, people who once respected me for my scholarship though I had never met them, and likewise had no answer, not a single one. I already told you how useless were my country's diplomatic representatives. . . .

I can feel a throbbing underground, that makes my prison tremble. My jailers attribute it to subway trains, but I sense it to be the working of a giant press, turning out copies by the countless thousands of the *Necronomicon*. Now I am no longer there to protect it, sooner or later Marsh and his victims will trace my Latin version and use it (better than computers!) to verify their text. Its translator, after all, was closer in time to Alhazred. . . .

All I can do, after so much struggle, is sit here and wait.

I pray occasionally to Nyarlathotep. At least he wears a quasi-human guise. . . .

Sometimes, especially at night, I hear faint words, not in any of the languages I've studied. Yet, thanks to my reading in the Peabody Bequest, I find I can make sense of certain phrases, and the sound of them strikes chill into my marrow. I hear eldritch voices moaning: "*Llllll-nglui, nnnn-lagl, fhtagn-ngah, ai Yog-Sothoth!*"

I know what it means! Yog-Sothoth is the Lurker at the Threshold! When fools broach the barrier He will be first to pass! But what I want to ask is a question none will answer:

Why me? Why me and no one else?

"Nyarlathotep, who bearest at least the guise of humankind: wilt Thou not answer — ?"

What a waste of breath! For this, above all, Alhazred taught about the Elder Gods:

They do not care, and that explains the universe. Ω

AMERIQUEST

There's a chalice blood red
In a white tower hid
Amid a forest of deep true blue.

Every summer we quest.
Somewhere far to the west
It waits (by definition
Just beyond the horizon).

So into the sunset
We ride.
We are not paladins.
All the white star-spangled knights are
  slain
And Camelot is fallen
    fallen
    fallen
Camelot is fallen
Only Alka-Seltzer remains.

We are therefore the RV pilgrims
Kneelers at sanitation stations
    Initiates
      To the mysteries:
The Paddlefish Capital,
The Jackalope Festival,
The Red River Valley Sesquicentennial.

We have long since accepted
That we will find
Only faint signs
A pebble red as wine
A white plastic cowboy
Blue Suede Shoes
On a tinny radio
All the long road home.

We cherish souvenirs.
They are for remembering
What hides.

We believe in the Grail
But this is the land
Where all heroes fail,
No blue is true.
Only Alka-Seltzer dares to promise
  rescue.

— **Nancy Springer**

WELCOMELAND

by Ramsey Campbell

Slade had been driving all day when he came to the road home. The sign isolated by the sullenly green landscape of overgrown canals and weedy fields had changed. Instead of the name of the town there was a yellow pointer, startlingly bright beneath the dull June sky, for the theme park. Presumably vandals had damaged it, for only the final syllables remained: . . . MELAND. He mightn't have another chance to see what he'd helped to build. He'd found nothing on his drive north that his clients might want to buy or invest in. He lifted his foot from the brake and let the car carry him onward.

Suppressed gleams darted through the clogged canals, across the cranium of the landscape. The sun was a ball of mist that kept failing to form in the sky. The railway blocked Slade's view as he approached the town. He caught himself expecting to see the town laid out below him, but of course he'd only ever seen it like that from the train. The railway was as deserted as the road had been for the last hour of his drive.

The road sloped toward the bridge under the railway, between banks so untended that weeds lashed the car. The mouth of the bridge had been made into a gateway: gates painted gold were folded back against the wall of the embankment. The shrill darkness in the middle of the tunnel was so thick that Slade reached to turn on his headlamps. Then the car left its echoes behind and showed him the town, and he couldn't help sighing. It looked as if the building of the park had got no further than the gates.

He'd bought shares in the project when his father had forwarded the prospectus, with Slade's new address scribbled across it so harshly that the envelope had been torn in several places. He'd hoped the park might revive his father and the town now that employment, like Slade, had moved down south. Now his father was dead, and the entrepreneur had gone bankrupt soon after the shares had been issued, and the main street was shabbier than ever: the pavements were turning green, the net curtains of the gardenless terraces were grey as old cobwebs, the displays in the shop windows that interrupted the ranks of cramped houses had been drained of colour. Slade had to assume this was early closing day, for he could see nobody at all.

The town hadn't looked so unwelcoming when he'd left, but he felt as if it had. Nevertheless he owed the place a visit, the one he should have made when his father was dying, if only Slade had known he was, if only they hadn't become estranged when Slade's mother had died . . . "If only" just about summed up the town, he thought bitterly as he drove to the hotel.

The squat black building was broad as four houses and four storeys high. He'd often sheltered under the iron and glass awning from the rain, but whatever the place had been called in those days, it wasn't the Old Hotel. The revolving doors stumbled round their track with a chorus of stifled moans and let him into the dark brown lobby, where the only illumination came from a large skylight over the stairs. The thin grey-haired young woman at the desk tapped her chin several times in the rhythm of some tune she must be hearing (dum-da-dum-da-dum-da-dum), squared a stack of papers, and then she looked toward him with a smile and a raising of eyebrows. "Hello, may I help you?"

"Sorry, yes, of course." Slade stepped forward to let her see him. "I'd like a room for the night."

"What would you like?"

"Pardon? Something at the top," Slade stammered, beginning to blush as he tried not to stare at her vacant eyes.

"I'm sure we can accommodate you."

He didn't doubt it, since the keyboard behind her was full. "I'll fill in one of your forms then, shall I?'

"Thank you, sir, that's fine."

There was a pad of them in front of her, but no pen. Slade uncapped his fountain pen and completed the top form, then pushed the pad between her hands as they groped over the counter. "Room twenty will be at the top, won't it?" he said, too loudly. "Could I have that one?"

"If there's anything else we can do to make you more at home, just let us know."

He assumed that meant yes. "I'll get the key, shall I?"

"Thank you very much," she said, and thumped a bell on the counter. Perhaps she'd misheard him, but the man who opened the door between the stairs and the desk seemed to have heard Slade clearly enough, for he only poked his dim face toward the lobby before closing the door again. Slade leaned across the desk, his cheeks stiff with blushing, and managed to hook the key with one finger, almost swaying against the receptionist as he lunged. Working all day in the indirect light hadn't done her complexion any good, to put it mildly, and now he saw that the papers she was fidgeting with were blank. "That's done it," he babbled, and scrambled toward the stairs.

The upper floors were lit only by windows. Murky sunlight was retreating over ranks of featureless white doors. If the hotel was conserving electricity, that didn't seem to augur well for the health of the town. All the same, when he stepped into the room that smelled of stale carpet and crossed to the window to let in some air, he had his first sight of the park.

A terrace led away from the main road some hundred yards from the hotel, and there the side streets ended. The railway enclosed a mile or more of bulky unfamiliar buildings, of which he could distinguish little more than that they bore names on their roofs. All the names were turned away from him, but this must be the park. It was full of people, grouped among the buildings, and the railway had been made into a ride; cars with grinning mouths were stranded in dips in the track.

Surely there weren't people in the cars. They must be dummies, stored up there out of the way. Their long grey hair flapped, their heads swayed unanimously in the wind. They seemed more lively than the waiting crowd, but just now that didn't concern him. He was willing the house where he'd spent the first half of his life to have survived the rebuilding.

As he turned from the window he saw the card above the bedside phone. DIAL 9 FOR PARK INFORMATION, it said. He dialled and waited as the room settled back into staleness. Eventually he demanded, "Park Information?"

"Hello, may I help you?"

The response was so immediate that the speaker must have been waiting silently for him. As he stiffened to fend of the unexpectedness the voice said, "May we ask how you heard of our attraction?"

"I bought some shares," Slade said, distracted by wondering where he knew the man's voice from. "I'm from here, actually. Wanted to do what I could for the old place."

"We all have to return to our roots. No profit in delaying."

"I wanted to ask about the park," Slade interrupted, resenting the way the voice had abandoned its official function. "Where does it end? What's still standing?"

"Less has changed than you might think."

"Would you know if Hope Street's still there?"

"Whatever people wanted most has been preserved, wherever they felt truly at home," the voice said, and even more maddeningly, "It's best if you go and look for yourself."

"When will the park be open?" Slade almost shouted.

"When you get there, never fear."

Slade gave up, and flung the receiver into the air, a theatrical gesture which made him blush furiously but which failed to silence the guilt the voice had awakened. He'd moved to London in order to live with the only woman he'd ever shared a bed with, and when they'd parted amicably less than a year later he had been unable to go home: his parents would have insisted that the breakup proved them right about her and the relationship. His father had blamed him for breaking his mother's heart, and the men hadn't spoken since her death. The way Slade's father had stared at him over her grave had withered Slade's feelings for good, but you prospered better without feelings, he'd often told himself. Now that he was home he felt compelled to make his peace with his memories.

He sent himself out of the room before his thoughts could weigh him down. The receptionist was fidgeting with her papers. As Slade stepped into the lobby the bellman's door opened, the shadowy face peered out and withdrew. Slade was at the revolving doors when the receptionist said "Hello, may I help you?" He struggled out through the doors, his face blazing.

The street was still deserted. The deadened sky appeared to hover just above the slate roofs like a ghost of the smoke of the derelict factories. Even his car looked abandoned, grey with the grime of his drive. It was the only car on the road.

Was the park somehow soundproofed so as not to annoy the residents? Even if the rides hadn't begun, surely he ought to be able to hear the crowd beyond the houses. He felt as if the entire town were holding its breath. As he hurried along the buckled mossy pavement, his footsteps sounded metallic, mechanical. He turned the curve that led the road to the town hall. Among the scrawny houses of the terrace opposite him, there was a lit shop.

It was the bakery, where his mother would buy cakes for the family each weekend. The taste of his favorite cake, sponge and cream and jam, filled his mouth at the thought. He could see the baker, looking older but not as old as Slade would have expected, serving a woman in the buttery light that seemed brighter than electricity, brighter than Slade had ever seen the shop before. The sight and the taste made him feel that if he opened the shop door he could step into memory, buy cakes as a homecoming surprise and walk home, back into the warmth of having tea beside the coal fire, the long quiet evenings with his parents when he had been growing up but hadn't yet outgrown them.

He wasn't entitled to imagine that, since he'd ensured it couldn't happen. His mouth went dry, the taste vanished. He passed the shop without crossing the road, averting his face lest the baker should call out to him. As he passed, the light went out. Perhaps it had been a ray of sunlight, though he could see no gap in the clouds.

Someone at the town hall should know if his home was intact. There must be people in the hall, for he could hear a muffled waltz. He went up the worn steps and between the pillars of the token portico. The double doors were too large for the building, which was about the size of the hotel, and seemed at first too heavy or too swollen for him to shift. Then the rusty handles yielded to his weight, and the doors shuddered inward. The lobby was unlit and deserted.

He could still hear the waltz. A track of grey daylight stretched ahead of him and showed him an architect's model on a table in the middle of the lobby. He followed his vague shadow over the wedge of lit carpet. The model had been vandalised, so thoroughly it was impossible to see what view of the town it represented. If it had shown streets as well as rides, there was no way of telling where either ended or began.

He made his way past the unattended information desk toward the music. A minute's stumbling along the dark corridor brought him to the ballroom. The only light beyond the dusty glass doors came from high transoms, but couples were waltzing on the bare floor to music that sounded oddly more distant than ever. In the dimness their faces were grey blotches. It must be some kind of old folks' treat, he reassured himself, for more than half of the dancers were bald. Loath to trouble them, he turned back toward the lobby.

The area outside the wedge of daylight was almost indistinguishably dim. He could just make out the side of the information desk that faced away from the public. Someone appeared to be crouched beside the chair behind the desk. If the figure had fallen there Slade ought to find out what was wrong, but the position of the figure was so dismayingly haphazard that he could only believe it was a dummy. The dancers were still whirling sluggishly, always in the same direction, as if they might never stop. He glanced about, craving reassurance, and caught sight of a sliver of light at the end of the corridor — the gap around a door.

It must lead to the park. He almost tripped on the carpet as he headed for the door. It was open because it had been vandalised: it was half off its hinges, and he had to strain to lift it clear of the rucked carpet. He thought of having to go back through the building, and heaved at the door so savagely that it ripped the sodden carpet. He squeezed through the gap, his face throbbing with embarrassment, and ran.

He was so anxious to be away from the damage he'd caused that at first he hardly observed where he was going. Nobody was about, that was the main thing. He'd run some hundred yards between the derelict houses before he wondered where the crowd he'd seen from the hotel might be. He halted clumsily and stared around him. He was already in the park.

It seemed they had tried to preserve as much of the town as they could. Clumps of three or four terraced houses had been left standing in no apparent pattern, with signs on their roofs. He still couldn't read the signs, even those that were facing him; they might have been vandalised — many of the windows were smashed — or left uncompleted. If it hadn't been for the roundabout he saw between the houses, he might not have realised he was in the park.

It wasn't the desolation that troubled him so much as the impression that the town was yet struggling to change, to live. If his home was involved in this transformation, he wasn't sure that he wanted to see, but he didn't think he could leave without seeing. He made his way over the rubble between two blocks of houses.

The sky was darker than it had been when he'd entered the town hall. The gathering twilight slowed him down, and so did sights in the park. Two supine poles, each with a huge red smiling mouth at one end, might have been intended to support a screen, and perhaps the section of a helter-skelter choked with mud was all that had been delivered, though it seemed to corkscrew straight down into the earth. He wondered if any ride except the roundabout had been completed, and then he realised with a jerk of the heart that he had been passing the sideshows for minutes. They were in the houses, and so was the crowd.

At least, he assumed those were players seated around a Bingo counter inside the section of the terrace ahead, though the figures in the dimness were so still he couldn't be certain. He preferred to sidle past rather than go closer to look. The roundabout was behind him now, and he thought he saw a relatively clear path toward where his old house should be. But the sight of the dungeon inside the next jagged fragment of terrace froze him.

It wasn't just a dungeon, it was a torture chamber. Half-naked dummies were chained to the walls. Signs hung around their necks: one was a RAPIST, another a CHILD MOLESTER. A woman with curlers like worms in her hair was prodding one dummy's armpit with a red-hot poker, a man in a cloth cap was wrenching out his victim's teeth. All the figures, not just the victims, were absolutely motionless. If this was someone's idea of waxworks, Slade didn't see the point. He had been staring so hard and so long that the figures appeared to be staggering, unable to hold their poses, when he heard something come to life behind him.

He felt as if the dimness in which his feet were sunk had become mud. Even if the sounds hadn't been so large he would have preferred not to see what was making them, wheezing feebly and scraping and thudding like a giant heart straining to revive. He forced his head to turn, his neck creaking, but at first he could see only how dark the place had grown while he had been preoccupied with the dungeon. He glimpsed movement as large as a house between the smudged outlines of the buildings, and shrank into himself. But it was only the roundabout, plodding in the dark.

He couldn't quite laugh at his dread. The horses were moving as if they could hardly raise themselves and yearned to fall more quickly and finally than they could. There were figures on their backs, and now he realised he had glimpsed the figures earlier, in which case they must have been sitting immobile: waiting for the dark? They weren't going anywhere, they were no threat to him, he could look away and make for the house — but when he did he recoiled, so violently he almost fell. The torturers in the dungeon were stirring. They were turning their heads toward him.

He couldn't see much of their faces, and that didn't seem to be only the fault of the dark. He began to sink into a crouch as if they mightn't see him, he was close to squeezing his eyes shut as though that would make him invisible, the way he'd believed it would when he was a child. Then he flung himself aside, out of range of any eyes that might be searching for him, and fled.

Though the night was thickening, he could see more than he wanted to see. One block of unlit houses had been turned into a shooting gallery, although at first he didn't realise that the six disembodied heads nodding forward in unison were meant to be targets. They must be, not least because all six had the same face — a face he knew from somewhere. He stumbled past the heads as the six of them leaned toward him out of the dark beyond the figures that were aiming at them. He felt as if the staring heads were pleading with him to intervene. He was so desperate to outdistance his clinging dismay that he almost fell into the canal.

He hadn't noticed it at first because a section had been walled in to make a tunnel. It must be a Tunnel of Love: a gondola was inching its way out of the weedy mouth, bringing a sound of

choked slopping and a smell of un-healthy growth. Slade could just distin-guish the heads of the couple in the gondola. They looked as if they hadn't seen daylight for years.

He swallowed a shriek and retreated alongside the canal, toward the main road. As he slithered along the over-grown stony margin, flailing his arms to keep his balance, he remembered where he'd seen the face on the targets: in a photograph. It was the entrepreneur's face. The man had died of a heart attack soon after he'd gone bankrupt, and hadn't he gone bankrupt shortly after persuading the townsfolk to invest whatever money they had? Slade began to mutter desperately, apologising for whatever he might have helped to cause if it had harmed the town, if anyone who might be listening resented it. He'd only been trying to do his best for the town, he was sorry if it had gone wrong. He was still apologising breathlessly as he sprawled up a heap of debris and onto the bridge that carried the main road over the canal.

He fled along the unlit road, past the town hall and the sound of the relentless waltz in the dark. The aproned baker was serving at his counter, performing the same movements for almost cer-tainly the same customer, and Slade felt as though that was his fault somehow, as though he ought to have accepted the offer of light. He mustn't confuse him-self with that, he must get to his car and drive, anywhere so long as it was out of this place. It occurred to him that anyone who could leave the town had done so — and then, as he came in sight of his car, he thought of the blind woman in the hotel.

He mustn't leave her. She mustn't be aware of what had happened to the town, whatever that was. She hadn't even switched on the lights of the hotel. He shoved desperately at the revolving doors, which felt crusty and brittle under his hands, and staggered into the lobby. He grabbed the edges of the doorway to steady himself while his eyes adjusted to the murk that swarmed like darkness giving birth. The receptionist was at her desk, tapping her chin in the rhythm of the melody inside her head. She shuffled papers and glanced up. "Hello, may I help you?"

"No, I want —" Slade called across the lobby, and faltered as his voice came flatly back to him.

"What would you like?"

He was afraid to go closer. He'd remembered the bellman, who must be waiting to open the door beside the desk and who might even come out now that it was dark. That wasn't why Slade couldn't speak, however. He'd realised that the echo of his voice sounded disconcertingly like the voice on the hotel phone. "I'm sure we can accommo-date you," the receptionist said.

She was only trying to welcome a guest, Slade reassured himself. He was still trying to urge himself forward when she said "Thank you, sir, that's fine."

She must be on the phone, otherwise she wouldn't be saying "If there's any-thing else we can do to make you more at home, just let us know." Now she would put down the phone Slade couldn't see, and he would go to her, now that she'd said "Thank you very much" — and then she thumped the bell on the counter.

Slade fought his way out of the rusty trap of the revolving doors as the bell-man poked his glimmering face into the lobby. The receptionist was only as sightless as the rest of the townsfolk, he thought like a scream of hysterical laughter. He'd realised something else: the tune she was tapping. Dum, dum-da-dum, dum-da-dum-da-dum-da-dum. It was Chopin: the Dead March.

He dragged his keys out of his pocket, ripping stitches loose, as he ran to his car. The key wouldn't fit the lock. Of course it would — he was inserting it somehow the wrong way. It crunched into the slot, which sounded rusty, just as he realised why the angle was wrong. Both tyres on that side of the car were flat. The wheels were resting on their metal rims.

He didn't need the car, he could run. Surely the townsfolk couldn't move very fast or, to judge by his observations, very far. He fled to the tunnel that led under the railway. But even if he made himself venture through the shrilly whispering dark in there to the gates, it would be no use. The gates were shut, and several bars thicker than his arm had slid across them into sockets in the wall.

He turned away as if he was falling, as if the pressure of the scream he was suppressing was starving his brain. The road was still deserted. The only other way out of the town was at the far end. He ran, his lungs rusty and aching, past houses where families appeared to be dining in the dark, past the town hall with its smothered waltz, over the bridge toward which a gondola was floundering, bearing a couple whose heads lolled apart from each other and then knocked their mouths together with a hollow bony sound. The curve of the road cut off his view of the far side of town until he was almost there. The last of the houses came in sight, and he tried to tell himself that it was only darkness that blocked the road. But it was solid, and high as the roofs.

Whether it was a pile of rubble or an imperfectly built wall, it was certainly too dangerous to climb. Slade turned away, feeling steeped in despair thick as pitch, and saw his house.

Was it his panic that made it appear to glow faintly in the midst of the terrace? Otherwise it looked exactly like its neighbours, a bedroom window above a curtained parlour beside a nondescript front door with a narrow fanlight. He didn't care how he was able to see it, he was too grateful that he was. As he fled toward it he had the sudden notion that

his father might have changed the lock since Slade had left, that Slade's key would no longer let him in.

The lock yielded easily. The door opened wide and showed him the dark hall, which led past the stairs to the parlour on the left, the kitchen at the back. The house felt more familiar than anything else in the world, and it was the only refuge available to him, yet he was afraid to step forward. He was afraid his parents might be there, compulsively repeating some everyday task, blind to him and the state of themselves — though if that was left of them could be aware of him, that might be even worse.

Then he thought he heard movement in the street, and he stumbled to the parlour door and pushed it open. The parlour was deserted, the couch and chairs were as grey as the hearth they faced, yet the stagnant dimness seemed tense, poised to reveal that the room wasn't empty after all. The kitchen with its wooden chairs that pressed against the bare table between the oven and the sink seemed breathless with imminence too, but he was almost sure that he heard movement, slow and stealthy, somewhere outside the house. He scrambled back to the front door and closed it as silently as he could, then he groped his way upstairs.

The bathroom window was a dull rectangle which gleamed faintly in the mirror like a lid that was opening. The bath looked as if it were brimming with tar. Even that was less dismaying than his parents' bedroom: suppose he found them in the bed, struggling to make love like fleshless puppets? He felt as if he were shrinking, reverting to the age he'd been when his father had shouted at him not to open their door. His hands fluttered at it now and inched it far enough to show him their empty bed, and then he dodged into his room.

His bed was still there, his chest of drawers, his wardrobe hardly wide enough for him to hide in any longer. He shouldered the door of the room closed tight and huddled against it. He felt suddenly as though if he went to the bed he might awaken and discover he had been dreaming of the town, just a nightmare about growing up. He mustn't take refuge in the bed, it would be too like retreating into his childhood — and then he realised he already had.

He'd been left alone in the house just once when he was a child. He'd awakened and blundered through the empty rooms, every one of which seemed to be concealing some terror that was about to show itself. He remembered how that had felt: exactly as the house felt now. He'd retraced the memory without realising. Then a neighbour who'd been meant to keep an eye on him had looked in to reassure him, but he prayed that wouldn't happen now, that nobody would come to keep him company. Surely his house couldn't be where they felt most at home.

"Never fear," the voice on the phone had advised him — but Slade had. The night couldn't last forever, he told himself desperately, pressing himself against the door. The sun would rise, the bars would slide back to let the gates open, and even if they didn't he would be able to see a way out. But he felt as if there was nowhere to go: he couldn't recall the faces of his colleagues, the name of the London firm, even the name of the street where he lived. He didn't need to remember those now, he needed only to stay awake until dawn. Surely the rest of the town was too busy to welcome him home, unless it was his fear that was bringing the movement he could hear in the street. It sounded like a wordless crowd which could barely walk but which was determined to try. They couldn't move fast, he thought like a last prayer, they would have to stop when the sun came up — but clearer than that was the though of how endless the night could seem when you were a child. Ω

STATEMENT OF OWNERSHIP, MANAGEMENT, & CIRCULATION, AS REQUIRED BY 39 U.S.C. 3685)
TITLE OF PUBLICATIONS: *WEIRD TALES*®. Publication Number: 0985703. Date of filing: 1 October 1991. Frequency of issue: Quarterly. Number of issues published annually: 4. Annual subscription rate: $16.00 [in the United States & its possessions].

Complete mailing address of Known Office of Publication, & of the Headquarters of General Business Offices of the Publisher: both at 4426 Larchwood Ave., Philadelphia [city], Philadelphia [county], PA 19104-3916 (P.O. Box 13418, Philadelphia PA 19101-3418.) Full & complete mailing address of Publisher is George H. Scithers, P.O. Box 13418, Philadelphia PA 19101-3418; of Editor: Darrell Schweitzer, P.O. Box 13418, Philadelphia PA 19101-3418; of Managing Editor: Carol Adams, P.O. Box 13418, Philadelphia PA 19101-3418.

Owner: Terminus Publishing Company, Incorporated, P.O. Box 13418, Philadelphia PA 19101-3418. Names & addresses of *all* stockholders: George H. Scithers, 4416 Larchwood Ave., Philadelphia PA 19104-3916. Mary Betancourt, 410 Chester Ave., Moorestown NJ 08057. Leslie Smith, 1209 Miller Ave., Ann Arbor MI 48103. David J. Williams III, 5079 Blacksmith Dr., Columbia MD 21044. Darrell Schweitzer, 113 Deepdale Rd., Strafford PA 19087. Yake F. Edeiken, 137 North 5th St., Allentown PA 18101. There are *no* Bondholders, Mortages, or Other Security Holders. This is not a Non-Profit Organization authorized to mail at special rates.

Extent & nature of circulation:
Average number of copies during the preceding 12 months: A. Total number of copies, 11,507. B. Paid &/or requested circulation. (1) Sales through dealers & carriers, street vendors, & counter sales, 4,071. Mail distribution (paid &/or requested), 4,090. c. Total paid &/or requested circulation, 8,161. D. Free distribution by mail carrier or other means, samples, complimentary, & other free copies, 47. Total distribution, 8,208. F. Copies not distributed. (1) Office use, left over, unaccounted, spoiled after printing, 2,682. (2) Returns from news agents, 617. G. Total (sum of E, F (1), & F (2)), 11,507.

Actual number of copies of single issue published nearest to filing date: A. Total number of copies, 10,666. B. Paid &/or requested circulation. (1) Sales through dealers & carriers, street vendors, & counter sales, 3,973. Mail distribution (paid &/or requested), 3,222. c. Total paid &/or requested circulation, 7,195. D. Free distribution by mail carrier or other means, samples, complimentary, & other free copies, 51. Total distribution, 7,246. F. Copies not distributed. (1) Office use, left over, unaccounted, spoiled after printing, 2,694. (2) Returns from news agents, 726. G. Total (sum of E, F (1), & F (2)), 10,666.

I certify that the statements made by me are correct & complete: George H. Scithers, Publisher

ALFRED VALE: A Cautionary Tale

Exposition

Young Alfred was a bright boy, as everyone concurred.
He could name the garden flowers and explain a puzzling word,
He could mend a fuse and polish his shoes and cook a simple meal,
And his tolerant dad occasion'ly had let him hold the steering-wheel.
But when he had to sit exams it was a different tale.
He never did his homework . . . so they called him Fail, not Vale!

Each night he vanished to his room and promised faithfully
That two full hours he would invest in maths and history.
He would open a book, and give it a look . . . and instantly grow bored,
And reach instead beneath his bed for figures, dice, and board.
He'd dream away his evenings on a nonexistent quest
Across a dragon-haunted land for ladies sore distressed.

One night as he was playing his game, his parents watching telly,
He felt a presence in his room, and ice-cubes in his belly.
When he glanced around to his shock he found a boy who was like his twin,
Wearing furs and hide, with a sword beside, and a scowl that was turning a grin.
"I'm here!" he cried. "I'd have come before, except that I always shirked
My studies . . . Still, no matter now. My latest spell has *worked!*

"I've escaped the world where monsters roam and wizards fight magicians,
Where you have to memorise foul grimoires to protect your acquisitions,
Where dwarfs kick shins and priests teach sins and gold coins shift to lead.
Here on this plane things are stable and sane — you have books that can simply be
  read!"
He went on like that till with delight his beardless cheeks were glistening,
But Alfred Vale, that foolish youth — he was no longer listening.

"I'll take your place!" he said with force. "I hate this world of mine —
I'd rather battle ogre hordes and drink enchanted wine.
To find them real has much appeal, far better than a game!
I'll swap at once, for I'm no dunce . . . By the way, what's your name?"
"Prince Bitterblade!" — "That's triff! I like! So now how do we do it?"
"Change clothes! And names!" — "Okay by me!" — That said, before he knew it . . .

He stood upon a misty street, with cobbles underfoot,
Saw bats, heard fighting from an inn, the twanging of a lute.
As soon as seen: "A place, I ween, where magic is abroad!
I Bitterblade am not afraid!" But, skill-less with a sword,
Knowing no charms such as most folk here recited out of habit,
He was promptly killed by a dragoncel no larger than a rabbit.

ALFRED VALE: A Cautionary Tale

Envoi

Prince, who changed places with sad Alfred Vale,
   Report holds, since you ploughed his next exam,
You crave return — of course, to no avail —
   For now you're loading dustcarts in East Ham.

Moral

Even magicians need to do their homework.

                    — **John Brunner and H*la*re B*ll*c**

BEWITCHING LESSONS

Two novice witches
Seek to practice at night,
Learning their spells
By candlelight.

They've learned their curses,
And their charms and all of the hexes —
But caution is the watchword;
Details never to be neglected.

A smile lights one's face
As she starts her incantation:
From a flame upon the floor
Begins the abomination.

Steadily it grows,
Until it fills the room:
A monstrous face with dripping teeth,
Red as a rose in bloom.

But no flower this!
Its stench is near o'erpowering.
But her pride is short-lived:
She has forgotten something!

One single passage,
The cause of her remorse:
"Should there be no victim named,
The fiend shall seek its source."

She has only a moment
To scold herself, though:
Red flash — and she is gone —
To serve someone Below.

One lonely novice witch
Seeks to practice at night,
Nervously learning spells
By candlelight.

                    — **Lynne Armstrong-Jones**

CONTINUING SAGA

Our hero, barbaric and grim,
   slays wizards and trolls to keep trim,
      and wades through the gore
       of dragons galore —
Already I've started to skim.

                    —**Darrell Schweitzer**

THE LILY GARDEN

by Tanith Lee

There is a wisdom to youth which later gives way to a different wisdom, of age. To have one usually precludes the other. Both are valid, and both, in their manner, sad.

When Camillo was young, and a student at the great university of Ravenal, he took a room which overlooked, as it happened none of the other apartments in that building did, an ancient garden belonging to an impressive but ruinous house of very ill-repute. I do not mean it was a brothel, nothing so simple. No, a magician was said to live there, whose name was known but seldom spoken. For general purposes he was called The Alchemist, and his dwelling The Alchemist's House.

At first Camillo was only interested in the garden, which was overgrown by oaks, ilex and a great pine, because it represented to his imagination, straying from his books, a wild forest. Late at night, when he had blown out his candle, he would stare upon the moon caught fast in the pine tree. If a dog howled from some neighbouring tenement, he would think of wolves treading the trackless undergrowth beneath the high wall. Sometimes strange sounds came from the garden itself. Doubtless owls, bats, rats, and hedgehogs caused them, but to Camillo, who had never left the city, they were the noises of a wilderness. He liked the garden very much, and if he had been four years younger, he would have found a way at once to get over into it. But now he was a student, a young man. Already responsibility had laid hold of him.

The Alchemist was reportedly never seen. But he had an elderly servant. One day Camillo saw this servant on the street leading from the marketplace, and recognized him from description. Accordingly he followed the servant, discreetly, and not unaptly, since he himself lived close by, back to the House. Sure enough the servant came to the building, but ignoring the great door fronting the street, went around to a smaller door set into the garden wall. This he managed with a key. As the door opened, Camillo was afforded a tantalising glimpse into the garden's forest: Vast trees of darkest green and coppery black, some rotted statuary.

Thereafter Camillo, when free from his studies, would loiter between the market and The Alchemist's House — there was a convenient inn.

Came an afternoon when the elderly servant, returning, dropped in the street a great package of some unguessable nature. Camillo hastened to his side. "Good sir, pray let me assist you."

"That is very kind," said the old servant, who was hunched in the back. Camillo retrieved the package — which felt pliable in a most unpleasant way, perhaps being a portion of a body purchased from some graveyard dealer for alchemical experiment.

They came to the door in the wall.

"Allow me to carry this inside for you."

"Alas, young sir, I must return a churlish response to your courtesy. My master — you may have heard of him —" and here the servant spoke the forbidden name — "does not permit any but myself to enter here."

"At least let me bear your burden up on to that terrace there. Who will know?"

"My master," replied the servant simply. He spoke without fear, but it was the fearlessness of one who needs not fear as never does he trespass.

So Camillo was once again shut out.

By now, of course, he was mad as the snake to enter the garden. On this occasion he had seen the terrace, mossy steps, a fountain of naked nymphs — and all about this clearing the enormous ravenous trees.

Someday I shall make myself rich. Such a garden, such land will be mine.

But he knew even then in his heart that these riches were unlikely, and here he was quite right.

Camillo began to brood on how he could get into the garden of The Alchemist.

He was not afraid of The Alchemist, this being an aspect of the wisdom of his youth. Yet also it was a figment of the *unworldliness* of his youth. There might have been much to tremble at. But Camillo discounted the dread name. He troubled only not to fall foul of the city's laws regarding property. And this meant that he must find a way to open the garden door by stealth, unseen, unknown, and doubtless by night.

Camillo therefore contrived to steal the key of the elderly servant. He did this by distracting the fellow at the wall with the gift of a pomegranate — a wicked deception, for the old man's eyes actually filled with tears at the supposed gift. The key was then removed from the door by Camillo, the old man ushered inside, already forgetting he had not retrieved it.

Camillo then took himself to a place where keys were copied, and had this service done for him.

Returning at dusk he cast up the original over the wall so it should land on the grass beyond — he had prudently locked up behind the servant — as if it had been dropped there.

Thereafter Camillo impatiently waited for one whole night and one whole day before daring his enterprise of invasion.

It was true that now and then a few dim lights might burn high up in The Alchemist's House, and on this night too they did so. Only when the last light, a very high and dim one in a narrow tower, was put out, did Camillo creep down through the lodgings and cross the street to the garden wall. It was by now three in the morning and from the old cathedral the wonderful clock with its figures of knights and maidens, imps and angels, was striking the dull dark hour. Camillo was not sleepy, he was wide awake, alert wit a light supper and a little wine. And with his fiendish curiosity, his actual *lust* to enter.

The key proved difficult. It had not been very well made, or else some extra bar was on the door. If so, ultimately it failed, and Camillo finally pushed wide the barrier, closed it soundlessly, and was alone in the moonlit garden of the magician.

The trees towered like steeples, and the house was all but lost in them, and anyway silent as death itself. But the terrace glowed under the moon, and the fountain of the nymphs with their grey-green night girdles of ivy.

Camillo crossed the terrace with caution, keeping to its shadow side. Something squeaked in the undergrowth, and Camillo did cross himself. But there again, though this was the wisdom of youth it was also a foolishness, for if any demons had been left on guard, what use that single lapsed gesture of a strong young mortal hand?

Then, besides, he jibed at himself. Only some little hog of the shrubberies was passing. And lo and behold up in the tall pine had begun to sing a golden nightingale. She was pleased to have a visitor, he had not heard her previously.

The garden had a night scent on it, but also now the perfume of flowers.

When he descended from the terrace, he found a new wall of yew, and in the wall presently an arch. Beyond lay a formal garden, as unlike the wild of the outer place as could be. It was a bower of flowers, of every sort of night-blooming lily known on earth, and perhaps the lilies too of Mercury and Venus and Saturn, so strange and fragrant was the odour of them.

In the middle of the inner garden was a patch of turf, with a sun dial, now a dial of the moon, and beyond this, under an awning of lilies, all of which were opened wide, sat a figure. Was it a statue — that of a young girl deftly tinted by paint, a faint rosiness to the lips discernible even in moonlight, a darkness to brows and lashes, and on the long and flowing locks, part plaited and part free, the faintest blondest hint of a colour almost pink? The robe of the being was fashioned like a dress, which gave proper evidence of all the feminine sweetness, yet slender and virginal. And indeed the robe flowed like the hair, down over the ground, decorously. The face was young and pure — Camillo thought — as that of an especially beautiful Madonna in the church.

Camillo stared some while, from behind the curtain of the yew hedge. He stared long enough that he expected no change, had come to the complete conclusion that the image was indeed a statue — when it moved. It moved actually very little. It raised one hand, and touched a lock of its own hair — no more, you might say, than the stirring of a petal. But Camillo jumped in his skin.

It must be remarked, there was something to the beautiful girl that was supernatural. Or so it seemed. After all, Camillo must have succumbed, in some form, to the idea of The Alchemist's House. He remembered now strange tales, most of them from books. The wizard in his tower. And in the bower, stolen forth by night, his daughter, or some princess in his thrall, who held the secrets of her slave-master's power.

Now, what should he do? In the story the hero stepped forth to confront the fair damsel. They were at once in love and in league. Camillo was not ready for either state. He therefore quickly, quietly, and, in later years he admitted,

most cowardly, stepped away instead.

Camillo left the lily plot, hurried over the terrace, and let himself out into the street. Here he locked up the door of the whole garden again.

No sooner was he back safe in his room across the street than a band of drunken carousers went down the way below, as if he and The Alchemist's House were of no import. *Let that be a lesson,* he thought. For the idea that all over the wall was not worldly had fastened on him. His was this world, of stones, and drunks, ink and paper, bread and warts and human things.

Thereby he sealed himself to the lily garden of the magician as Eve did to the Apple Tree when first warned it was not for her.

Some days and nights then passed, and Camillo did not think of the garden. That is, he would not allow thoughts of the garden to remain. But thoughts of the girl did stick to him. What had she been? What? And some book-memory of a life-size doll, or statue enabled by magic to move, began slowly and insidiously to obsess him.

It was no use. He must return, and look for her, and see of what sort she was.

Probably, thought he, some pretty servant of the house, perhaps the magician's secret mistress, who mooned herself by night for fear of the prying eyes of day.

So Camillo took the key from where he had hidden it from himself, which was up the chimney, and on a night of no moon at all he went down, a little cool and unsettled, hearing the cathedral clock strike only for two, but all the lights out, as it seemed not only in the two houses, but everywhere in the city.

Oh, it was like a night of the dead. Such utter blackness. And Camillo commended his own bravery, and opened the door to the forbidden garden.

The key went more easily on this

occasion, as if now it were familiar with the lock.

Beyond was a darkness that might have been black space itself, if space were filled by leaves, and spotted only here and there with the blue-white specks of stars. Nor did the nightingale sing. Nor did anything squeak in the undergrowth. The garden too had been put to bed.

But Camillo resolutely crossed the sombre terrace, glad of its concealment and uneasy at it, and came down on the black prickles of the yew hedge.

In the faint starlight, scent alone might have guided him. How glorious, how overwhelming, how almost rotten the exquisite perfumes of the lilies were. They were like a fermenting wine no mortal would dare drink — nectar.

And there among the pale forms of the flowers, the pale shape of the sun dial. And there, in her arbour, as before, *the girl*.

He saw her lighted as if by holy rays and almost cried out. Until it came to him that a little lamp was burning on a hook in the arbour wall just behind her head. And by this glimmer, she was sewing a piece of white cloth with purple and rose and red. He caught the flash of her needle. It was so ordinary — a thing he had seen women at since he could recall — and yet, how strange.

And then, she looked, it seemed, straight at him. The look, although not she herself, said: *I know you are there. Come forth, or do you wish to frighten me?*

No! Never, thought Camillo, and got into the archway as fast as he might, for he was afraid in that moment she might scream and summon what help he could only guess at.

She must indeed have seen or sensed him, for now she did not start. Her large eyes, blue-grey as irises, gazed up at him.

"You must pardon me," said Camillo. But she was young too, it would be best to try her mercy. "I should not be here.

But — curiosity. I saw you once before. Forgive me if I offend."

"No," said the girl, "you do not offend."

Her voice was very strange. It was as if she seldom used it, husky, dusky, a whisper, a shadow. But then she said, "How did you come in?"

"Oh, I have a key to the door." This bluff pleased him. If he had a key, as a visitor he was legitimate. But then, she did not seem to mind that he was here by night.

"Do you seek him?" she asked simply.

"Your — The Alchemist?"

"My master," she said.

A slave then, a *slave*. Just like the fearful, foolish, and fascinating books.

"I would not dare," confided Camillo. And thought himself a fine fellow, fit enough to dazzle her, and so perhaps he was. "I came here for another glimpse of you."

"Well you have it now."

"So I do." Camillo was at a loss. Honesty was a new game. He said finally, "But why are you out here in the garden by night? Does he allow you no freedom by day?"

"I am always free," she said. "At any hour after dusk you may seek me here. But," she hesitated, she was modest, "by day I sleep."

"I must change my habits," said Camillo.

"But you too are awake by night. And I have heard others in the streets. And there is a great clock. He told me of it. It wakes all night and strikes the hours."

"But the clock is not alive."

"But it has men and angels on it."

"They are clockwork" said Camillo. A shiver of cold ran down his back. He thought, *Truly, like knows like. She is The Alchemist's doll.*

Just then a moon rose up in a tree. It was arched in shape and high up it had a pane of ochre glass: A window come alight.

The girl looked away at it. "He has woken too," she said.

Camillo said passionately, "If he finds me, he may punish me. I must leave you at once."

She seemed dismayed. He was pulled back and forth between panic and pleasure.

He left her with a pledge of return. "Tell him *nothing*."

"If he asks, I must," she said. "But he will not ask."

Camillo fled, imagining all the while the sounds of footsteps behind him, slow, onerous, and sure. A bramble snagged his sleeve and almost he shouted. He escaped the garden a second time, unscathed, except perhaps by Cupid's arrow, the worst scratch of all.

Camillo sought the worst help he could find, that of strong drink and old volumes.

For three days and three nights he did not venture to invade the garden, and all this absence fed his senses, as the wine and the books did. Soon he was in love with the mysterious maiden, the magician's doll; lost. For he was in the story now, and what else might happen? I can make no further excuses for him. He was young and life had not been unkind. Those are two weak schools in which to learn the first reality.

On the third night, Camillo returned to the garden, and his plan was made. He would seduce the affection of the maiden — already he suspected her enamoured of him — and then he would induce her to flight. How he should shelter her God knew, he did not. What would become of them, likewise. Some instinct told him that if only he could get her out of the garden, vengeful pursuit would not travel beyond the wall. In this he was partly correct.

It was now a night of new moon, a slender silken light, like thin water.

The key turned with ease, the garden opened. There was no nightingale, but as he descended from the terrace Camillo saw all the lights of the house were out

for sure, and the lamp in the arbour lighted.

The girl sat reading from a great book. He was impressed and pleased she had been lessoned in the wise arts. Probably she too had powers.

"Lady," he said at once, "I'm here to entreat you. To come away with me. My heart is yours!" (Oh, did he not even once tremble at the fulsomeness of those special words? — No he did not.) "You must leave this place of your captivity."

"I cannot," said the maiden.

"Yes, if I am your protector. Fear nothing. The holy church is stronger than any dark gambit of *his*."

"But all I need is here," replied the obstinate girl, turning another page idly. "Here I first saw the light, and grew, and here I live."

"His slave."

"Perhaps. I do not mind it."

"Mind it! You must. We are made free by God. Only trust in His name." (He meant in the name of Camillo, which he had not even told her.) "Trust, and I can take you from this loathesome spot."

This too was a lie. Never had the lily garden seemed so mystically fair or smelled so lovely.

The girl looked sad. She put the book aside and clasped her hands.

"Tell me of the world beyond the garden."

Camillo then became the book. He told her of the world — or all he could, for he too had never left the walls of the city.

He spoke of the streets and houses, the mansions of the rich, the churches with their goldwork and the great cathedral. He spoke of the university of Ravenval, its courts and chambers and the library. He spoke of hunting on the hills, which he had never done, the racing of horses and sailing of hawks. He went further. He described vast blue seas with ships on them, and dusty tracks, and deserts where one tree marks a well, and of the caravans of the Road of Spice, and the distant East where obelisks tower, lamps

are rubbed to produce demons, girls dance with their faces veiled but otherwise naked, and carpets fly through the air. He spoke of lands where men are black and men are golden, and where men are blue and carry their heads under their shoulders. For Camillo had read what he had not done.

And when he had finished, the maiden sat enraptured, and he thought it was as much with him as with his tales. In the pine the nightingale did not sing, but a vast planet, silver-green, had come between the oaks and stared on them like the eye of a cat.

"These are the dreams of day," said the maiden.

"You will learn to endure the day," said Camillo. "Only the evil things of night fear sunlight, and you are pure and good."

"No, the day is not my time. I do not think I could bear the sun. It is a ball of molten matter about which the earth spins."

"No, no," Camillo hastened to reassure her, "the sun moves about the earth, passing over, and under us during the darkness."

"I must shield myself from day. I must cover up my head and sleep."

"Then so you shall," decided Camillo magnanimously. "I will guard you. And by night I will show you the world."

"It is not to be," said the girl sorrowfully.

And as if summoned by her words, a second planet, small and dully red, lit the wall of The Alchemist's House.

"*Damnation.*" Camillo moved rapidly towards his prey. "I shall be discovered. Come now. Am I to live life without you? I offer you my heart, I offer you holy marriage."

"What is that?"

Disbelieving, Camillo reached her and raised her gently to her feet, and her long gown spilled upon his shoes, and he thrilled at the touch of it even as at the touch of his hands upon hers. How

smooth and douce she was. No doll, surely, though magical.

"Trust me and trust in God. We must fly at once."

"I cannot."

"Yes!"

"No, it is impossible."

"In love, all things may be!" cried Camillo softly, between fright and dominance. And he moved his hands to her waist meaning to lift her straight up in the air and off the spot, meaning to carry her if needful.

But when he lifted her he heard the oddest sound. It was a sort of snapping, like the noise a vegetable makes when it is broken. And then the girl gave such a dreadful scream, a scream of such horrible agony, that only once had he heard anything like it, and then from a square where an execution had been taking place.

Camillo let her go. And for a moment he forgot what her scream might bring upon him, for he saw something that made all his organs change to ice.

From below her gown, long streams of thick blood were running out.

Then she fell, directly down, like a branch, and her gown tore open. And he saw that she was a maiden to the knees, and from beneath that juncture she grew together and she was a stem, a stem like that of a lily, greenish and furred, and where the stem went into the ground below the arbour were the roots of her, and like entrails they had been torn up. They writhed there, ripped in half, dying, and the blood ran from them.

And in the house other lights lighted.

But Camillo saw the face of the girl, and it was white and empty and already dead.

He spewed once, and then he choked himself to contain it, and he turned and rushed away.

Nothing did he afterwards remember of his journey through the garden, save that he must have left wide the door in the wall. Nothing did he remember of the streets he ran through. Not until he heard the great voice chime above him for five in the morning, the hour before the dawn. And looking up he saw the iron angels pass over his head with their swords upraised, and the iron knight upon his iron unicorn. And then Camillo hammered on the penitents' door of the cathedral and after many years it seemed they let him in, and he fell in a sort of swoon under the altar of the Virgin.

For a month Camillo lay very sick in his sister's house. But he told no one, beyond the first priest, anything of why, or of what he had done, or seen. His sickness was the war in him between revulsion and guilt, and not understanding either, he was ill for longer than a wiser man would have been.

Then, when he had recovered a little, he went to his lodging to take back his few possessions, and when he passed the wall of The Alchemist's garden, he grew so faint that a passerby helped him into the lodging house.

There he recovered, drank some wine with the landlord, and for the first time said to himself, *I must not think of this any more.*

Then Camillo hurried to put together his books and papers and the other items that had been kept for him in his room. While he did this, up came the landlord again.

"Young sir, there is a priest below who wishes to speak to you."

"Yes, send him up then, if you will," said Camillo, thinking the church had come to collect its fee for a kindness to him, and glad enough to pay, for the payment of dues seemed a part of his healing.

Presently then into Camillo's room, which overlooked as the other apartments did not the tall trees of the wild garden, there came a robed and hooded figure, that Camillo might also have taken for a priest or a friar, except that there suddenly looked out on him, as if from behind a mask, a face entirely remarkable. It was a face centuries old, yet unlined. It was a face young as morning, with the no-eyes of a skull. It was cruel, and compassionate. It was like, Camillo dared to think long, long after, the face of God — or the Devil. It was the face of The Alchemist.

"Camillo," said The Alchemist, and Camillo did not wonder how his name was known, "I am not here to rebuke you. What was mine you wantonly destroyed, and took from it also its own life, which I had given it, but which it valued for itself. This you realize, I believe. I only ask you that in future you do not meddle. Do you suppose that you have learned a lesson?"

And in Camillo's mind there was a sort of shudder, or crash, quite mild and painless, but as if all the jumbled pieces of his doubts and fears had fallen home into their proper places. And suddenly he wept, but without shame, eight burning tears. And he said: "Yes."

"Then I am content," said The Alchemist.

And with no more than that, he left him.

I am old today, and can write of Camillo who was my younger self, now as unlike me as a summer tree to a winter stick, with distance and perhaps with fortitude. He is almost a stranger, and it is easy to speak of *he* and *him,* of *Camillo,* as though truly he were another. But the lesson has remained of the venture in the garden. And even now my old body would weep, if it had moisture left enough, at the wrong it did, in total innocence, as so many wrongs are done. But there is no more to say. Ω

LITTLE BOY BLACK AND BLUE

by Robert J. Howe

Eddie sat on the stoop, a knot in his stomach, waiting for his father to come down and take him to Dr. Kline's office. He sat hunched on the steps, his too-short pants hiked up almost past his socks, his arms wrapped miserably around his schoolbag. He picked at a knee of his corduroys, wishing they would tear so he wouldn't have to wear them anymore, and Raymond Vesi wouldn't call him a clamdigger.

The door opened behind him and he heard his mother's voice, too loud, talking to his father.

"Make sure he gets the whole hundred," she said.

"He'll get it, don't worry," Eddie's father said, making the money disappear into his pocket like a magic trick.

Eddie stood up and slung his bookbag over his shoulder.

"Don't hold it up like that!" his mother snapped, "You'll tear off the straps. How many times do I have to tell you that?"

He dutifully slipped the bag off his shoulder and tucked it under his arm.

"I *asked* you a question . . . ," his mother said.

Eddie looked down at the toes of his Buster Browns. "I don't know," he muttered.

"Nobody knows anything around here," she said, and slammed the door.

Eddie let his father take his hand, even though he was in the third grade, and too big to hold hands unless he was crossing the street, and they went down the block to the bus stop. His father's hand was rough from handling crates and things down at the pier, even though he hadn't gone to work at the pier in a long time. Eddie wished his father would go back to work on the pier, then maybe his mother wouldn't be so mad all the time. Eddie had gone to work with his father a couple of times, usually on Saturdays. He liked seeing the ocean and all the different ships.

The bus wasn't coming yet, and Eddie's father lit a cigarette, only letting go of his hand long enough to shield the match from the wind. Cars went by on Myrtle Avenue, and if one went too fast, or came close to the curb, Eddie's father would pull him back and curse under his breath.

The bus came and they stepped on after his father flicked the cigarette away. His father put in just one fare, even though Eddie was really too big to ride for free anymore. The busdriver gave them a mean look, but didn't say anything. Once they sat down, Eddie put his schoolbag on the seat next to him and scrambled up on his knees so he could look out the window. Every time the bus started and stopped, his father would reach over and grab the back of Eddie's coat, until he finally said, "Turn around and sit straight, for chrissake, or you'll fall."

"I won't fall," Eddie said, but he turned around and sat in his seat.

They got off the bus at Kent Avenue, and walked halfway down the block to Dr. Kline's office. Before his feet even touched the steps, Eddie's stomach started to hurt again. By the time they were in the waiting room with the white tile floor, he felt like throwing up. Because it was early, no one else was in the waiting room, and Eddie sat close to his father on the couch. He wanted to crawl inside his father's big reefer coat, up against the old flannel shirt and the Old Spice smell, where it was safe and warm.

Dr. Kline came into the waiting room

a few minutes later and smiled at Eddie under his scraggly black mustache.

"Hi, Eddie," he said, bending over and sticking his nose right in Eddie's face. "How do you feel this week?"

"Okay," Eddie muttered into his chest.

"Good," Dr. Kline said brightly. He straightened up and looked at Eddie's father. "Will that be cash or check, Mr. Logan?"

"Cash, Doc," Eddie's father said. Dr. Kline made a face at the *Doc,* but didn't say anything.

Eddie's father slipped the money out of his pocket and counted out the bills with a thumb and forefinger.

"There's seventy there," he said. "I'll give you the rest next week."

Eddie wanted to say that his mother had said to pay the whole hundred, but he couldn't look up into Dr. Kline's face.

When Dr. Kline gave his father the receipt, he took Eddie by the shoulder and steered him toward the inner room.

"About forty-five minutes," he said over his shoulder to Eddie's father, who was already buttoning up his coat.

Eddie wanted to cry and run back to his father then, but he was afraid that he'd just have to stay with Dr. Kline anyway. Then it would be worse.

With tears already stinging in his eyes, Eddie went into the room — what Dr. Kline called the "playroom."

Sister Margaret took Eddie's hand from his father and led him toward the bathroom. It had been much worse today than ever, and Eddie had thrown up on his white shirt. The whole way over from Dr. Kline's office to school he'd cried and begged his father not to make him go back. His father had finally said okay, but Eddie knew his mother would say no, and that would be that.

He stood passively next to the sink while Sister Margaret scrubbed his shirt with a wet paper towel. Everybody would notice the spot on his shirt, especially since he was late. He wished he could just go home and hide under the covers.

"Eddie, I can't clean it like this. You're going to have to take your shirt off."

At any other time, taking off his shirt in front of a lady, especially a nun, would have horrified him, but he felt so sick and miserable just then, he didn't have the strength to object.

"You'll be a little late for reading, but I'll tell Sister Catherine . . . *Mother of God!* Eddie, what happened to your back?"

The shock in Sister Margaret's voice scared him more than anything else. There were fresh tears welling in his eyes as he looked over his shoulder into the tin mirror. Starting at the middle of his back and disappearing into the waistband of his navy-blue corduroys were dozens of shiny red welts, each one the width of a small leather strap.

"I forgot [sob] my tee shirt [sob] at th' doctor's office," was all he managed to get out before he burst into tears again.

Eddie sat on the couch in Sister Margaret's office, dressed again and hugging his bookbag against his chest while she talked on the phone.

"Your mother isn't at work yet, and no one's at your house. Do you know where your father is right now?"

Eddie looked at his shoes. His father was at Ack's Bar, that was where he always went after dropping Eddie off at school.

"I don't know," he said.

Sister Margaret drummed her fingers on the table. "Do you know the name of the doctor?"

Eddie nodded.

"What's his name?"

"Dr. Kline."

"What kind of doctor is he?" Sister Margaret asked, taking a phone book down from her shelf.

"A shrink." Philip Mussberger had told him that. Philip talked to him sometimes if no one else was around, and he never called Eddie a clamdigger, though one time he said, "Jeez, Logan, get your old lady to get you some pants that fit, huh?"

"A psychiatrist?" Sister Margaret wanted to know.

"I don't know," Eddie said to his shoes. "A shrink."

He never had thought to ask Philip Mussberger what that meant. There were a lot of things Philip said that he didn't understand, but he *knew* what a shrink was.

Sister Margaret was leafing through the phone book.

"Is his office on Kent Avenue?" She said avenue like *avenew*.

"Uh-huh."

Before she picked up the phone, Eddie had the urge to tell her everything; about the belt, and the shrink, and the doll family. But then she was dialing the phone and it was too late.

While she stood silently, holding the phone next to her ear, Eddie's stomach began to cramp up again. He hoped Dr. Kline wasn't there — he hoped Dr. Kline had gone away and wasn't coming back.

"Hello. May I speak with Dr. Kline, please?"

The knots in Eddie's stomach tightened. *Please don't let him be there,* he prayed.

"Sister Margaret Thole, from the Nativity School. One of our pupils is a patient of Dr. Kline's . . ."

"Edward Logan."

"Yes. He had an appointment this morning."

"I'll hold."

Sister Margaret smiled at him while she waited with the receiver next to her ear.

"I think I'm going to be sick again," he said.

"Go ahead," she said, putting her hand over the mouthpiece. "You can do it in the washbasin."

Eddie stood with his back to her, his knuckles white around the rim of the white porcelain sink. His stomach contracted hard, but nothing came up. He shook with the violence of the spasms that made his eyes water and his vision blur. Behind him, Sister Margaret spoke quietly into the phone. He tried to still his stomach to hear what she was saying, but was only partly successful.

". . . very sick little boy."

"Yes, all over his back. He's sick to his stomach . . ."

". . . without his parents' consent . . ."

Sister Margaret hung up the phone and came over to him. "I'm going to take you to the hospital, Eddie. I'll leave a message at your mother's job and she'll meet us there."

"I don't want to," he said, panting out the words between heaves.

"It's all right. I'll stay with you until your mother comes, and Dr. Kline will be there . . ."

"Nooo!" Eddie cut her off with a wail. "I don't want to!"

He bolted toward the door, but she caught him in two steps and wrapped her arms around him.

"You don't have to be afraid . . ."

"I don't want to go," he wailed, thrashing wildly against her.

"Eddie, I'll stay with you, but you have to go."

In the end he was just too weak to resist.

He had only ridden in a car once before, his uncle's green Cadillac with the red plastic horn hanging from the mirror. Sister Margaret's black Buick was much newer, and the leather seats and dashboard felt like butter under his fingertips. While they were driving, he could pretend he was a normal kid, out for a normal drive, even though he didn't know any kids who went driving with nuns. But too soon they were pulling up next to the blue sign for Cumberland Hospital.

His stomach hurt, but he was all cried out. He walked numbly up the ramp and into the hospital, his hand gently imprisoned in Sister Margaret's.

Dr. Kline wasn't there yet, and they sat together on orange plastic chairs in the waiting area. Eddie sat quietly with his hands clenched in his lap, his face pale and sweaty with tension. He wanted to tell Sister Margaret about the doll family; he wanted her to take him away before Dr. Kline came, but he couldn't force the words out. Every time he heard steps in the corridor his heart would swell with terror.

He was staring at the cracked floor tile when he heard Dr. Kline's voice. The shock of it was so unexpected that he let out a stifled little scream.

"Eddie, what's wrong?" Sister Margaret asked.

"He's had a rough time, the little man."

Eddie was frozen in his seat by the doctor's stare.

"Hello, Eddie," Dr. Kline said, putting his face too close to Eddie's.

Out of the corner of his eye, Eddie could see Sister Margaret's polite, slightly confused expression.

"You are Dr. Kline, I imagine?" she said.

"I'm sorry, yes," he said, looking away from Eddie.

When they shook hands, Eddie bolted. It wasn't a conscious decision. He was halfway down the ramp toward Willoughby Avenue before he realized what he was doing.

Someone opened the glass door just as he reached it, and Eddie flew out past a blur of surprised adult forms. As he skidded around the corner onto Whaley Street, he heard the furious **tap tap**, **tap tap** of Dr. Kline's loafers slapping against the pavement behind him. Suddenly Eddie was horrified by the magnitude of the bad thing he'd done by running away. His guilt and fear went to his legs, slowing them until he felt Dr. Kline's hand close on his collar and jerk him from his feet.

He walked back with the doctor's hand clenched around his collar, eyes directed at the pavement to avoid grown-ups' curious stares. Sister Margaret was coming down the street toward them when they turned the corner, and one look at the anger in her face sank Eddie's spirits even lower.

"You don't have to lead him like a *dog,* for heaven's sake," she said when they were a few feet apart.

"I don't want him running into traffic, Sister."

She crouched down to be at eye-level with Eddie.

"You have to go with Dr. Kline, Eddie. Do you understand that?"

"Yes," he mumbled into his chest, unwilling to meet her gaze.

"And you're not going to run away again."

"No."

"All right." She straightened up and took him gently by the shoulder. "You can let him go, Doctor. He'll be all right."

Dr. Kline made a face, but unclenched his fist from around Eddie's collar. The three of them walked back into the emergency room with Eddie like a prisoner between them.

His mother came into the emergency room while they were filling out papers.

"What's wrong with you?" she shot at Eddie.

He wanted to run into his mother's arms and beg her to take him away, but her rigid, angry posture forbade him.

"I don't know," he said.

"What do you mean, you don't know?"

"Mrs. Logan," Sister Margaret said, "Eddie has marks on his back. He looks like he was beaten."

"What? Let me see."

Eddie, horrified at the thought of taking his shirt off in front of all these people, clenched tighter into himself.

"I said, let me *see,*" his mother repeated.

"Mrs. Logan . . ." Sister Margaret began, giving Dr. Kline an impatient look as if she expected him to come to Eddie's defense.

"Are you listening to me?" Eddie's mother asked as she pulled off his coat in angry little tugs.

Eddie went completely limp as him mother peeled back his shirt to reveal the reddish-brown stripes on his back.

"Who did this to you?" she demanded angrily. "Did your *father* do this?"

Eddie didn't want to cry; it felt as if the whole room was staring at him, but hot salty tears welled up in his eyes, and his shoulders started to shake.

"Stop crying and *tell* me," his mother said, shaking his shoulder.

The dam broke then, and for the next few minutes he saw and heard everything through a filmy blur. The next time he was able to take stock of his situation, he was being led into a playroom with deep orange carpeting on the floor, and a doll family just like the one in Dr. Kline's office. When he looked more carefully, in fact, he saw it *was* the family from the office; the mother doll's head was sewn in the same place, and the father doll had the same magic-marker stain on its foot.

Eddie stared at the dolls, feeling as if he'd swallowed a ball of ice. His mother and Dr. Kline sat in the tan armchairs across from him, along with another man who had come in behind them.

"Eddie," Dr. Kline said in his terribly concerned voice, "I want you to tell us who hurt your back."

Eddie looked at his mother, who sat across from him smoking with angry gestures, and at the other man. They were all looking at him intently. His eyes filmed up again and he stared at his feet.

"Eddie," Dr. Kline took him by the arm. "This is Detective Kehoe. Do you know what a detective is?"

Eddie nodded. He watched *Hill Street Blues* every Thursday night.

"I want you to tell us who hurt you. You don't have to be afraid."

The detective smiled wanly at Eddie and tugged at the waistband of his Levis.

Eddie looked at the detective and his mother with a sinking heart; they would never believe him, no matter what he told them. Philip Mussberger hadn't believed him, and he was only a year older and left back in the fifth grade.

"Eddie," Dr. Kline said. "Are you listening to me? You have to tell us who hurt you, Eddie."

The doctor got up from his chair and squatted on his haunches in front of him, close enough so that Eddie could smell his bad breath.

"Eddie . . ."

"All right!" Eddie fairly levitated off the orange carpet. "He did it, *he* did it!" he screamed, kicking the small father doll across the room.

"*Who* did it?" Eddie's mother wanted to know.

Dr. Kline stood up and faced the two adults.

"I'm afraid he's saying Mr. Logan beat him."

"No! Daddy didn't do it. It was *him*," Eddie cried, pointing to the doll.

Dr. Kline puffed out his cheeks and threw Eddie a mean look that the others couldn't see.

"Children, especially little boys, are terribly loyal to their fathers," he said. "Even if they are physically abused. Eddie is resolving that by blaming the doll for his hurt. It's a very common defense mechanism, actually. That's what the dolls are *for*."

"Did your *father* do that to you?" Eddie's mother snapped. "Sick bastard!" she said, and without waiting for an answer, stormed from the room.

The detective got to his feet as if he were very tired.

"Are you *sure* that his father beat him?"

Nobody was paying any attention to Eddie anymore.

"Yes, I am. He's a heavy drinker, you know. A very common pattern, unfortunately."

"All right. Don't let them wash him or anything until my partner comes by with

the social worker to take the pictures and all that."

"And how long will that be?"

"I dunno. She's over in the projects — some woman threw her infant into the back of a garbage truck. Maybe an hour or so. We'll try to get back as soon as we can."

"Fine. I'll wait here until then."

The detective looked down at Eddie.

"You're going to be all right, fella. I'll be back in a little while, okay?"

Eddie stared at the cop's white Reeboks and nodded dumbly.

Dr. Kline walked out with the detective and locked the door behind him. Eddie hesitated a minute, then got up and put his ear against the door. He could hear Dr. Kline and Sister Margaret and the detective talking, but the door was too thick, and they were talking too quietly for Eddie to make out what they were saying. When he heard them say goodbye, Eddie returned to his seat.

A moment later he heard a key in the lock, and Dr. Kline came in with a short nurse who looked Chinese.

"Cora is going to give you something to make you relax a little, Eddie. I want you to take the injection like a big boy."

Eddie was afraid of needles, but he was more afraid of what was going to happen to him when he was alone with Dr. Kline. His stomach knotted so hard he barely noticed the nurse swabbing his arm with the alcohol pad and sticking him with the needle.

They made him lie down on the carpet, then the nurse left. After a few minutes he started to feel fuzzy, and the knots in his stomach started to dissolve. He felt awake, but he was too lazy to do more than wiggle his fingers and toes a little. He almost forgot Dr. Kline was there until he smelled the magic marker.

Dr. Kline was kneeling over him, the red marker uncapped in his hand. Eddie badly wanted to jump up, or kick his legs, or scream, but the best he could do was a slight mewling sound. When he felt the soft, fuzzy tip of the marker run wetly across his forehead, his bladder let go.

Dr. Kline pulled away from his wet pants with a grimace of disgust, but continued to draw the sign on Eddie's forehead with slow, meticulous strokes. When he was done, he stood and capped the marker, and tossed it on the red plastic play table.

Eddie felt queasy from fear and the magic-marker smell.

Dr. Kline looked down at him and made a smile that wasn't a smile.

"Shrink!" he said.

Eddie's stomach rolled over as he felt his clothes loosen.

"Shrink!" Dr. Kline said again.

Eddie's shoes slipped off his suddenly too-small feet.

"Shrink, shrink, shrink!"

Eddie disappeared down into his clothes, his uniform shirt blocking out Dr. Kline's ugly smile. He stopped getting smaller only when his clothes were like a collapsed tent atop his naked body.

He was now the size of the little boy doll.

Dr. Kline picked up his pants legs and dumped him rudely out of his clothes. Eddie found enough strength to pull himself to his knees and cover his privates.

Dr. Kline went across the room and set the three dolls, Father, Mother, and Boy, all in a row along the wall.

"Wake," he said to each of them. "Wake, wake!"

The three dolls stirred and looked up, their cloth hands and faces now smooth, pale skin. Eddie tried not to look at their eyes. They were the worst: just black holes in their faces.

"Eddie was bad today," Dr. Kline told the doll family.

"Nooo . . . ," Eddie moaned, staggering to his feet.

"Eddie kicked Mr. Doll, didn't he?"

The man doll stood up and took off its leather belt. Eddie stood and took a step backward, then caught one heel in the deep orange carpet pile and toppled, arms windmilling frantically. Before he could scramble to his feet, the man doll was on him with the strap.

The sound of it slapping against his naked skin hurt almost as much as the blow. Tears sprang to Eddie's eyes as a welt rose from his navel to his neck.

Twice more the strap came down, the biting pain of it making his skin contract. Eddie blindly groped for something to put between himself and the stinging leather, his hands flailing the carpet around him until his fingers closed on a Lego block.

Without thinking about it, he brought the block up from behind his head with both arms, smashing it into the man doll's face.

The doll let out a liquid shriek and dropped the strap, its face a mask of watery red blood. Dr. Kline slapped Eddie aside angrily and scooped up the man doll.

"Sleep," he said through gritted teeth. Then to the other dolls, "Sleep, sleep."

The three dolls sagged back into cloth and kapok stuffing, the same as before except that the man doll now had a jagged tear down the middle of its face.

Eddie lay balled up on the carpet, terrified of what Dr. Kline would do to him now that he'd hurt the man doll. He pushed himself away from the doctor with his heels, not daring to look up until he heard the heavy wooden door **whoosh** open and shut, then **snick** locked.

This was the worst it had ever been — first the beating before school, with the strap, and now new welts on his face and chest. Dr. Kline had never left him shrunk before, either. He'd told Eddie he would, if Eddie was ever *really* bad, but he'd never left him alone like this.

Eddie sat, half buried in the deep carpet, his whole body weak and trembly. He heard footsteps in the corridor and held his breath, both hoping and fearing that someone would rescue him. When

the footsteps receded, light **click-click** ones like his mother's, he almost started to cry again. He realized then, with a little shock of fright, that nobody was going to come and save him. Not Sister Margaret, or even his father or mother. Dr. Kline was the "Big Man" in the hospital, Eddie's father would say, and no one else could do anything.

It wasn't fair, he thought. *He hadn't told anybody about the doll family. It wasn't his fault if Sister Margaret had seen the marks on his back.*

"I hate them!" he shouted, his voice sounding tiny and echoing in the huge room. "I didn't *do* anything!"

A man's voice in the corridor made him start, and he realized that he hated Dr. Kline most of all for making him be afraid. He knew what Dr. Kline was going to do with him — he was going to make him like the doll family. Maybe his mother and father, too.

Another, louder, man's voice passed outside the door. Eddie scrambled to his feet, too afraid and too mad to be ashamed of his nakedness. The mother and boy dolls stared blankly at him from across the room.

He looked around the room for something to keep Dr. Kline away from him, but there were just a few more Lego blocks and some crayons and paper. Even if he wasn't shrunk, there was nothing he could hurt a grownup with. Then he saw the barrel of the red magic marker on the plastic table.

There was power in the marker, that was why they called it magic.

Eddie reached up onto the table, standing on tiptoes to stretch his arm toward the middle where the marker was, but it lay just out of his reach. There was nothing in the room he could use to reach it, either. The only thing long enough to reach it was one of the dolls, but they were too heavy for Eddie to lift.

While he stood on tiptoe, staring at the marker, he heard Dr. Kline's voice somewhere down the corridor. He sounded mad, which made Eddie's stomach knot.

Eddie tried shaking the table, but as small as he was, and as firmly as the thick carpet held its legs, he couldn't move it very much.

He stood there for several minutes, his ears cocked for the doctor's voice, staring at the marker just out of reach. A thought came to him then, and he stooped, sliding under the table until his shoulders were at the edge, then all at once he straightened, jogging the table upward slightly.

The marker rolled from the center of the table to the far side, held at the edge by the slight lip. Eddie backed out from under the table and tried to squeeze between it and the wall to reach the marker.

He was wedged in that position when he heard Dr. Kline's voice coming down the hall. He jerked against the table in a panicked rush, nicking his neck on the sharp plastic edge.

He heard the doctor push against the door, then mutter a curse as he rebounded heavily off of it. There was a jingle of keys — Eddie had pulled away from the table and was scrambling under his tent-like shirt — then another muttered curse, followed by fast, deliberate footsteps away.

Eddie stayed crouched under his clothes until the doctor's footsteps receded down the corridor, then he shrugged them away and scrambled under the table.

He could just barely get his arm through the space between the wall and the edge of the table, and his fingers pounded with the pressure as he groped for the marker. When he finally grabbed down on the thick barrel, it felt like a baseball bat in his hand.

The size of the marker and the awkward angle his arm was at kept him from sliding it through the small space. When he heard footsteps in the corridor again, he gave a last, desperate jerk. Instead of

pulling the marker free, however, he hit his funnybone on the wall and dropped the marker back on the table.

It clattered noisily on the plastic, then rolled to a stop just at the other side. With more footsteps echoing in his ears, Eddie scrambled back under the table and out on the open side. He grabbed a marker from the edge with both hands and dropped it on the floor.

He almost wailed with despair then: the cap was on too tight for him to budge it, even with all his strength. He looked around the room for something he could use to loosen the white knurled cover, but the Lego blocks, the only things hard enough to use as a wedge, were too fat to fit in the narrow space between the cap and the barrel of the marker.

Eddie picked up the marker by the thick end and swung it clumsily at the wall, hoping to knock the cap loose. The impact jarred his arms, but the cap stayed tight.

He heard Dr. Kline's voice outside, loud and angry. A wave of pure terror swept through him, and he tried batting the cap off the marker again. Nothing.

Keys jingled somewhere down the corridor. Eddie resisted the temptation to hide under his clothes again.

His arms were weak with fear and the effort of swinging the awkward barrel around his head. He set the marker against the wall to catch his breath, and while he was staring vacantly at the rug, an idea came to him.

Eddie made sure the marker was wedged firmly into the rug and against a crack in the molding, then he backed up and jumped with both feet on the middle of the barrel. His feet slipped off, sending him crashing painfully on his hip. The marker flew a foot across the floor, spinning to a stop with the white cap slightly askew.

Dr. Kline's voice was suddenly loud just outside the door.

"What *is* it now?" he said.

A woman's voice murmured some-

78

thing, then it was quiet again.

Eddie scrambled to his feet and set the marker against the wall again, unmindful of the pain in his hip. Twice more he jumped on it, until the cap finally went spinning into the air over his head.

He dragged the boy doll away from the wall by its feet until it lay flat on the rug. He then picked up the marker in both hands and, straddling the doll's chest, began to draw the sign on its forehead.

Eddie had never *seen* the sign himself; there were no mirrors in Dr. Kline's office, or even in the bathroom. He drew it, using the big, unwieldy marker, in slow deliberate strokes, drawing on his memory of how it felt when the doctor drew it on his own forehead.

He was so absorbed in his work that he never heard the key in the lock, or the door **whoosh** open.

"Eddie is a very *smart* boy, isn't he?" Dr. Kline said, tossing the sutured man doll onto the rug.

Eddie started and dropped the marker at the end of the last stroke.

"Eddie won't be so smart when we cut his brain cord, right?" Dr. Kline said, holding up a tiny silver blade with a blue plastic handle. "Eddie is coming to join the doll family, aren't you, Eddie?"

Eddie slid backwards along the carpet, giving himself rug burns to stay away from the silver knife.

"Wake up . . . ," he half whispered.

The silver knife whickered through the air in an invisible arc. Eddie didn't feel anything, but the blade dripped a tear of blood onto Dr. Kline's hand. Behind the doctor, the boy doll shook itself awake.

Dr. Kline stepped on Eddie's foot, crushing it painfully into the rug.

"Grow," Eddie moaned. "Grow, grow grow grow . . ." the last syllable ending on a high note as the blade drew a thin red line across his chest.

Dr. Kline put all his weight on his foot, and Eddie screamed as he felt the bones crunch. Dr. Kline grabbed a fistful of hair with his free hand and brought the knife to the back of Eddie's neck.

Something in his face gave it away at the last second, but it was too late for the doctor to do anything but let go of Eddie's hair.

The huge, pale hand closed over Dr. Kline's, pulling it effortlessly away from Eddie's neck. Eddie watched in fascinated horror as the boy doll, now too big to stand straight up in the room, forced the doctor's knife hand back and across the front of his throat.

The splash of hot, red blood on his face was the last thing he remembered.

Eddie woke up to the sound of Sister Margaret's voice.

"I *knew* something was wrong when he said he left his undershirt in the doctor's office," she was saying.

Eddie was on his back on the rug with a hospital gown covering him up to his chin. He was normal size again. There was a black rubber sheet with legs sticking out from under it. The same detective with the white sneakers was looking under the sheet and shaking his head.

"I don't give a shit that he cut his own throat," the detective said, "but did he have to do it in front of the kid?"

Sister Margaret noticed that Eddie was awake and shushed the detective.

"It's all right, Eddie," she said. "No one's going to hurt you."

He looked around until he saw the little boy doll slumped in a small, lifeless heap under the table.

Uh-huh, Eddie thought, closing his eyes, *nobody's ever going to hurt me again.*   Ω

BEHIND THE REALITIES:
The Fantasies of John Brunner

by Mike Ashley

When Terri Windling introduced John Brunner's "The Fable of the Farmer and the Fox,"[1] which she and Ellen Datlow had selected for their first *The Year's Best Fantasy* (1988), she remarked that Brunner's was "not a name one expects to encounter in an anthology devoted to fantasy . . ." I suspect many think that, and would wonder why an issue of *Weird Tales* has a special section for Brunner who is regarded by many, after all, as the consummate English science-fiction writer. The author of some eighty books, including such intense dystopian works as *Stand on Zanzibar* (1968), *The Sheep Look Up* (1972) and *The Shockwave Rider* (1975), and such far-reaching adventures as *Enigma from Tantalus* (1965), *The Avengers of Carrig* (1969) and *The Dramaturges of Yan* (1972), is so closely linked with science fiction that his name is not immediately associated with weird or fantasy fiction.

Yet, when John Carnell introduced Brunner's novelette of parallel worlds, "A Time to Rend,"[2] back in 1956, he remarked that despite Brunner's "versatility . . . we feel that the fantasy story will eventually be his best medium." After forty years as an author, John Brunner is perhaps, at last, about to receive due recognition for the many strange and off-trail stories he has written.

In fact the closer one looks at Brunner's output, the harder it is to classify some of his fiction. As he remarked to me in a recent letter, many of his writings cross the boundaries between science fiction, fantasy, and horror. There is an unreality or uncertainty about much of them. Undeniably some of his dystopian SF may genuinely be regarded as horror fiction, whilst some of his fantasies may also fit happily into the realms of science fiction. It is a sign of Brunner's versatility that he is able to use themes and ideas redolent of one genre to clever effect in another.

For instance his early story, "The Biggest Game,"[3] is essentially a story of alien hunters on Earth seeking out fine human specimens, but its treatment is much more in the horror vein, so much so that the story was later reprinted in *Startling Mystery Stories* (as "The Men in Black") and the macabre anthology *Splinters,*[4] without the raising of an eyebrow. Then there is the example of "No Future In It,"[5] which I regard as fantasy and which Brunner firmly calls science fiction. It's about an alchemist trying to prove his abilities, who attempts to summon a demon. Instead he traps a time-traveler in a stasis field. To the alchemist, of course, the man from

1   *Omni,* June 1987; reprinted in *The Year's Best Fantasy: First Annual Collection* edited by Terri Windling & Ellen Datlow, New York: St. Martin's Press, 1988.
2   *Science Fantasy,* December 1956.
3   *Science Fantasy,* February 1956; collected in *From This Day Forward,* Garden City: Doubleday, 1972.
4   *Startling Mystery Stories,* Fall 1966, and *Splinters,* edited by Alex Hamilton, London: Hutchinson, 1968.
5   *Science Fantasy,* February 1956; included in collections *No Future In It* (London: Gollancz, 1962 and New York: Doubleday, 1964) and *The Best of John Brunner,* New York: Del Rey, 1988.

the future can be nothing other than a demon. It's a science-fiction story in fantasy trappings. So is "Father of Lies,"[6] one of my favorite Brunner stories, in which a child possessed of powerful psychic abilities creates a fantasy world around him populated with creatures and people from myth and legend. So is "Earth Is But a Star," perhaps better known in book form as *Catch a Falling Star*.[7] This delicate tale is set in such a far future that science is like magic, and the whole story has the atmosphere and mood of fantasy. Then there is "The Gaudy Shadows,"[8] a relatively straightforward science-fiction story about a powerful hallucinogenic drug which allows the taker to experience fully a tangible dream world. But when the drug is combined with a strong depressant, the dream world becomes a nightmare. Brunner uses this potential in the story's climax to create a terrifying personal hell.

This ability of Brunner's isn't solely a product of his early years. "A Case of Painter's Ear"[9] reads every bit like a developing horror story, though its denouement is undeniably science fiction. A struggling painter seeks the help of a failing doctor to rid him of voices in his ear. When the doctor cleans the ear he finds within it creatures or machines of metal constructing a metal web. "The Clerks of Domesday"[10] is marketed as a horror story in an anthology by Ramsey Campbell billed as "stories that scared me," yet it's a fairly routine science-fiction story, about scouts from a post-nuclear future who return to measure ancient ruins so that they can be reconstructed. The horror comes from the violence of the man who discovers this secret, but refuses to believe it.

You see, there is much that is fantastic and terrifying in the enigmatic fiction of John Brunner. One reason it has been so overlooked is because no single collection reflects the bulk of his weird and fantastic tales. I've added copious footnotes to help readers track down the stories. But let's turn to a simpler, more readily available example.

Possibly the one direct work of fantasy for which Brunner is known is *The Traveler in Black* (1971), more recently expanded as *The Compleat Traveler in Black* (1987). This comprises a sequence of five stories written over the period from 1960 to 1979. They recount the exploits of the Traveler, who works to establish order from chaos. Over unmeasured time he fights a constant war against entropy, though most of his battles are against the ignorance and greed of the populace. He has no choice but to grant people their wishes, though these frequently do not lead to their expectations. Most telling is the climactic tale, "Dread Empire," where the Traveler has to unleash the elemental forces in a battle against chaos. Only then does he learn that despite mankind's natural inhumanity, the desire for love will ultimately win out and chaos will never totally dominate order.

The *Traveler in Black* stories share a theme with Brunner's harder science fiction, about mankind's treatment of itself and of the Earth, and of the need for the rational to always challenge the irrational.

The first *Traveler in Black* story, "Imprint of Chaos," appeared in the British magazine *Science Fantasy,* which, in the 1950s, was the only regular source of fantasy and weird fiction. Brunner was one of its most prolific contributors. His

6 *Science Fantasy*, April 1962; in book form as *Father of Lies*, New York: Belmont, 1968.
7 *Science Fantasy*, June 1958; revised in book form as *The 100th Millennium*, New York: Ace, 1959; expanded as *Catch a Falling Star*, New York: Ace, 1968.
8 *Science Fantasy*, June 1960; in book form as *The Gaudy Shadows*, London: Constable, 1970.
9 *Tales From the Forbidden Planet*, edited by Roz Kaveney, London: Titan Books, 1987.
10 *Fine Frights*, edited by Ramsey Campbell, New York: Tor Books, 1988.

earliest fantasy was "The Talisman,"[11] about an artist who discovers an egg-shaped object which releases the true genius of its owner. Unfortunately that genius can as equally be a curse, as both the artist and a poet discover. On the lighter side is "Proof Negative,"[12] about a man who unknowingly meets Father Christmas.

"Death Do Us Part"[13] is a ghost story, one of only two Brunner has written. This one is humorous, about the ghost of a long-dead man at last free to roam the Earth during a drought (because spirits cannot cross running water). He seeks the services of a living lawyer to help in obtaining a divorce from his shrew of a dead wife. Brunner's more recent ghost story, "The Fellow Traveler,"[14] is darker and more sinister. An unscrupulous Russian bureaucrat, on an overnight express, meets his fate in a haunted compartment.

The lead novel slot in *Science Fantasy* gave Brunner the space for some of his best fantasies. "This Rough Magic,"[15] which was later expanded in novel form as *Black is the Color*, is a powerful story about a black magic coven in London. It bears some similarities to his later, non-fantastic psychological thriller, *The Devil's Work* (1970), about the evil doings of a modern Hell Fire Club.

"The Kingdoms of the World"[16] is one of his most intriguing early novellas. It features the disturbing character Mr. Bell, who, it transpires, is a representative of a race of beings that once ruled the Earth and who are remembered as creatures of legend. Bell is one of the vanguard in an attempt by the creatures to dispossess mankind and reclaim the Earth.

"All the Devils in Hell"[17] is among the most effective of these early stories. It's about a beautiful woman who has made a pact with a demon to ensure her irresistibility and power over men. She eventually meets her match with the inevitable consequences.

In all of these stories the lead character is faced with the dilemma of distinguishing the real from the unreal. Brunner constantly unsettles us by reminding us to probe behind everyday normality to the suppressed chaos within.

Several of Brunner's early stories were optimistic and light-hearted. Take his Tommy Caxton series. Caxton is the leader of a jazz band which frequently experiences the bizarre. Written in a hip-jazz style, the stories are rather ephemeral, but can be amusing. In the first, "The Man Who Played the Blues,"[18] a gifted blues pianist turns out to be an alien. In "When Gabriel . . .",[19] a trumpet turns out to be genuinely heavenly. "Whirligig"[20] has the band whisked into the future to play at the birthday party of a debutante. In "Djinn Bottle Blues,"[21] which is the most openly fantastic, the group find a bottle reputed to contain a captive djinn, who ends up playing percussion on the group's new record!

As the sixties progressed, however, Brunner's short fiction took on a more

11 *Science Fantasy*, September 1955.
12 *Science Fantasy*, February 1956.
13 *Science Fantasy*, November 1955.
14 *The Magazine of Fantasy & Science Fiction*, October 1986.
15 *Science Fantasy*, May 1956; expanded as *Black Is the Color*, New York: Pyramid, 1969.
16 *Science Fantasy*, February 1957.
17 *Science Fantasy*, December 1960.
18 *Science Fantasy*, February 1956; and the collection *Out of My Mind* (London: New English Library, 1968 — British edition only).
19 *Science Fantasy*, August 1956; and the collections *Out of My Mind* (1968, British edition only) and *The Book of John Brunner* (New York: DAW Books, 1976).
20 *Beyond Infinity*, November 1967; and the collections *Out of My Mind* (1968, British edition only) and *Time-Jump* (New York: Dell, 1973).
21 *Fantastic Stories*, February 1972.

sinister form. "Orpheus's Brother"[22] starts after the death of pop star Rock Careless, torn apart by his adoring fans. The star's brother seeks revenge on the brother's agent. The agent reminds the brother of how Orpheus's music drove the Bacchantes wild, and how they tore him to pieces. Orpheus was thereafter worshipped as a god, and this may also be the fate in store for Rock. Brunner has in some ways here foreseen the posthumous idolatry of a number of rock stars. This story is spoiled by a rather unnecessary ending, when the agent suddenly looses two encaged panthers on the brother, and they likewise tear him to shreds.

"The Nail in the Middle of the Hand"[23] is a particularly thought-provoking story. Decius Asculus, a Roman soldier, is noted for his skill when it comes to crucifixions. However, after he nails Christ to the cross, he undergoes a spiritual decline.

Although Brunner has written less of this type of story of late, he showed he had not lost the skill with "Moths,"[24] an especially dark story, in which one half-sister seeks revenge on the other. In anticipation for her half-sister's marriage, the other agrees to repair her mother's wedding gown, but in the preparation she weaves into the dress the larvae of moths, which have a devastating effect at the wedding ceremony.

One of Brunner's most enigmatic stories is "Dropping Ghyll."[25] Since that story is reprinted in this issue I shall reveal none of its mysteries but, as you will discover, it is a perfect example of how Brunner peels back the unrealities of this world layer by layer to reveal the mysteries beneath.

"Dropping Ghyll" is written in a form

Brunner has adopted more frequently of late. It is ostensibly a narrative, a story within a story, the events being related by someone who was a party to them. Brunner had used this form as early as "Oeuf du Coq,"[26] a tongue-in-cheek tale about a womaniser who goes too far with one girl. She invokes a cockatrice, which turns the libertine to stone. His "statue" is seen on a local dump.

More recently Brunner has used that form with particular effect in his most enigmatic series to date, the Mr. Secrett stories. Mr. Secrett is by profession the Head Librarian at the Royal Society for Applied Linguistics, but by experience he seems to have been involved in almost every bizarre and abnormal event of the last fifty years. Mr. Scrivener is a rather luckless writer, who usually has to earn his money from ghost-writing for a playboy author who seldom has an original idea but receives all the glory for his books. At the point when Scrivener is at his lowest ebb, or is in a particular mess, Secrett miraculously appears on the scene and narrates a tale of some relevance to the situation.

The series began with "The Man Who Could Provide Us With Elephants."[27] Secrett relates how, during World War II, he was one of a special command sent into darkest Africa to build a landing strip for aircraft. Their deadline is ridiculously short, and even with the help of local natives they are doomed to failure. That is until one particular native turns up who has mastery over the African elephants, which are known to be untameable. Not all of the series (which runs to eight stories, with a final ninth soon to appear) can be classified as fantasy or horror. In fact most of them

22 *Magazine of Horror*, April 1965; also in *Out of My Mind*, British and American editions (New York: Ballantine, 1967).
23 *Saint Mystery Magazine*, July 1965; also in both editions of *Out of My Mind*.
24 *Dark Voices 2*, edited by David Sutton & Stephen Jones, London: Pan Books, 1990.
25 *Dark Fantasies*, edited by Chris Morgan, London: Legend Books, 1989.
26 *Science Fantasy*, February 1962, where it appeared as "Ouef du Coq."
27 *The Magazine of Fantasy & Science Fiction*, October 1977.

are unclassifiable. Take "The Man Who Saw the Thousand-Year Reich,"[28] which on the surface seems to be a time-travel story. The body of a wartime SS officer, General Wentschler, is found frozen in a Swiss glacier. Secrett relates how Wentschler is let into an SS secret about plans to send officers on short trips into the future to discover developments and their cause and to return with that information, to allow the Nazis to change the course of events. But this turns out to be an elaborate hoax to humiliate Wentschler and unbalance his mind. There's something of a hoax, too, in "The Man With a Taste for Turkeys,"[29] about a secret society established in the thirties with the aim of financing dreadful films, thus explaining the reason for the existence of so many "turkeys."

The most powerful of the Mr. Secrett stories is "The Man Whose Eyes Beheld the Glory."[30] Set on a small and fairly remote Greek island, it tells the story of a priest investigating a local religious group. Here he finally sees a vision of the glory of a local deity, and thereafter blinds himself. The story might be symbolic of all of Brunner's weird fiction, which reminds us that the realities we believe we see around us may only be masks for the unrealities for which we are unprepared.

In contrast to these bizarre stories, it is almost hard to believe that Brunner has also been writing some fairly straightforward fantasies. Two of these appeared in the shared *Thieves' World* series of anthologies edited by Robert Lynn Asprin. Brunner was quick off the mark when the original stories were commissioned, delivering his manuscript way ahead of schedule and thus establishing some of the series basics that others had to follow. His first story, "Sentences of Death,"[31] stands well on its own. It's about a coded and accursed message which comes into the hands of a translator. He discovers it relates to a sentence of death, and he needs to do some double-dealing in order to resolve the matter and help his young assistant seek her own revenge on a man who raped her in childhood.

Elsewhere, Brunner has sought the fantastic in his adopted home county of Somerset, with a new series of stories loosely connected by the locality. In "An Entry That Did Not Appear in Domesday Book,"[32] the clerks compiling the Conqueror's survey find that the magic that protects Avalon thwarts them from discerning its existence. "The Dragon of Aller"[33] tells of a young man, whose family are murdered by Vikings, who encounters and does battle with one of the last surviving dragons. A third story in this series, "In the Season of the Dressing of the Wells," is due to appear in a centenary tribute to J.R.R. Tolkien.

The record shows that John Brunner is not solely the leading science-fiction writer that the world recognises, but is also a formidable and long-standing writer of enigmatic and turbulent fantasies. And as his career stretches into its fifth decade, I'm sure he'll now start to cement the reputation that John Carnell predicted so long ago. We all forgot to look beyond the writer's façade. Now Brunner the Fabulist stands revealed. Ω

---

28 *The Magazine of Fantasy & Science Fiction,* November 1981; and in the collection *The Best of John Brunner,* New York: Del Rey, 1988.

29 *The Magazine of Fantasy & Science Fiction,* May 1989.

30 *New Terrors 2,* edited by Ramsey Campbell, London: Pan Books, 1980.

31 *Thieves' World,* edited by Robert Asprin, New York: Ace Books, 1979. The sequel, "A Mercy Worse Than None," is in *Aftermath (Thieves' World #10),* edited by Robert Lynn Asprin & Lynn Abbey, New York: Ace Books, 1987.

32 *Amazing Stories,* March 1988.

33 *Amazing Stories,* March 1991.

UP TO NO GOOD

by Sue Robinson

"Of course I'll let you go," said the old lady.

His hand quickened around the knife. This was going to be easy. He stood, tensed in the dark, waiting for her to unlock the doors.

"It's partly my fault," she said.

There was the gritting sound of metal on metal, one bump at a time, and then a heavy thud against the tin doors that caused one Hell of an echo. Until he reached up and touched them from the inside to stop the palpitating tremor. Damn, that sudden noise was aggravating! Now he was angry. His thumb running over the carved indentations on the knife handle felt good. So good. "Pardon me," he said politely, "Is there a chain on the door, ma'am?"

"And a padlock, too," confirmed the old lady. "George must have done this."

"Can you open the door, please?"

"Yep, you're locked in there pretty good," said the old lady.

"Can you get me out, now?" he said again.

"I said I would." She sounded a trifle peeved, so he just waited. And waited. And waited for the sound of the key in the padlock.

Instead he heard a dull thud, followed by the sound of something being dragged, then some quick, sharp sounds he couldn't identify, an "Oh, dear," from the old lady, and then a steady scraping sound.

"Er, ma'am?" he asked. "What are you doing?"

"Are you still there?" asked the old lady, sounding surprised.

Oh, Christ, was she senile?

"Yes, ma'am," he said.

Scrape, scrape. That sound again.

"My name is Edna," she told him.

He gritted his teeth. "Well, what's that noise, Edna?"

Scrape, scrape. *Scrape, scrape*.

"Noise? What noi— oh. It's just the potting soil," Edna explained matter-of-factly. "I spilled some of my potting soil and I'm havin' to scrape it up off the concrete. With the hand shovel."

Shit! The old bat was crazy. Or senile. Or both. It was that stuff he had seen piled against the side of the shed, before he had slipped through the open doors to hide. Bags of dirt, little plastic containers all stacked up, and cardboard boxes full of inch-high, green things. *She was fooling with a bunch of plants instead of getting him out! Cool, that was the thing.* He could have cursed her from New York to China, but he had to stay cool, in spite of this set-back. He didn't want to blow it. And anyway, it might not be a setback. If she was a little dotty, it might even help. The better to scare you with, my dear.

His fist against the tin roof of the tin shed made a tremendous, shattering crash, followed by her startled, high-pitched scream. He liked the scream. Perfect. Not bad for starters.

He could hear her rapid breathing and just imagine her removing the wide-brimmed sun hat from her head, wiping the sweat from her forehead with one garden-gloved hand, while putting the other to her chest.

"Well," she said, short of breath, "that darn near gave me a heart attack."

He thought so. He knew people. And he had this old bag figured out. Typical gray-haired, too old to wear those sandals, too plump to wear those pedal-pushers, naïve, nagging, stupid, old lady. Deservingly stupid, probably. No doubt particularly in need of Jayce Earl-Roy Hawn's justice, the kind he habitually meted out to older, trusting individuals who moved too infuriatingly slow and thought too slow to catch on. Before it was too late.

He had seen her that morning, up on the hill in her own front yard, as he walked along the road below, the rotting dufflebag with all his possessions heavy on his back. With any luck, it would soon be heavier. With silverware. Jewelry. All the little antique knicknacks her type would have. And the cash. Her type always kept a wad stashed somewhere, "safe" from the bank. He would make her tell him where it was. Before she begged for her life.

"I want OUT, Edna," he yelled. Forcefully. That ought to make her jump. He listened. Nothing. There was no sound at all. Jesus, had she really had a heart attack? Maybe he had overdone it. If she had — Christ, if she had, he would rot in here.

"Why, of course you do," came the old lady's voice finally. Hawn was relieved.

"All cooped up in there. It bein' hot, and damp, and dark, and muggy. I've been in there before, I know how it is. Why, of course you want out. That's only natural."

Something about her voice bothered him. It wasn't the rattled, fainthearted, overwhelmed voice he was expecting.

"After all," continued Edna, in the sweetest, most reassuring, grandmotherly tones he had ever heard, "it's partly my fault."

"That's right," he agreed quickly.

"If I hadn't just left the doors to this silly, old garden shed wide open, you wouldn't have been — tempted — to wander around in there, would you?"

"No, ma'am."

"And if I hadn't left the doors open like that, you wouldn't have thought about this silly, old rattletrap of a shed as a place to — what was it, now — sleep?"

"Yes, ma'am." Hawn went through the whole spiel again. About how he was homeless. How all the earthly possessions he owned were in his backpack. How he had finally found work in a tiny town, just two dots over on the map, some place he had never heard of, what was the name of it? Yes. Hadleyville, he agreed, when she volunteered the name. And how he was on his way to the job, on foot. But it got so blamed hot, and he got so sweaty, the heavy pack on his back and all, that when he saw the open doors to the shed, it looked so cool there in the dark, so inviting, and how, seeing as he hadn't slept inside in so very long —

"Why, of course," the old woman interrupted him. "You just couldn't help it."

"That's right," he said. Any more than he could help noticing the neat, tidy house with the neat, tidy garden down the hill a ways, the whole place set off by itself, a good country mile away from the last place he had passed. And probably a mile away from the next one. With a granny in the front yard who could scream all day and all night for a month and no one would hear her. And the perfect hiding place in the back. Until "George," whoever that was, had slammed the doors shut, instead of stepping inside them.

"Can you let me out, now, Miss Edna?" he asked.

"Well, I could," Miss Edna hesitated, ". . . if I had the key."

"You don't have the key?!" his voice exploded.

"My, my, temper, temper," fussed the old lady. "Didn't I tell you? I thought I told you. The key is up at the house, way at the top of the hill."

"Well, go get it," Hawn ordered icily, all patience gone from his voice. "I want out — now."

"Well, the thing is," explained Edna

slowly, her voice a contrast in patience from his own, "it's such a long walk up that hill for an old lady. You really wouldn't mind if I just finished what I came down here to do, would you? That way, I wouldn't have to make two trips."

Hmph. Two trips. Godalmighty, what kind of way-out, off-balance old fool was he dealing with here? The rage shot through his body all the way down to his clenched fists. He began banging on the doors with both hands, making a real racket, and screaming.

"*Make* two trips, dammit!" he yelled. "Don't you understand, lady? I've been locked in here for almost an hour, already. It's dark, and it's hot. And I want *out!* Go get the *key!*"

Scrape, scrape. Scrape, scrape.

"Now look at that," said Edna. "What a shame. I've spilled more potting soil."

Jesus, thought Hawn.

"What's your name?" said Edna.

Oh God. This was not going to be as easy as he thought.

"Jayce," sighed Hawn. He couldn't stand this. Not even telling her his name was easy. He had to answer fifty million old-lady questions. What an odd name that was. Well, how did you spell it? How? No, no one in his family had that name. It was shortened from Jason. No, he wasn't spelling it wrong. He spelled it that way on purpose, because it looked better, fancier. Made him feel more — important. Of course he hated her for making him admit this. If she would just open the damn doors, it would all be over in a flash, in an instant!

"Now, Jayce," the old bat was saying, grandmother-sweet again. "I couldn't possibly go all the way up the hill, all the way to the house to get the key right now, even if I wanted to. Because of George. And the police, silly."

"George?" inquired Hawn, focusing on the letter of the two evils.

"My husband. Now I know, Jayce, that you're a perfectly decent young man who just got — tempted — but I'm afraid my George isn't so understanding. And if I was to go up there before George leaves for the afternoon shift, why, I'm afraid George would want to call the police. George is silly about things like that. He always thinks the worst. He'd think that, just because you were in our shed, that you might want to — hurt me."

"Oh, I wouldn't do that," Hawn began protesting. "It was an accident, lady, honest. All I want is to be out of here and on my way, and you'll never see me again," he said truthfully. The panic in his voice sounded almost genuine.

"I liked it better when you called me Edna. May as well," recommended the old lady, "seein' as we'll have time to chat for a few hours."

"A few hours? Er, what time do you suppose it's safe to go get the key, Edna?"

"Hmmm — I suppose it would be all right around three-ish, just to be on the safe side. George leaves just after two."

"And what time is it now?"

"Do you have a watch, Jayce?"

"No."

"It's just about noon."

Funny, he could have sworn it was later. It was already late morning when he had spotted the place, and by the time he had walked around and up the hill a ways, and hidden for a while, and waited to hear the footsteps that never came . . . well, he could have sworn noon was long gone.

"The best thing for you to do, under the circumstances," Edna speculated, practically reading his mind, "is to just calm down and take it easy."

Hawn despised her for being right. The thought of another three hours in this place made his skin crawl. But he didn't want to blow it now. Let George leave. Let the old woman "chat" her brains out. He could wait another three hours. For the jackpot. Then the whole, beautiful, deserted, nest-egg of a place would be his. He might even have time to come back with a car and really clean out the place. Or a truck. A truck would be better. There must be one within a couple of miles that he could steal. Wait, was he crazy? A stolen truck, in these small-town parts, would be recognizable for miles around. Too easy to trace. Jayce Earl-Roy Hawn, for once in his life, would go the high-class, A-number-one route and maybe even pay to rent a U-Haul. Being as he hadn't stumbled across anything this good in years, it would certainly be worth it. Provided he could swing it before old George came home and found the body.

Wait a minute! What an ass he had been. Hell, he didn't have to be afraid of old George. Two for the price of one was certainly a tempting thought. It was just a question of what was safest, get-away wise. Hawn could feel that he was letting himself get far too worked up about this. But it was so exciting and all. He couldn't decide if it was worth the extra time to stick it to ol' George, slit his throat, for instance, or just get the Hell out fast, as usual, and let George find his bloody artwork with the knife . . .

"I think organic fertilizer is best, don't you?" Edna's voice cut into his thoughts.

"Yes, ma'am," Hawn agreed politely, slumping down to sharpen the knife. The old lady began to rattle her trap about the asinine garden. How all the neighbors who came to visit said she had the best garden around for miles, and what was her secret, and how she didn't have a secret, not really, but if she did, she wouldn't tell them, anyway, now would she, and weren't the fucking petunias healthy this year? Blah, blah, blah. Boring. Hawn "yes-ma'amed" and "no-ma'amed" at all the appropriate places, sharpening all the while. Thank God he would be out soon. There was just enough light left to see the blade and that was shifting. The light came in as tiny cracks underneath the shed's interlocking metal partitions. The interlock jutted inward and then outward from the shed wall just far enough, some three-quarters of an inch, to allow the tiny shafts of light to come through underneath.

But something was wrong. The tiny cracks of light were beginning to disappear from underneath several of the partitions. That didn't make sense. The old bat had said it was noon. He had been slumped here, sometimes listening, sometimes sharpening, and sometimes just staring at the four walls for a couple'a'three hours now. That meant it should be two, maybe three o'clock at the most. Hawn had been walking with his face to the sun long enough to know just where it ought to be. At two o'clock, for instance, it should have been just over the "hump" on the horizon. At three o'clock it should have been a little ways down into the sky, but still huge, still an uncomfortable fact of life, and still burning into his eyes. And still bright enough to have lit up those cracks. But it wasn't lighting up the cracks anymore. And now he noticed, his eyes having adjusted to the dark, that there were only four little cracks of light left. Way down at the end of the wall.

"Hey!" Hawn's fists were thunderous on the metal doors as he interrupted Edna's nonstop monologue. Four cracks. Jesus! Four cracks of light. That meant the sun had to be far down in the sky. It meant the sun had to be . . . setting.

"Hey!" Hawn screamed again. "You lied to me!" Real panic choked his voice now as he realized it wasn't so hot anymore.

"Now, why would I do that?" Edna asked patiently, as soon as Hawn stopped screaming.

"I don't know, lady. You tell me."

"What on Earth are you talking about, Jayce?" inquired Edna sweetly.

"You know what I'm talkin' about!" he yelled, his fists pummeling the doors again. "It's later than I thought."

There was a pause, a long pause in which he heard nothing but his own rushed breathing.

"Yes," agreed Edna finally. He could hear in her voice how pleased she was. "Yes, oh my, yes. It is much later than you thought."

Then she laughed. A big, hearty, booming, woman's laugh came pouring out of her, as if she had been wanting to laugh all day, the sound of it cutting through the shed, the chilling sound of it cutting all the way through to his heart, more penetrating than all the thunderous echoes of his fists against the metal walls.

"Why," Hawn asked cautiously, "why would you want to lock me in here?"

"So you won't hurt me," the old lady told him.

Hawn began the spiel again, but she cut him off.

"Seems to me," the old lady sniffed, "that if you really had work, you'd at least know Hadleyville was Hadleysville. And if you don't know that," she continued, "then you must be up to no good. Yep. No good."

"Edna," he reasoned, cautious again, "you're making a mistake. It's all a misunderstanding. I'm innocent."

"Hmph." said Edna.

"Look," said Hawn. "I'll prove it to you. We'll go ahead and let George call the police. I wouldn't want to see the police if I wasn't innocent, would I?"

"George? How could George call the police?" Edna snapped indignantly. "George is dead!"

Oh God Ohgodohgodohgodohgod. No. This couldn't be happening to him.

"George should have called the police," said Edna. "A long, long time ago. He really should have called them. I seen 'em coming. They had packs on their backs, just like you. Dirty jeans. Filthy. Not clean-cut at all. Up to no good."

"But no. He just came walkin' down the hill. Always thought he could reason with folks. Poor George."

She was crying softly.

"And when they started beating on him like that, I h-h-hid." She was sobbing now. "Right in that shed where you are now. Did I mention that? I've been in there before. Where it's all dark and dank and muggy. Oh, it was awful. And I had to hide in there for hours. I darn near lost my mind . . ." she said, her voice faraway.

"Edna," he said, "I'm sorry about George. But you've got to let me out. I'm begging you," he pleaded. Was this a trip? He, Jayce Earl-Roy Hawn, was begging for his life. Just like the old ladies he liked to bump off. That's what this old witch had done to him. She had made an old lady out of him. God, how he wanted her to pay!

"I seen you comin' this morning, you know. You had a pack on your back, just like them. Not clean cut. Not clean cut at all. I see everyone coming up here on this hill. Not a one of 'em got by yet."

"Let me go, Miss Edna, please?" begged Hawn respectfully.

"Please?" he said again, when there was no answer.

"Please," he begged, realizing that the choking sound in his throat was a sob.

Edna was all business again. "So you can hurt me the way they hurt George? Not a chance."

Hawn kept sobbing, unable to stop himself. Then suddenly he got a hold of himself. He stopped sobbing in midgasp. Why hadn't he realized? This was a shed, a garden shed! There would be tools, probably a shovel, a rake, a hoe, or whatever. He could break out! He threw himself onto the ground and rooted feverishly through the dufflebag for his flashlight.

As if she could read his mind, Edna said, "There aren't any sharp instruments or tools or anything in there, you know. Keep 'em all up at the house, in the utility room."

With a sinking feeling, and with the light from the flashlight overpowering the last two tiny cracks of light, Hawn took a closer look at some of the very things he had been staring at all afternoon. She was right. There were some bags of fertilizer, some plastic bottles of insecticide and weedkiller and such, tomato cages, and those green sticks that you stake vegetables with. Nothing sharp. Nothing that would really help. "Oh, I figured you might have a pen knife, or even a hunting knife, maybe, but that won't really help you much."

Hawn slumped again, thinking.

"You know, Jayce," Edna said, "it would help me, really help me if you were to go over to that one corner. Where the leaves are? And the concrete is missing? Right there in the corner, it's about, oh, four foot by three foot. And three foot deep. It's full up with leaves, now, but it would really help me if you were to just go sit down in there."

"Three feet deep?" said Hawn. "You mean, where those leaves are, it's like a — pit?"

"Uh-huh," she said.

That was it! Three feet deep. He could dig himself out. He had his hands and his knife. He could dig himself out! He knew she was telling the truth. He had seen the leaves piled high in the corner, but just hadn't paid any attention. Frantically, he groped for the flashlight that had slipped from his hand and made his way to the corner, digging madly through the leaves. Until the flashlight struck the post. And then he found a second post. And another. And another.

It was a pit, all right. But it had iron posts driven into the ground, all around it. At three-inch intervals. The kind supermarkets erect to keep customers from stealing shopping carts. He hadn't seen the posts before because the leaves had covered them.

Jesus. Oh God. Why, he asked himself, still not wanting to realize, his clammy hands scratching at the itchy sweat that bathed his face, and his neck, and his chest, why would anyone dig a pit inside a tool shed, and put posts around it, no less?

"To keep 'em from digging themselves out of the compost pit," Edna answered, anticipating his unspoken question.

"You bitch," Hawn half-screamed, half-sobbed.

Then he saw the lime. There was an open bag of it right next to the leaves. And more bags of it, stacked up in the corner. Hawn knew what lime was for. Gardeners used it in compost heaps to take the smell away from things that were — rotting.

"I first began to notice the difference," said Edna, "when I buried George. He's over there under the lilies. Well, my gosh, there were so many of them that year, so many blooms, and the leaves so green and bright. That's when I got the idea. With so much scum passing through the county, up to no good, with their filthy jeans, and backpacks and all. Why not, I thought, put the — pardon the pun — 'scum' to use?" She laughed delightfully.

"And it worked like a charm, of course. Why, you'd be surprised at just how much 'scum' the bait of an open door can trap. And the next year? Why, you should have seen the roses. Did I tell you what the neighbors say about my garden? And how they're just dying to know my secret?"

"Let me *outtt,*" Hawn wailed, banging the walls with all his might.

"Good Lord. I knew you'd start making a racket sooner or later."

Hawn kept yelling.

"Oh, shut up. Won't do you any good. Don't you realize you could scream all day and all night for a month out here and no one would hear you?"

Hawn realized. But he kept it up.

"I could have told you hours ago, you know. It wouldn't have made a blamed bit of difference. But I just couldn't have stood that racket while I was trying to get my gardening done. I didn't want my transplanting disturbed."

Jayce Earl-Roy Hawn was calmer now, much calmer because he realized it had to be a joke. She was an old lady, for Christ's sake. She wouldn't, couldn't do this to another living, breathing human being. Could she? She was definitely dotty all right. He realized it was completely dark now, and there she was, still out there in the dark, still rambling on about her garden.

Hawn found the flashlight and then grabbed one of the vegetable stakes. He made his way to the pit again, and with the help of the flashlight began to sift through the leaves with the stake. *See? Nothing to worry about.* Except for the soup at the bottom. At the bottom, under all the leaves and rotting banana peels, underneath the orange skins and cucumber peelings and slimy leftovers of God-knows-what, there was this foul-smelling soupy gunk. And then the stake hit something solid. *Oh, no. Oh, Jesus, no, no, no, no. It couldn't be. Clear the leaves,* Hawn told himself. *That's it, yes, clear the leaves, with your hands, the light, anything, because it's just not possible.* Hawn shined the light deep down where he had cleared. It was a rounded, grayish-white, bony object, with all manner of slimy gunk floating out of the sockets where the eyes had been.

Hawn screamed. He screamed more loudly, agonizingly, pathetically than he remembered any of his victims ever had. He screamed again and again and again. Until it hurt. Until the air, rushing in to fill his lungs, cut like a knife all the way down into his chest.

"There, there, now," said Edna, comfortingly, when all the screams eventually degenerated into sobs, "can't do that all night, now, can we? And Jayce? Would you please do me one, little, itsy-bitsy favor?"

Edna paused, listening to the deep, labored sobs emanating from the shed.

"When you go over there to sit down in the pit," she continued, "the compost pit in the corner over there? Would you mind taking your clothes off first? It always so messy havin' to fish the clothes out once decomposition begins."

Another agonizing scream echoed through the night air. From somewhere far away Hawn heard it, but now he could no longer distinguish: was the scream a reality? Had that come from him? Or was it just a memory?

"Good," said Edna. "That's very good, Jayce. Just get it out of your system," she said soothingly. She waited a little. "Now, where was I?" Edna continued. "Oh, yes. Yes, indeed. I think organic fertilizer *is* best, don't you?"   Ω

FEAR

All is imp fear, goblin fear, terror of darkness.
Peasant wench I scurry, mine is a hard life
Amid danger of pixies, elf-peril, troll-peril.
Hand in pocket I finger my lucky charm.
May Will-o'-the Wisp not beckon me,
Witches not harry,
May Lady Death keep to herself her cold sudden clutch.
I beg of faerie,
I propitiate the unseen gods,
O princes of evil
May I be spared yet awhile
The wail of the banshee
The yelp of Hell's hounds.
In the air always I fear the ringing of harebells.

All is AIDS terror, cancer fear, fear of heart disease.
Careful I walk, a modern woman
Amid dangerous cholesterol, high blood pressure, peril of unprotected sex.
In my purse I carry my prophylactic.
Every day I pray
May diet and exercise suffice me
May passion not entice me
May radon gas, asbestos or dread virus never enter me.
I eat oat bran; may my arteries flow free.
I beg the powers that be
O gods of education and research
O mighty ones of Pap smear and mammogram
May I be spared yet awhile
The blood test
The mastectomy
In the air always I fear the ringing of harebells.

—Nancy Springer

DROPPING GHYLL

by John Brunner

Fifteen miles of heather, bracken, rock, and bog — twelve it should have been as the crow flies, but I had to detour round the wettest stretch — brought me over the grey-green shoulder of Postle Bar, whence I had my first sight of Foldertoft, some hundred houses of the harsh local stone, a church, three shops, and blessedly a pub.

I had planned to carry on to Wakeworth, another four miles, but a storm that had been threatening since noon chose that moment to break and changed my mind.

However, when I reached the pub — it turned out to be called the Horse and Cart — I found it locked, opening time not being due for another hour. I had to knock.

"A room?" said the plump sixtyish woman who appeared at last. "Well, we don't usually, except in high summer, but — Here, you'd best come in the dry. I wouldn't turn you away, not in this weather. *Sally!*"

Sally proved to be a sullen teenager in jeans, who condescended to show me to my lodging, cramped but clean, and listlessly promised to make the bed and bring a towel. I dumped my pack in a corner, hung up my anorak, changed my fell boots for sandals — that was a relief — and left her to get on with it.

Downstairs, the only public room appeared to be the bar, long and narrow like the house itself, with a fireplace in the middle of the back wall, so I sat down in a wheelback armchair and listened to the beating rain, glad I'd found shelter in the nick of time. From one of the private rooms drifted the sound of radio or television, but I couldn't make out what the programme was.

The landlady bustled in shortly with an armful of logs and in a moment had them ablaze. Rising, dusting her hands together, she invited me to draw my chair nearer the fire and then suggested, "Would you like a drink?"

"I thought you weren't open," I countered in surprise.

"Ah, but now you're a resident, and that's legal, isn't it?"

"In that case," I said gratefully, "I'd like a whisky mac." I'd just realized how the wind on Postle Bar had chilled me to the bone.

"To warm you inside like the fire outside?"

"Yes, exactly. Make it a double!"

Having brought the drink, she showed no inclination to depart. Thinking she wanted to know whether it was mixed to my taste, I assured her it was, and she took that as an invitation to start chatting.

"You're not from round here, are you, sir?"

"No, I'm from London. But I come to Yorkshire fairly often. I was evacuated here during the war — not exactly here, but over Scourby way — and took a liking to the area. I suppose I must have walked almost every track in the county by now. Though this is my first time over Postle Bar."

"Funny!" She scrutinized me intently. "You don't look old enough to have been evacuated."

She didn't intend it as a compliment; Yorkshire people tend to be direct. I said with a shrug, "Well, I was only a little

From the anthology *Dark Fantasies* edited by Chris Morgan

boy . . . Do you get a lot of walkers like me around here?"

Shaking her head, she sat down on a chair the other side of the fireplace. "No, hardly any. Foldertoft is in a kind of no-man's-land, really. Matter of fact, when I was a girl, we didn't have any visitors at all."

"You're local, then?"

"Born three miles from where we're sitting, up at Wallside Farm. Never met anyone from outside the Riding till I were twelve. That was an evacuee like you and he came from London, too. Cuthbert, they called him. Cuthbert Swann."

I started and almost spilled my drink — or as much as was left of it.

"Good lord! He was a cousin of mine!"

An expression crossed her face that I could not define. Perhaps one might say it mingled shock with wariness and suspicion. After a moment she said, "Was?"

"He disappeared. Several years ago, not far from here. They never found a trace of him. That day there was a fog on the moors, so presumably he lost his way and tumbled in a pothole."

"Dreadful!" she said with no discernible sincerity. "I *am* sorry."

The whisky mac, which I had now finished, had loosened my tongue with remarkable speed. I said, "I wasn't!"

She stared a question at me.

"I wasn't sorry," I emphasized. "I couldn't stand the little — blighter. Sorry to be so blunt, but he was a sarcastic knowall, always putting other people down. I hadn't seen him in years, and I'd never known him well. His father was my mother's brother, and she and he didn't get on, so . . . In the end Cuthbert and I had a row, a real shouting-match. I'd told him I was coming up this way — come to think of it, that was my first proper walking-tour — and he said some awful things about Yorkshire folk, and in the end I . . . Well, I hit him to shut him up. I never saw him again."

Rising, she took my glass and refilled

it. Watching her press it to the whisky optic, then measure out the ginger wine, I wondered whether I'd been too open; after all, what landlady would be pleased to learn she'd let a room to someone given, on his own admission, to violence? I waited a little nervously for her return.

But as she sat down again she said musingly, "He never changed, did he?"

"How do you mean?"

"That's just the way he were as a kid — like you said, a sarcastic knowall. And conceited with it. And he never changed."

"You mean you — well, you met him in later life?"

"Oh, yes. He came back now and then. Not what you'd call regular, but — oh — five or six times."

"That's incredible!" I exclaimed. "Hearing him talk, you'd have thought he hated Yorkshire so much, after his time as an evacuee, that he never wanted to set foot here again. When they said he'd disappeared in this area I could scarcely believe it."

"He never told you about his visits?"

"Never. As I said, we weren't exactly close."

"Well, I don't suppose he'd have wanted to make a fuss about the reason he kept coming back. Oh, how I hated it every time he walked through yon door with some fancy bit of gadgetry, saying, "Rosie" — that's my name, Rosie Thwaite as was, Mrs Gosling as I became when I married Tom, rest his soul — 'Rosie *you bitch*, I'm going to prove it this time! I'm going to have the last laugh!' "

The storm had darkened the windows, but by the light of the fire I could read as much bitterness in her face as I heard in her voice. Tensing, leaning forward with my elbows on the arms of the chair and my glass clutched tightly in both hands, I said, "What did bring him here?"

There was a pause. Eventually she made a long arm and switched on a wall-mounted lamp that scarcely broached the gloom. Then, folding her hands, she said as though to herself, "Well, it were a long time ago, and now Tom's gone, who were t'only one I ever told . . . And you are his cousin, aren't you?"

She fixed me with piercing eyes.

"I am indeed. My name isn't Swann — it's Harris, Roger Harris — but as I said his father was my mother's brother, and Swann was her maiden name."

"Well, then, I suppose . . ." She sighed deeply. "If anybody has a right to t'truth, it's one of his kinfolk. So I'll tell you what became of Cuthbert. Somebody ought to know apart from me.

"Not that I expect you to believe the tale."

There weren't too many kids of our age around Foldertoft in the forties, but then there hadn't been for quite a while. Times were right hard before the war, and few of the young people cared to stick it out on the land like my dad. He used to say, "So long as you own land you can get food." And he practised what he preached. He was canny, was my dad. He bought up four abandoned farms, though he didn't have anyone to work them until the Land Army sent us half a dozen girls, and I never went hungry, nor my brothers, when they brought in rations. But it took the war to change things. Sad that, wasn't it?

Then all of a sudden it was "Feed the Forces!" and "Dig for Victory!" and farmers were vital to the war effort, and kids from the big cities were being sent away to escape the German bombs, and the government paid money to people whose evacuees wet the bed. Did you know about that? Mam did. That's why she applied for one. She said we could rinse the sheets in the beck and it wouldn't cost a penny, and the mattress could dry by the kitchen stove.

Funny, you know! I never told anyone but my Tom before — not this story, in this way . . .

Still, like I said, he's gone. Two years come Michaelmas, it'll be. And I don't

like not sharing it with anyone at all . . .

Where was I? Oh, yes! We got this evacuee kid: *Master Cuthbert!*

I could hear the contempt in her voice. It summed up everything I myself had felt about my loathsome cousin.

Why he wound up in Yorkshire, 'stead of being sent to some cushy hideout in Canada or Australia like most boys from rich families, *I* don't know. But there he was, and inside a week all on us wished he were dead.

Why? Because of his airs and graces! He made out that coming from London he had a right to sneer at Foldertoft as if it were the back of beyond. I remember most of all how he mithered about not being able to go to t'pictures the way he was accustomed — two or three times a week, if we were to believe him. Back then we had a film-show every other Saturday at the parish hall, and were glad of it, but the films were mostly old 'uns and if he'd seen them he took spiteful pleasure in describing the plot beforehand so as to spoil it for everybody else.

He had to come to school with the rest of us — we had our own school then, here in the village, though of course now the children have to take the bus to Waith — and the very first day he got up and contradicted our teacher. Mr Denny was his name, brought out of retirement when Mr Pickles joined the navy. 'Course some of his ideas were a bit oldfashioned, but in wartime you have to mek do, don't you? And it wasn't any kid's place to tell him off in front of the class!

Oh, I forgot to say. My mam didn't like Cuthbert either. He complained about her cooking all the time, and what's more he didn't wet the bed, not once, so she didn't get the — what did they call it? — the enuresis allowance, that's it. But that's by the bye.

I suppose, thinking back, he was brighter than the rest of us. Certainly he'd read lots of books, and he were good at his studies, and in the evening he'd get through his homework in fifteen minutes when it took me an hour — and I were older than him. Three years older. Once I dared to ask him for help, and we had a right to-do. What were it he said? Said my brain must be as damaged as my face. The cheeky beggar!

I must have betrayed astonishment at that point, for Mrs Gosling broke off her tale and leaned back to let the wall-lamp shine full on her.

Without a trace of self-consciousness she said, "Back then I had a harelip, and I talked sort of funny. They mended it when the National Health came along, but you can still see the scar. When I got to courting age" — here a chuckle — "I remember wishing I were a boy so I could grow a moustache and cover it! Never bothered my Tom, though, rest his soul . . .

"Where was I? Oh, yes."

Spite of all, he and I had to put up with each other, living under the same roof. The other children at the school — even my brothers — wouldn't keep company with either of us, him for his snobby ways and me for my silly looks, so we spent a lot of time together.

And I could have welcomed that, after being alone so much, except he was so full of himself! He was forever lecturing anyone in earshot. Like, "Do you know how far it is all round the world?" And I'd say, "No," and he'd say — no, he'd crow! — "Thought not!" And then he'd say, "It's however many thousand miles, and it would take such-and-such a time to walk it if you could, and you're ignorant like all these other horrible people!"

And then again he'd point at the moon and say, "That's nearly ten times as far from here as the distance round the world," and I'd say, "How do you know?", and he'd get angry and say he read it in

a book, and I'd say not everything you read is true — I learned that off my dad, who knew the news was being censored to disguise how badly the war was going for us — and Cuthbert would storm off in a rage.

'Course he came back. Wasn't anyone else around who'd even talk to him, even my mam and dad, even my brothers. Mainly 'cause he wouldn't listen. Too full on hisself, like I said . . .

Well, this dragged on for months, past Christmas and New Year, right into the spring. It were a miserable time. They kept calling people up, so one day there they were and next day gone, and then no news for months on end. I got my first grown-up kiss and cuddle around then, from a boy off to the army —

Didn't mean to say that. Afterwards I reckoned he must have been too drunk to notice what I looked like, but it felt nice, any road . . . Never came back, that Jack. North Africa it were that did for him. Tanks.

I'm rambling. I was talking about Cuthbert.

Well, I put up with him as best I could, for lack of anybody else save mam and dad, and they were busy, and by then we had the Land Girls, and mam was jealous of them with their city ways and suspicious of what dad might get up to with them in the barn, so there were rows at home and even Cuthbert was better than that.

Until one day when he tried to tell me something really silly. Really stupid! He said light things fall as fast as heavy things!

We were up on Postle Bar after school and the wind were blowing — not as hard as now but pretty hard — and there was an empty magpie's nest with some feathers stuck to a broken eggshell, so I took a feather and a stone and let both of them go, and the stone fell and the feather blew away, so I said he was talking rubbish.

He got all red in the face and said it

was because of the air. So I said to him, I said, "All right, take me where there isn't any air." And he said it'd been proved in some — what's the word? laboratory, and I said, then you do the same!

And he said he couldn't, not without the right equipment, so I laughed (he never could stand to be laughed at), and he really went wild. He said it was all in the books at the library because it had been demonstrated by a famous scientist in Italy, and I said, well, we're at war with the Italians, aren't we? Maybe that's one of the reasons — they're crazy over there!

And he said this happened a long while back when Mussolini hadn't even been thought of, and it was proved by dropping two sizes of cannonball and they always reached the bottom at the same time.

So I asked where they did it from, and he said some tower that was so badly built it wasn't upright but leaned at an angle, and by that time I'd had enough and I wanted to go home for my tea, so I said it was a shame they didn't try the same at Dropping Ghyll.

And he asked why, and I said, because it's bottomless, and he got so angry that he started calling me names. I jumped up and ran from home, him chasing behind. When I got there my brothers were outside — mam was busy getting the tea and she'd told them to stay out of the kitchen till the parkin were ready — and they asked why I was laughing so hard.

And I said, "This lummock won't believe that Dropping Ghyll is bottomless!"

All of us knew it was for solid fact, you see.

Dropping Ghyll? Oh, you came by it. It's on the north flank of Postle Bar. They've put a wall round it, partway broken down so you could take it for a disused fold, but they built it to keep sheep out, not in. And toddling children, of course. Since we were old enough to talk we'd all been warned to stay away.

Once I asked Parson about its name, and he said it doesn't mean what it sounds like. He said it started out as "Dry Pen Ghyll" because a stream that wore it through the rock was diverted by a landslide and now runs down the west of the Bar . . . Just as well, happen.

Any road, my brothers looked at me as if we'd never met before. Could be they'd heard about me being kissed by Jack — I never dared to ask, but I always wondered. And Barrie, who was the older on 'em, said, "So Cuthbert is that thick. Well, there's a while before tea. Let's show the stupid —" I better not repeat exactly what he said. Anyway, he's dead. Bomber-crew over Germany. Later on Joe got his in the submarines . . .

Still, it was all a long time ago.

It took us only a few minutes to reach the spot and scramble over the wall. Knowing better than to walk close to the hole, we laid us down on us stummicks and wriggled the last couple of yards. Cuthbert didn't want to — it were undignified! — but when Barrie told him bits might break off and take him with them he did in the end. With our heads over the edge, we peered down.

"It's certainly deep," Cuthbert said at last. "But so are lots of other potholes, aren't they?"

"So how would you measure it?" Joe asked.

"Well — drop a stone down the middle and count the seconds till you hear it hit the bottom."

"Go on, then," Barrie said.

I don't think I mentioned, but Cuthbert had a wristwatch with a seconds hand; that was rare for a youngster in those days and he was terribly proud of it. Well, he'd been challenged and he couldn't back down, so he found a stone and lobbed it into the middle of the hole and started counting. The rest of us stayed quiet as mice so he couldn't say he'd missed hearing the stone because of us.

When a full minute had gone by

and there was still dead silence, mam shouted to come in for us tea, so we ran back. Cuthbert followed very slowly, looking grim.

Later that evening, when I'd finished my homework and gone back to the kitchen to listen to the wireless a while before bed, I expected to find Cuthbert there. He wasn't. Mam was puzzled too and went to see if he was all right. She came down and told us that he were busy with something in his room. Sums, she said. Well, I never knew him that bothered wi' sums before.

'Course, later we figured it out. He was trying to work out how deep the hole must be if a stone took more than a minute to reach the bottom. Tom did show me once how to calculate it, but I've forgotten what he said the answer was.

Didn't matter, of course.

After that Cuthbert stopped being such a knowall. He spent more and more time wandering off by himself. I didn't mind. Suddenly I was getting on better with my brothers. And seemingly mam's mind had been set at rest about the Land Girls, so life was a lot easier.

And down south the bombing let up and one day the next summer Cuthbert went back home. He made no secret that he'd rather be in London, bombs or no, than among idiots who believed in impossible things like a bottomless pit. We all laughed behind his back, never expecting to see him again.

'Course Joe and Barrie never had the chance . . .

Mam and I did, though. After t'war. He was waiting to be called up for the army — national service — and we got this letter asking if he could come and stay a day or two before he was due to report at Catterick. I wasn't overjoyed, no more was mum, but after so many years . . . I remember saying, "Well, maybe he's changed like the rest of us."

And at first we thought he had.

Certainly he was more polite. But then, when he got the chance to talk to me alone, I found out what his reason was for coming.

He'd got hold of some new kind of very thin, very light cord — nylon, I suppose — so light you could carry a mile of it on a reel. His father owned a chemical works or summat, I believe. And he proposed to let it down Dropping Ghyll. On the end of the line he'd fixed some kind of gadget that would make a howling noise when it touched bottom. He showed me all this with pride. And he said, "I only wish your stuck-up brothers could be here!"

Both dead by then, like I told you . . . I'd never liked him. That was when I started to loathe him.

I don't think he expected me to say yes when he asked if I wanted to watch him carry out his "experiment." But I did, and I sat on the wall and waited. And waited.

'Course he let all the line out and the howling gadget didn't make a peep.

Dark-faced, he looked at me as though suspecting I'd sabotaged it somehow, but he made the best of things and wound up saying, "Well, I know it's at least as deep as the length of my line."

Next day he went off to recruit camp and I hoped we'd seen the last of him.

I were wrong.

During his time in the army he served in the engineers, and next time he came back, about three years later, he brought summat different, some sort of government surplus echo-sounding device. Same as before, he invited me to witness his proof that Dropping Ghyll did have a bottom. I was engaged to Tom by then — they'd mended my lip the year before — so it weren't quite right for me to go off alone with a man, but we had known each other since we were kids, so . . .

And things turned out the same way. No signal from the echo-sounder. This time he got right mad wi' it, claiming the bloody thing must have got broken on the way — pardon my French — although when he tried it on everything else in the area, like the stone walls, it worked fine.

Once again I hoped that would be the end of it.

Time passed. Dad died, and mam didn't long outlast him, so t'farm passed to me, and I decided to sell it so Tom and I could take this pub. He'd always fancied the licensed trade, and though I wasn't too keen I didn't feel I could stand the loneliness of a farmhouse stuck out there on the hillside. Besides, we wanted a family, and children need other kids to play with. I didn't want mine to be ignored the way I was by my brothers. We've — I mean I've — been here ever since.

And, a handful of years later, up turns Mr Cuthbert Swann again, this time with — what was it? So heavy he took most of a day setting it up ... He always came by himself. I don't suppose it was because he didn't know anyone he could have asked to help. I think more likely it was because he was afraid they'd laugh when he explained the reason for his visits.

This time he'd managed to get his hands on surplus radar gear. He brought it in a jeep complete with its own generator. I was expecting him, of course; he'd written to the farm as usual, and Mr Wardle the postmaster knew I wasn't there and redirected the letter. I wanted to run and hide, but you can't just shut the only pub for miles ...

So I let him stay, in the same room you have, and passed him off to Tom the way I had before, a wartime friend, and he didn't mind my going out to watch the experiment, as usual. Though he did have his suspicions about the black mood Cuthbert came back with, thinking maybe he had tried summat on. Still, obviously I'd refused, so not to worry.

Any road, the radar didn't find bottom, either.

Once again I hoped he'd given up, and as the years slid by I more or less forgot about him. We had kids to raise by then, twin girls first, and later on a boy, and the war was far in the past.

But he came again, and again, each time with some new sort of measuring device. One was like a tiny helicopter that was supposed to fly down the exact middle of the hole, keeping its distance automatically from the sides. He was specially proud of that. Said he'd designed and built it himself. By then he had a job with an aircraft company.

When that one didn't work any better than the others he had to invent brand-new excuses. This time he said the hole couldn't be straight; there must be a kink in it, and some kind of metal in the rock absorbed the signal his toy plane was broadcasting when it got to the lower side. He was beside himself when he lost it, though — and even madder when I pointed out that, if there were any kink like that, the very first stone he dropped, all those years ago, would have hit it and we'd all have heard the noise.

Funny! I haven't thought of this in ages, but it must have been around then that I found out he'd been right on one score: without air, light and heavy things do fall at the same speed. Remember one of them Americans took a feather to the moon and demonstrated? When I saw that on the telly I started to laugh and Tom wanted to know why, and I couldn't explain that I was laughing at myself.

And then Cuthbert turned up for the final time.

He arrived in an ordinary car, and what he had with him was a laser coupled to a battery-powered computer. The whole lot, plus an aluminum pole that folded up like a telescope, fitted into a nylon haversack, and he couldn't help boasting about how everything was being made smaller and more efficient every year. I don't know much about that sort of thing, but my lad Jerry does, and he asked Cuthbert lots of questions and did his best to translate the answers into plain English. Cuthbert had to admit that he was trying to measure the depth of — he didn't say Dropping Ghyll, but he did say underground caves — and Jerry, all innocent, asked why he wasn't working with the country caving club, instead of around here where they never used to come. Well, Cuthbert wriggled out of that somehow. But he made sure to time his experiment for a school day, when Jerry would be safely on the bus to Waith.

By now I'd grown resentful of the way he seemed to feel he was entitled to march into my life whenever he chose, take over our only spare room, and promise to show me up, and my dead brothers, for having fooled him for so long. I told you he talked about having the last laugh, didn't I?

And — well, I think by then he was a bit touched. I mean, nobody in his right mind would let something like this turn into an obsession, would he? I'm sorry to say it to his own cousin, but there it is.

So . . . Maybe it was malice, but I hope not. I'd simply had enough of him and wanted him to go away and stay away. So I had a word with Jerry and learned some tricky questions I could put when he invited me — more sort of ordered me — to come and witness his new experiment.

For once rather looking forward to it, I turned out first thing next morning, and we walked through fog to Dropping Ghyll. I waited until he'd explained about his laser, this beam of very pure light that would hit the bottom, no matter how far down it was, and bounce back to be caught in an electric detector, so the computer could measure the time it had taken to travel both ways. Then I surprised him by asking, "What if the material it hits absorbs light at just the right frequency?"

That took the wind out of his sails! He hadn't thought what an education

it is for folk like me to have a bright fifteen-year-old studying subjects that weren't even invented when I were at school . . . He said crossly, "No question of that! I detoured via Dropping Ghyll yesterday and threw down some of this stuff."

He produced a bag and showed me a handful of crystals. Faceted, he said they were. They were supposed to act like mirrors. Whichever way up they landed, at least some of them would reflect the light straight back the way it had come. And he wound up by saying, "It's more than a day since I chucked the first lot down. No matter how deep the hole is, they *must* have reached bottom by now!"

I bit my tongue to stop myself from asking what he'd do if they hadn't . . .

So he set up his laser on the collapsible pole, so it hung square over the middle of the hole, dancing around and rubbing his hands and muttering about how he was going to settle the matter once for all, and took a deep breath and switched on his computer.

"There!" he said, pointing to a line of green numbers, the kind you see on a video-recorder or one of them alarm-clock radios. "That's the computer's measurement of the distance to what's reflecting the laser beam —"

That was as far as he got. Because he suddenly realized what I'd already noticed. The numbers weren't staying the same. They were getting bigger. And bigger. And bigger.

He started to whimper. He said, "They can't still be falling! They can't! Not after more than twenty-four hours! Oh, the damned thing must have gone wrong like all the others!"

And then he rounded on me. He had a devil's look on his face, lips pulled back, eyes wide and staring, and a spray of spittle flew from his mouth.

"It's your doing, isn't it?" he screamed. "Every time I come you pull some sort of trick on me! Well, I don't know what you do or how — I wouldn't be surprised if you call it magic! — but I've had my *bellyful!*"

And he slapped me. Hard. Hard enough to knock me off the wall where I was perching.

I tumbled on my back in the wet heather, more furious than hurt, and picked myself up shouting at the top of my voice — not of course expecting anyone except Cuthbert to hear, which was as well because I was so angry I used language I didn't know I knew!

But when I looked for him — there he wasn't.

Nor was the aluminum pole.

Nor the laser, nor the computer that had been tied to it by an electric lead.

And it wasn't just that they were hidden by the fog.

I stopped shouting. I felt very cold.

Eventually I climbed back over the wall, finding it harder than when I were a youngster, and just as we used to in the old days I dropped on my stummick and crawled the last few yards to the edge of the hole.

Far below, faint and getting fainter, I heard Cuthbert screaming. Now and then there were a bang as one of the machines he'd dragged down with him crashed against the wall.

It was a long while before I were able to go home. By then the fog were so dense I almost missed my way. Me!

Naturally Tom was horrified at the state I was in, and — well, in the end, I had to explain. I'd just about finished when it came opening time, and I had to pretend to the customers that everything was fine.

But Tom must have done a lot of thinking while he was serving at the bar, because when we closed that afternoon he had it all worked out.

He said we shouldn't worry about anything until nightfall. Then we'd have to let slip a few hints during the evening, about our lodger that was overdue; then

after we'd called time at ten-thirty we'd ring up P C Russell and tell him we were worried, and leave it to him to decide whether to call out a search team.

Weren't many folk in here that night, as I recall. Fog grew thicker and thicker . . .

Next afternoon, throwing to the chickens the sandwiches I hadn't sold that dinnertime, I thought about sending some after Cuthbert. But I didn't. Like he said, light and heavy things fall at the same speed, except where there's air, when light things do fall slower. Either way they'd never have caught up, would they?

I suppose he starved. Well, maybe not; once, looking right over the edge of Dropping Ghyll with an electric torch, I noticed mushrooms growing on the wall. He could have picked some of those. And there's always water oozing from the rock.

Still, if he didn't, he must be awful bored by now . . .

A dozen questions were on the tip of my tongue. I knew there had been a search, and inquiries by the police, and I wanted her first-hand account of both. But I was forestalled by a bang on the door. Mrs Gosling gathered herself with a start, glancing at the clock above the bar.

"Lord, sir, it's way past opening time! Can you see to the fire while I unlock? *Sally!*"

The rest of the evening passed on a drift of slow country conversation, the sort where there always seem to be pauses yet one can never introduce a new subject. I was fed — a lamb chop with mashed potatoes and beans, some kind of freezer package warmed in a microwave oven — and I drank more beer than was good for me, and my legs complained more and more loudly concerning the toll that fifteen miles over the moors had taken of them, and in the end I gave up and turned in, having ordered an early breakfast.

But I lay awake for a long while.

Next morning broke dry and bright. Yawning Sally served me tea and cereal in the empty bar. I said, "Can I have a word with Mrs Gosling before I go?"

She answered with a shrug. "You'll have to wait. Never gets up before nine, her."

It was seven, and I had four overdue miles to make up. I hesitated, torn two ways. At length I said, "You see, she told me she used to know a cousin of mine who fell into Dropping Ghyll trying to prove it wasn't bottomless."

"Must have been a long while back!" Sally exclaimed.

"What do you mean?" I countered in amazement.

"Why — !" She rubbed sleep out of her eyes and pointed at a scroll hanging on the wall behind the bar, that somehow I had overlooked the previous night. I rose and inspected it. It recorded an achievement of the West Riding Spelunkers, who for the first time on such-and-such a date had plumbed the depths of Dropping Ghyll and made a safe return, and celebrated the fact with a party in the Horse and Cart.

I stared at it numbly. At long last I said over my shoulder, "Do you come from around here, Sally?"

"Spent all my life in Foldertoft," was her muttered answer. "Deadest place on earth, I reckon! Wish I could get away!"

"Were you brought up to believe that Dropping Ghyll was bottomless?"

She burst out laughing.

"When I was a kid gran used to try and scare me and my cousins by making out it was. But it's like believing in Father Christmas! Stands to reason, don't it?"

Nodding, I chose my next words with care.

"When the cavers reached the bottom,
did they find anything? For instance, bones?"

"Bits of a sheep, it said in the paper . . . Finished with your breakfast, have you? I haven't had mine yet and I wouldn't mind."

"Nothing else?" I persisted.

"Such as what?"

"Well — broken scientific equipment."

She shrugged. "Not that I heard about."

"No human bones?"

"They said just sheep's. Must have been some other pothole your cousin fell down . . . *Can* I clear away?"

"Yes, go ahead. And bring my bill."

When I returned home, one of the first things I did was write a letter to Mrs. Rosie Gosling at the Horse and Cart Inn, Foldertoft. It came back with a scrawled note on the envelope from one of the local postmen saying, yes, there was a pub in Foldertoft but it was called the Barn Owl, and the last people in the village named Gosling had emigrated to Australia in the fifties.

I wrote to the Yorkshire Spelunkers and they said they could find no reference to Dropping Ghyll; would I kindly furnish its co-ordinates because they were running short of new potholes to explore?

Since then I haven't found time to make another walking tour in Yorkshire —

No, that's less than honest. It's more that I seem always to be able to find an excuse not to go back. You see, if I did, I'd feel obliged to pursue inquiries into the fate of my loathsome cousin, Cuthbert Swann.

But what the hell did become of him? And, come to that, of Rosie Gosling? Maybe you can work it out. I can't.

If you can, though, I would rather not be told.   Ω

THE CLASSIC HORRORS

... Coeurl leaped out of
hiding. With ravenous speed, he
smashed the metal and the body
within it to bits. Great chunks of
metal, torn piecemeal from the
suit, sprayed the ground. Bones
cracked. Flesh crunched. ...

BLACK   DESTROYER
by A.E van Vogt

ALLEN K. '91

HUNTING THE LION

by S.P. Somtow

I have never liked eunuchs. I must confess a certain queasiness in their presence; in this I fear I am behind the times, and possessed of a kind of naïveté most unsuitable for one who practices the craft of the private detective in this modern world, this Ninth Century since the founding of the greatest nation on earth.

It was nevertheless a eunuch who was ushered into my triclinium at the hour of cena. I was drinking a goblet of undiluted Falernian and attempting to disentangle a dish of calves' brains sautéed in egg and honey, all the while dictating a letter to the steward of my Sicilian estates. I did not take kindly to being interrupted, but the creature whose presence now graced my dining room was not the kind of person one could ignore if one had any regard for one's political prospects.

He had the singularly inappropriate name of Eros. He wore a gold-fringed tunic dipped in purple (making up in ostentation for what he lacked in virility) and, when I showed him the couch, waddled towards it like an animated blood pudding.

"Rejoice," he said in his clipped demotic Greek, "O Publius Viridianus! I trust I find you in good health? Ah, but I see you are at dinner; perhaps I should come back at a more convenient hour."

"No hour could be more convenient," I said with practiced insincerity. I made to proffer the Falernian, then changed my mind and called for an amphora of Lesbian wine. Eros hemmed and hawed until I dismissed the scribe and whisked aside the arras to show that there were no spies. Even then he stared about like a caged beast. At last I said, "Come, come; I know you didn't come here to admire the murals. You just had your own house in Baiae done by the same artist, though I understand the mythological scenes you selected weren't quite as tame as the ones here — the rape of Ganymede, was it not?"

"How did you know? — but of course, such is your business — I imagine you've a thick dossier on me by now."

"You flatter me," I said. Not to mention yourself, I thought. "I am not nearly as omniscient as is rumored. Nevertheless, it delights me that I am deemed capable of providing service to no less a figure than the — third? — undersecretary of the — privy purse, is it? — division of Cæsar's household."

"You will be well paid," Eros said. Wine dribbled from his lips. He took another swallow. There is nothing more unnerving than a fidgety eunuch. "That is, if you — ah — accept the commission." He emptied a purse full of aurei onto the dining-table. One of them skittered into the brain omelette. "An advance, perhaps." I did not look at the money, though I wondered where such a supply of gold could have come from, what with the recent debasement of the coinage. I did not imagine that many of the coins would bear the image of Nero Claudius Drusus Germanicus, our current God of State.

"You haven't told me what the commission is."

"Haven't I?" He looked around again.

"My good man," I said, "I think you can see from my surroundings that I do not lack money; why, the very idea of your offering me so much seems not a little vulgar — I no longer make my living by spying on the mistresses of the nobility, tracking down the changeling heiresses switched at birth by inattentive nursemaids, children running away to join the foreign legionaries, and the like. Now and then, as a favor, I might essay a little investigation, but. . . ."

"Name your price, Viridian! I've no time to haggle. . . ."

I smiled. "There will be a price. I take it we are not speaking of some petty patrician whom it would be politically expedient to embarrass. You want me to hunt . . . nobler game. The lion rather than the jackal."

"Q. Drusianus Otho, to be precise," said the eunuch, his voice dropping to a whisper. "Now that I've revealed this, I may as well tell you that, should you refuse the assignment, I have been given authorization to order you to commit suicide."

Probably a bluff, I thought, shrugging. And even were it not, it would not do to appear overly concerned. After all, I am a real Roman and not some freedman's son . . . at least, not since I bribed a palace scribe 8,000 sesterces to "purify" my birth papers. Pity I had to kill him afterwards, but one can't be too careful nowadays.

He immediately began to imbibe the Lesbian and, though I had not asked him to share my cena, to attack my homely brain-and-honey omelette with gusto. I let him eat while I pondered my prospective target.

This Drusianus was an influential man. He was related by adoption to the Imperial family and also, by the marriage of his cousin to the Lady Octavia, to the Emperor's discarded ex-wife and through her to the Julian Divinity himself — thus he could claim, with more justification than many would require, to be descended from the goddess Venus on both sides. He was extremely rich — had served as editor of the games on a number of occasions, and owned both a gladiatorial school and a menagerie most noted for its abundance of lions — but had kept his nose remarkably clear of politics, apart from serving as consul once or twice. He didn't indulge in loose women or little boys — at least no more than was politically correct under our artsy-fartsy régime — and his home life was a model of uxoriousness and probity. A lion indeed, I thought. No wonder they want to bring him down.

"Why?" I asked at last, after giving Eros a chance to sit around quivering for a few moments. "He seems harmless enough. Why, he wasn't even part of the Pisonian conspiracy."

The eunuch pulled a little scroll from his tunic and handed it to me. It contained a poem that purported to be by Petronius, although I could tell by its stylistic infelicities that it was some second-rate imitator. The poem extolled the virtues of this Drusianus while castigating the Emperor's excesses; clever little thing actually, in a mindless sort of way — the sort of ditty one might compose while squatting in the communal shit-house at the public baths.

"If you don't mind my saying so," I said, "this hardly seems something to get all flustered about. The man obviously had nothing to do with this poem; what's more, it's abysmal. I can dig up dirt for you — you know my reputation for finding merda in unlikely places — and undoubtedly I will be able to discover something, however picayune, to bring about the downfall of this member of the Noble Order of Equites. But why bother? You know how expensive my services are; it is well known that I have many scruples, and that I charge by the scruple. How many scruples will I have to overcome to finger the most honorable man in Rome? More than this," I said, clapping my hands for someone to come and gather up the gold pieces scattered all over my triclinium table.

"But Cæsar is annoyed," said Eros. "And you know what he's like when he's annoyed."

And that, of course, was that.

I spent the evening scouring through my files on Drusianus. I knew him only by reputation — we did not go to the same sort of parties — and his reputation was amply backed up by my researches. His wife Volumnia had been one of the Christianoi for a while, but after being interrogated by the secret police had done the sensible thing and turned in all her contacts; I doubted it was anything more than an indulgence in the cult-of-the-month fever that infects our city in the summer heat.

I had a lot more information about Eros. Castrated though he was, he had slept with everybody who was anybody in Rome. He was a Syrian of some sort, born a slave into the household of one Polycrates, owner of a chain of brothels that promised uniform prices and service from Gaul to Gaza; as a boy had first attracted the attention of the Lady Claudia Procula, wife of Pontius Pilate, procurator of Judæa, by his acrobatic skill with his tongue; brought back to Rome; several bills of sale later, earned his freedom and ended up buying out his former master Polycrates, whereupon he lost his entire fortune in a venereal disease scandal, and ended up working for the imperial house under an assumed name. . . .

Exciting reading, almost as good as an evening at Petronius' house.

Drusianus was editor of the current spectacle season. Opening day was tomorrow, the Kalends of August . . . auguries pointed to a steamy, hellish day. With the Great Fire and its subsequent Grand Spectacle only two years past, the games were bound to be lavish, but I did not doubt that Drusianus had paid for them out of pocket, without a qualm; he was not the sort of person who ever needed to ask the price of anything.

Perhaps the Lady Volumnia would be a likelier target; she had fallen prey to the treacherous Christianoi once; perhaps she was still tainted by the bloody Oriental rites they were known to practise.

It was time to don the first disguise of the evening.

I spent a few minutes propitiating the household gods by the hall entrance, lighting incense and wringing the neck of a small dove in expiation for the impieties I was about to commit. I took a last look in a bronze hand-mirror and had to admit that my handiwork was impeccable. I had built up my nose with a liberal application of clay, applied a false beard, put on a white robe, and wrapped around my head a prayer-shawl such as the Judæans use.

Of course, it would not do to be seen after dark in this costume, here in the old-money south side of the Palatine, so I called for my litter, drew the curtains tightly shut as though I was a cloistered Greek matron slipping off to a night-time tryst, and proceeded downhill toward the seamy side of town. The bearers moved at a brisk trot and I was pleased not to have to quirt them. I avoided the great squares and took only back streets.

It was a quiet night — many had gone to bed early, doubtless anticipating the early morning commencement of the games — but now and then a link-boy ran down a passageway waving his torch to light the way for some drunken reveller, and once I spied, through the peephole I had made in the curtain, a group of centurions gang-raping a slave-woman against a bakery storefront. A graffiti artist scrawled "Arrius is a nefarious retiarius" along a wall while his friend pissed noisily alongside.

At length we reached a taberna by the Judæan quarter on the other side of the Tiber, and I abandoned my litterbearers there with a bag of copper and the admonishment that they were not to get too drunk or they would feel the lash on my return. The litter was parked in one alley, and from another alley I emerged in my Judæan garb, shawl about my head, mumbling to myself in what I hoped was a passable imitation of the Aramaic tongue.

The night life was in full swing. The tabernæ were open; whores in whiteface walked the streets, as did young children with their tunicæ hitched up above their buttocks; the smell of bread being baked for the morning rush mingled with the odor of animal blood running into the street from a slaughterhouse that practised ritual killing in the Judæan fashion. There was an all-night bank across the street — for the Judæans engage in moneylending at all hours of the day or night — and I went there to deposit my bag of aurei, for the Judæans are the only people in Rome with whom I would trust my money, and I have accounts under different names in Jewish banks from Rome to Alexandria, all earning a hefty rate of interest.

"Rejoice, Ioannes!" The voice was a resonant bass. Quickly, I allowed myself to flow into my persona: Ioannes of Damascus, physician, philanthropist, thrower of good parties — thoroughly Hellenized on the surface, thoroughly subversive at heart.

I was not surprised to find the banker, an Alexandrian by the name of Chrysolithos (he found his true name, David ben David, too ethnic for his social aspirations) still up, doing his accounts by lamplight; he was only too happy to take my money, and smiled as he counted it out.

"It must be a good life," he said, "this specializing in the diseases of the rich."

"The rich have many slaves," I said, affecting an expression of wounded piety, "and those who have nothing are most likely to need riches in heaven."

Chrysolithos cackled. "Converting the heathen is all very well," he said, "but I'm glad you're lining your pockets too . . . it's the Roman way, after all. . . . "

"Roma terra opportunitatis," I said.

I pocketed the receipt and, looking furtively from left to right, made the sign of the fish in the air.

Chrysolithos immediately became defensive. "Look, you're not going to go on about *that* business again, are you? Ever since the secret police cleaned up the catacombs for spectacle-fodder two months ago, you won't find much —"

"I'm looking for the Lady Volumnia Drusiana," I whispered. "She's in terrible danger! Her husband has angered Cæsar — *anything* could bring about his political downfall — especially her involvement with *us* —"

"Don't say 'us,' Ioannes, please! Oh, I know my wife talked me into this New Age nonsense for a while, but —"

"By Jupit— I mean, by the blessed Paraclete!" I said. "Do you mean to deny your savior, as did Simon Cephas the fisherman? Reprobate! Do you still cling to Earthly things when you should be thinking of the life to come?" I rather enjoyed giving that speech; I must admit that I was really getting into the role.

It was at that moment that the Lady Volumnia walked into the room.

I gasped, for she was every bit as sensuous as I last remembered her — her features delicate, her nose aquiline, her dark hair luxuriously bunned, her gazelle-eyes imbued with fragility and a certain coldness. Though she was past forty, her breasts had not succumbed to time, and the robe she wore was designed to reveal more than it concealed.

She looked at me guiltily — it was, of course, because she thought I was this Ioannes fellow, an elder of the banned cult to which she had once subscribed.

"Daughter Volumnia! — but what are you doing here? — at this hour, unchaperoned, in a dangerous sector of town?"

"I am not entirely unattended," she said. Behind her stood a black man of impressive height, clad only in a leopard-skin. I had not realized that Lady Volumnia's taste ran to Numidian gladiators; perhaps this was going to be an easier job than I thought. After the austerity of the Christianoi, she could not be blamed for wanting to have a little fun.

"This is Babalavus," she said, "a mage of the Iorubæ, a tribe that dwell in the yet-unconquered regions where lies the source of the Nile."

I smiled. There's a charlatan on every block in Rome, waiting to hoodwink a credulous rich woman out of a few million. Such a charlatan, in fact, was *my* role that night. "Have you abandoned then, Volumnia, the faith of the Christianoi? Have you ceased to attend the love-feasts?" I had to know.

"Oh, Ioannes," she whimpered, falling to her knees before me, "forgive me for being such a weak woman! Would that I were a slave, and had no position in society to lose for belonging to a subversive religion! Then I would gladly go to a thousand love-feasts every night. Really, I didn't mean to denounce anyone in the faith, it's just that — well — most of them weren't really our kind of people anyway, so I suppose they were more or less expendable. . . ."

I made the sign of the cross over her and mumbled a few nonsense words, hoping that she and Chrysolithos would take them for the Christianoi ritual of "speaking in tongues." It must have worked, for the two of them immediately placed their palms together in an attitude of reverence, their glazed eyes fixed on me like a pair of village idiots. By the Pudenda of Venus! How I hate these weird Oriental cults!

We stood in a moment in a sort of tableau of religious ecstasy, and then Lady Volumnia, all business, got up and said to the banker, "Listen, the reason I came is — I have to make a rather large withdrawal."

"Precisely how large, O Clarissima?"

"Well, you know I've no head for figures, but — well, a round one million sesterces?"

"Such a sum might be rather difficult to come by in cash —"

I was all attention now, even as I stood there mimicking the servile unctuousness of a preacher of the Christianoi.

"Perhaps eight hundred thousand —"

"My Lady, you will bankrupt me! Of course, bearing in mind the substantial penalty for early withdrawal from your interest-bearing equity account —"

How well I knew this ploy of Chrysolithos's! By the time Volumnia received her money, she would end up owing him more than she'd ever paid in; such were the perils of high finance in a world in which our Emperor has melted down the very vestments of the statues of the gods to help eke out a currency that is, at best, half silver and half lead.

"I'll have to give it to you in gold, Clarissima," Chrysolithos said, "and of course, there'll be an exchange rate deduction. . . ." He called for a slave to bring out some bags from his vaults.

Meanwhile, my attention was drawn to the mage Babalavus. He stood with his arms crossed, every bit the bodyguard. I would wager that he was not a Christianos, for the followers of that sect have a look about them, a strange cross between the hangdog and the insolent. They have a complete disregard for human life, even their own, for they believe that they will shortly be resurrected and the world will end in an apocalyptic conflagration. There was something distinctly unnerving about him, for he stared back at me and would not be stared down, even though it is customary for the lower classes to be a tad more circumspect in the presence of patricians. I could well believe that Lady Volumnia had taken him for her lover, though eight hundred thousand seemed a steep price to pay for the services even of so stallion-like a physical specimen.

Unless it was hush-money . . . a coverup . . . unless this were only the epigraph to a veritable epic of scandal in high places. . . .

Then again, Volumnia and the Numidian were not exactly lovey-dovey; a practised eye like mine can almost immediately tell if two people are involved in a clandestine intimate relationship, but with these two I had the distinct impression that something else was going on . . . some darker secret.

"Please, Ioannes, holy man," Volumnia said, "do not be too harsh with me for my lack of faith! I have a plan that will redeem me in your eyes . . . that's why I need the money, you see. . . ."

What a stroke of luck! She was going to incriminate herself. I would have no trouble at all arranging for her husband's political demise if I could uncover some kind of bribery scandal. . . .

At that moment I felt a sneeze coming on. I knew that my clay nose would be turned into a projectile if I stayed another minute. It was time to retreat. "May the Sacred Paraclete guide you and comfort you," I said in sacerdotal tones. "I must go now and tend to my lost sheep. Rejoice, O Volumnia Drusiana, Chrysolithos, and Babalavus!"

"Such a model of Christian piety!" I heard Lady Volumnia remark as I passed from the hall into the street. It was getting toward the ninth hour. Keeping to the shadows, I made my way back to my litter, rousted the bearers, and returned to an alley next to the bank to await the emergence of my prey.

An hour later — it was not yet dawn, but the sky was already tinted red, for in the summer the night hours are shorter — Lady Volumnia and her companion emerged from a side door, the latter slinging a jingling sack over his shoulders. Babalavus whistled and two litters appeared: a plain one and one bearing the minotaur-crest of the Drusiani. Side by side, they made off down the alley, curtains open wide so I could see they were deep in conversation as they rode.

"Follow them!" I whispered to the head bearer. "And be as inconspicuous as you can!" We started to move. I peered through my peephole while wrestling with the elaborate garments and make-up for my next charade. It was good to be able to sneeze at last.

The litters moved slowly. They were easy to follow at first. Whenever they stopped, we ducked behind a convenient pillar or fountain. I did not think they were lovers now; else why would the Lady Volumnia be so brazen about being seen in public with this so-called mage, not even bothering to keep the curtains of her litter drawn?

Another alley now — a street of smithies — I could hear the clank of chains and the clink of hammer on anvil — and somewhere in the distance, a slave being noisily chastised. The mage looked at the moon, which, though full, was paling fast in the impending sunrise; a look of concern crossed the Lady's face . . . the litterbearers went into a trot, and a lead-tipped quirt materialized in her delicate little hand.

"Faster!" I said. "But stay out of sight!" My litter swerved to avoid a chamberpot that was being emptied from an upper window.

My quarry took a left turn and suddenly we were in a fish market. Though it was the dead of night, the square was bustling. Dozens of carts were lined up, with slaves and peasants hastening to unload their wares before the dawn deadline — for horse traffic is not permitted in the city from dawn to sunset — and the smell of fish and horsedung was overpowering. Already the cooks from the great houses on the Palatine were out in force, snapping up the best fish for the evening's orgies. I followed the two litters closely as they weaved in and out of the stands. The litterbearers were moving briskly, purposefully. Suddenly they stopped in front of a stall and purchased a few fish. Lady Volumnia did not even bother to have them wrapped. She said something and the bearers began sprinting back downtown, toward the Old Forum.

It was harder to follow them now. The avenues were broader and there were fewer monuments to duck behind. We collided with a bevy of partygoers, garlanded, drunk, and singing lewd songs, and weaved in and out of a procession of Cybele-worshippers on their way to the Temple of Magna Mater. A beggar tried to climb into my litter, and had to be shaken off. At last the two of them turned sharply into a narrow passageway. It was difficult not to be seen, and my front bearers were literally pronging

the buttocks of the aftmost litter-slaves of the Lady Volumnia when our way was blocked by an old plebeian, wheezing as he tried to push a cartful of chickens out of a rut. I braced myself for a collision. It came.

I barely had time to take in the spectacle of the three-litter pileup. Chickens ran amok. A fishy projectile had landed in my lap. It was, I noted ruefully, the common pufferfish, hardly a delicacy, and poisonous besides. Lady Volumnia screamed as she attempted to disentangle herself from the Numidian, the chicken vendor, and the chickens, and litter-slaves were rolling about in the excrementa, their livery ruined.

Fortunately, I had already finished donning my next disguise, and when I emerged, veiled and forbidding, from the litter, the Lady and her Negro witch-doctor were both aghast to discover that they had collided with the litter of the Clarissima Julilla Juliana, the aged, prim, severe and intractable second high priestess of the College of Vestal Virgins.

It is one of my most convincing disguises.

"Dear me, my children," I said, brushing the pufferfish off my stola, "you really ought to watch where you're going."

Even my own slaves were impressed, and many of them quickly kneeled and began muttering every formula of aversion they could think of.

"O sacred one! Forgive me for profaning — I had no idea —" the Lady Volumnia began, and then suddenly, inexplicably, winked at me with a kind of nudge-nudge informality that suggested some kind of womanly conspiracy of concealment. Meanwhile, the black mage seemed to have gone into a trance, for his eyes had rolled up all the way into their sockets, and he was looking from side to side in the manner of a hungry lion, occasionally muttering the phrase "Oba kosó, oba kosó."

In the distance, a cock crowed.

Lady Volumnia roused herself in alarm. A shaft of predawn halflight made the dust dance in the noxious air. "Hurry, Babalavus!" she said, trying to shake him out of his ecstasy. "We're losing the moon!" Turning to me, she said, "By your leave, Clarissima," and bowing, added, "I will see you at the games, perhaps." Then she clambered back aboard with her pufferfish under her arm and, tossing a purse to the disgruntled chicken vendor, quirted her bearers uptown. Babalavus set off with equal dispatch toward the gates of the city. I could not follow both; besides, it would be undignified for a Vestal Virgin to go charging through the streets at night.

What was I to do? I bade my bearers run alongside Babalavus for a few minutes, doffed my robes and, making sure that I could be seen turning in the direction of the Capitoline, slipped out of the far side of the litter, now garbed in the loincloth of a common slave.

I ran behind Babalavus's litter. It was hard to keep up as we raced downhill. Past the rickety insulæ of the impoverished, the many-storied slum buildings whose roofs leaned across the alleys and blocked out the twilight, where dirty immigrant children played amid piles of refuse . . . past dingy temples of unfashionable cults, where priests with scruffy tonsures prayed in empty vestibules in unfamiliar tongues . . . past whorehouses frequented by washed-up gladiators and slumming patricians . . . I could see where we were heading . . . a catacomb whose entrance lay just beyond the walls behind the intersection of the Appia and Nomentana.

I tapped the hindmost bearer on the shoulder. Ran up alongside him and showed him an aureus that I had had concealed in my mouth, and explained to him what I wanted. The other bearers, panting as the leader called out the rhythm, were concentrating so hard that they did not notice when, without skipping a beat, I changed places with the slave and — thanking the gods that it was still pretty dark — changed loincloths with him also, for the bearers wore a matched set. I was counting on the mage having hired the litter rather than owning one, so that he would not notice me, for one hired litterbearer is much like another.

The litter stopped at the entrance and Babalavus stepped out. He was carrying an amphora under his arm which appeared to be in the shape of a human skull. He seemed already to be drifting into one of his trances. He called for a torchbearer. As luck would have it, that torchbearer was I.

We descended. The steps were steep. The stench of rotting plebeians filled our nostrils. I held the torch high for him but he seemed to need no light, for he moved about as one possessed, rocking his head from side to side and now and then springing like a panther. We went deeper. There were white flowers and mushrooms and strange herbs growing from cracks in the floor. Once he paused to pluck some leaves from the eye-sockets of a human skull. Always he sang to himself. Sometimes his voice was high-pitched, like a child's; other times he appeared to be answering himself in a mellifluous bass. Now and then he paused to gather his roots and flowers and to throw them into the skull-amphora.

I was beginning to suspect that this was no Christianos.

Dead bodies lined the walls. Some niches were occupied by two or three corpses. Some had been incompetently mummified; others were just skeletons; many were fresh, and bore on their limbs and torsos evidence of the torture that must, by law, be inflicted on all slaves who give evidence in a court of law. The odor was nauseating, but I had a rôle to play.

Babalavus danced and chanted for a while longer, then stalked up and down a passageway looking for something. At length he selected the skull of a child and slipped it into his amphora. He motioned to me to go on up.

I was not displeased when we once more achieved the upper air. The sun was just rising now, and I could see, along the Appian way, the long line of horsecarts hastening to leave the city before their owners were arrested for disobeying the ban on daylight equestrian traffic.

It was a simple matter to change places with the slave once more — he had been waiting in the portico of a nearby temple of Mithras — and to slip back to my own litter, wherein, once safely ensconced, I could once more assume the apparel of the Lady Julilla. I had lost a few hours. Nevertheless I made it to the Temple of Vesta just in time for the ceremonial blessing of the hearth and was able to go through the motions of the rite without any of the other Vestals noticing either my excessive perspiration or my inappropriate gender.

As soon as it was over I retired to the chamber of the Lady Julilla — fortunately I had a duplicate key — just in time to see a shadowy figure slipping out of her window.

"By the Sacred Mysteries!" cried the Lady Julilla, springing from her bed with astonishing alacrity for one of her years, and sprinting behind the nearest arras. "I have been profaned — my honor violated —"

"Relax, O Clarissima!" I said, as I sat down on a tripod next to the window. "It is only me." I squinted as I looked out, but all I could see was a rather corpulent figure waddling at top speed through the garden, now and then bumping into a stone Silenus or satyr. Once more, I hadn't arrived quite in time to discover the identity of the Lady's paramour.

The Vestal — who, upon realizing it was only me, had come out of hiding and was now seated upon a couch, powdering her face and looking at me with hauteur — said, "Ah, Viridianus. I trust the morning service went smoothly?"

"Most smoothly, Clarissima. No one suspects that you are in your bedroom trysting with —"

"Be nice, O Publius Viridianus!" she said, peeling an apple. "You know very well that if I am ever discovered, my life is forfeit; the virginity of the Vestals is inviolable. But I've been stuck in this dump since the age of sixteen, and a girl gets to wondering what it's all about, if you know what I mean . . . you won't gain a thing by turning me in, you know that. I'm a Roman of the Julian gens, and descended from the goddess Venus; I know how to die properly."

"True, Clarissima, but a certain curiosity —" I glanced once more at the garden, but the priestess's fat lover had managed to escape.

"Curiosity was not part of our deal, Publius Viridianus," she said, relapsing into that sternness of demeanor for which she was well known. She pulled a bag of silver from under the couch and threw it to me. "Our arrangement still stands, I trust. I need you to impersonate me at the games as well today; I have . . . ah . . . a business meeting to attend to . . . a little matter of the Temple archives."

"As you wish, Clarissima," I said, noting with satisfaction that her plans jibed perfectly with my own.

I was, I confess, rather tired when I finally reached the Circus of Nero and staggered up to the Vestals' balcony. A venation was in progress, but the heat and the humidity had rendered the mob restless, and only the distribution of the lunchtime lottery tickets had been able to prevent them from getting ugly. There are only so many gazelles, wolves, jackasses, ostriches and hippopotamoi one can watch being slain on a sweltering day in August without being driven insane with boredom. The Vestals' balcony was only half full; after showing me the deference due my putative rank, my fellow virgins mostly gossiped or licked their snow cones or nibbled at a tray of succulent kebabs assembled from thrushes' tongues, finches' gizzards, and the like.

I was able to observe the editor's box at my leisure, since it was next to the Vestals' and separated from me only by a marble frieze.

There was my quarry at last, in full view, every inch the lion. Q. Drusianus Otho was reclining on a gilded couch, with slaves and dancing girls at his feet. Suckling pigs stuffed with figs and apples sat ignored on silver platters; oiled Nubians wielded impressive peacock-feather fans; a couple of centurions squatted, rolling the bones, under a makeshift canopy put together from three javelins and a cloak.

Sitting next to him was Volumnia, heaving prettily. Behind them stood the Ioruba mage. They weren't sweating one bit after the adventures of the previous night. I was not surprised to see that Eros was there too, looking shiftily about. He was the only one to show any interest in the suckling pigs.

There was another woman there too, with gold dust in her hair, her face powdered to the color of packed snow, wearing a king's ransom in purple silk, plucking idly on a kithara. She was singing, and everyone stopped now and then to applaud.

I was somewhat bemused when I realized that this Lady was none other than Himself the God of State, His August Divinity, L. Domitius Ahenobarbus to his friends, Nero-666-The Beast to his treasonous and godless detractors, many of whom were fated to perish before our eyes that very day. The aria he was singing was none other than the fiendishly virtuosic *Hecabe's Lament*

from Euripides' *The Trojan Women*. I'm no critic, but there seemed to be a number of wrong notes in his rendition.

As the carcasses were dragged off, the Emperor launched into a rousing rendition of something of his own. I was thankful that I knew nothing about modern music; I could not tell the wrong notes from the right. I was however saved from having to comment by the miraculous emergence of the face of Petronius Arbiter from the thighs of a voluptuous Celtic woman; he made some pronouncement, the Emperor nodded daintily, and everyone clapped.

I took out a wax tablet and began making notes as the Amphitheatron was being filled with water for a simulated sea-battle. I kept an ear cocked, for one of the occupants of the editor's box might well reveal something I could use.

What had I found out?

Imprimis: the tableau of glorious dissipation that was visible in the editor's box was a mere simulacrum; in fact, I was witnessing a viper's nest of seething intrigue. Someone had written a poem in a blatantly inferior pastiche of Petronius's style in order to discredit Drusianus; Lady Volumnia, guilt-ridden over turning in so many Christianoi, had dug deep into her pockets to form an alliance with a bizarre African magician; Eros was watching everybody, hoping someone would fall from grace so that he could move up the ladder of power; Petronius was not long for this world, for I had been invited to his suicide party later in the week; the Lady Julilla — that is to say, myself — was fooling around and decidedly non intacta; none of the pieces were falling into place for me.

Had the Emperor really sent Eros to destroy Drusianus, or did the eunuch have his own agenda? Should I deliver the innocent patrician up on a platter, or was I risking my own downfall by essaying something that the Emperor had *not*, in fact, commanded?

Was it not entirely possible that the entire thing was a ruse, and that it was I — the knower of secrets — who was the quarry? Had one of my thousand disguises finally been seen through?

These are the kind of questions a detective must wrestle with daily, and I fell into a kind of reverie.

A theological argument was now going on in the editor's box, and now and then a phrase penetrated my miasma of self-examination. . . .

"Resurrection of the body!" the Emperor was saying. "What a curious concept. These Christianoi must be quite, quite mad."

"It is not as uncommon as all that, Divinitas," — I recognized the resonant bass of Babalavus — "for amongst the Iorubæ, and also the Kikongii, our neighbors, malefactors are often sentenced to become *nzambi*, the Living Dead . . . they are first poisoned with a powder whose active ingredient is the ground-up liver of the homely pufferfish. . . ."

Pufferfish!

I came to all at once. Resurrection! and pufferfish! Were the Christianoi poisoning themselves in the hope of coming back to life? Was not their sign of recognition a fish? And had I not last seen the Lady Volumnia climbing onto her litter with a brace of pufferfish tucked under her arm?

In the arena below, two ships were having at each other with catapults. In a humorous touch, the projectiles were neither rocks nor flaming brimstone, but political prisoners — Christianoi of dwarfish stature, each one bundled and trussed into a compact sort of ball. Since catapultæ are not really designed for hurling humans about, it was impossible to aim them. The crowd screeched and hooted as Christianoi crashed into the sea or brained themselves against the embankments. Now this was not only purest entertainment — full of human interest as the prisoners bobbed up and down, trying to extricate themselves from their bonds only to find themselves being devoured by the crocodiles which were now being released into the waters — but a practical thing too, since the flooding of the arena also functioned as a rudimentary air conditioning system, and the water was constantly being cooled with cartloads of Alpine snow.

I was really beginning to enjoy the show when a man was catapulted right into the Vestals' pavilion. His head struck the marble floor and his brains spritzed my robes, my wax tablet, and my eyelashes. Fortunately I had the presence of mind to scream in falsetto.

I had seen and heard enough for the day. "I have been profaned!" I cried. "I must return at once to the Temple of Vesta to be purified!"

I turned and made for the secret passageway by which the Vestals may come and go as they please without being subjected to the indignity of plebeian frottage. I was more upset than I wanted to admit to myself. I had seen the dead man's face, in the split second before the big splat. To my astonishment, it was the face of someone I knew — someone who ought have been able to afford to buy his way out of this unholy mess.

I was going to have to get myself a new bank account.

I was finally getting a moment to myself, taking a postprandial soak in my private tepidarium, when the nomenclator announced the arrival of Lady Volumnia Drusiana. She stalked into the bathroom and flung a purseful of gold at my head. The two Spanish masseuses fled in panic.

"Take this!" she screamed. "You vulture! You parasite! You — you open-sphinctered catamite!"

"The first two I allow, Clarissima, but really you do go too far in accusing me of —"

"Oh!" she turned away from me and began weeping copiously, and I availed myself of the opportunity to slip into something decent.

"There, there," I said, "let's hear all about it now." I escorted her to the library, where three of my scribes were in the process of reproducing Petronius's *Satyricon* in triplicate — for the novel makes a nice gift for someone on whom one has amatory designs. I shooed the scribes away and offered Volumnia a drink from the jug of best-vintage Lesbian I kept on my desk.

"You've got to help me!" she said, flinging herself onto the nearest couch. "My life is in ruins — my husband's political future has been horribly compromised —" She pulled a little scroll from her bosom. I was not surprised to see that it was a copy of the insulting poem that had been attributed to the Arbiter of Elegance himself.

"Oh, I've already read that," I said. "And eight hundred thousand sesterces won't be enough to overcome my scruples —"

"Eight hundred — ! How could you possibly —" She stared at me, for in my demeanor and accent there was absolutely no trace of Ioannes of Damascus, the fanatical prophet of the Christianoi.

"Yes," I went on, "you were consorting with an elder of the banned sect last night, weren't you? One" — I pretended to consult my notes — "Ioannes of Damascus. And you were visiting the offices of another Christianos, a certain Chrysolithos, were you not? Who is now —"

"Dead," she whispered. "I'm going to have to open another bank account."

There was a pause while I took out a tablet and prepared to take some more notes.

"Anyway," she said, "I don't have all the money anymore. He took a twenty percent commission, the poor dead soul! And there were other — expenses. I can only offer you what I threw at your feet — if you'll only call off the hunt. Don't say you're not after him — I was told this by no less a figure than the third undersecretary of the Emperor's privy purse!" So Eros was playing both sides against the middle! So much for him! "My husband, as you well know, is innocent of all wrongdoing. Never has a man been more loyal to his Emperor. It is I who have been weak, I who have gone from faith to faith, never finding certitude in this complex modern world!"

As she shrugged out of her clothes, I realized that there was also to be compensation of another kind. The Lady Volumnia, though not young, possessed a statuesque voluptuousness which certainly lived up to her name. She palpitated curvaceously against the harsh right angles of my shelves of papyri.

"My dear Clarissima!" I said, tossing down the last of the Lesbian. "This display of your not unappetizing charms renders me quite inarticulate," I added, stooping to litotes in my confusion.

She smiled. There was nothing for it but to bed her, on the instant, in the half hour or so before my next appointment. She clawed, whinnied, and bounced about with such enthusiasm and vigor that I was glad I had recently had all the lecti cubicularii in the house reupholstered.

Afterwards, I assuaged my guilt by leaving a nice juicy leg of lamb as an offering to the house gods.

It was time for me to return to the games, this time as myself.

Cæsar too was Himself by the time I arrived. Garbed once more as a man, wearing a towering diadem of solid gold and a floor-length purple robe embroidered in gold thread with suns and moons, Himself was enthroned on a chair of state, with the outrageously beautiful Statilla Messalina at his side. I was glad to see that he was getting over the apotheosis of the Empress Poppæa, whom he had accidentally kicked to death one drunken evening.

It was almost the hour of cena, and the day was cooling off; a Greek tragedy, put on at the Divinity's behest, had just been booed off the stage, and the stage manager had been forced to bring on some Christianoi as an entr'acte. They were being eaten by lions, but as no one ever pays much attention to last year's hits, they were being watched only by the most devoted fans of Christianoi-bashing.

I hastily paid my respects to the God of State. "Ave, Divinitas," I said, and quickly switched to Greek, for the Emperor hated the uncouth jangle of the vulgar tongue. "Rejoice, Autokrator," I said. "I didn't have a chance to pay my respects earlier. . . ."

"Pity; you missed my new poem. I'd sing it again, but I'm not dressed for it anymore."

"I am crushed," I said. "But maybe I'll have a chance to borrow it from the Library; I know it's not the same as hearing it from your Divine Lips, but —"

"Poor little Viridian," said Nero. "As tone deaf as can be, yet he still attempts, in his small way, to sit at the feet of the Muse."

The reason I had come back to the games was because I was sure I was missing some vital piece of information. I noted that Drusianus and Eros were deep in conversation, and that Lady Volumnia and her curious magician were absent; Petronius, on the other hand, was leaning on the balcony, watching the Christianoi being eaten with profound fascination. I supposed that, since he was about to die himself, he was finding something in common even with this most tedious of spectacles. I was really looking forward to his suicide party; it's not every day that a patrician decides to go out in style.

Since Petronius was as good as dead, I decided I might as well whip out the scurrilous poem and show it to the Emperor.

"What do you think of this, Divinitas?" I said. "It — ah — came to my attention last week."

He took it from me, looked at the first few lines, and began to chuckle. I became uneasy. I looked at Drusianus, but he was still deep in conversation with Eros.

"What a terrible thing!" said Nero, looking deep into my eyes. "Who do you think could have perpetrated such blasphemy?"

"Well, it *looks* like Petronius, and yet there's something — ah — something — ah —" I wanted to protect Petronius from the imputation that he might have written this inferior piece of doggerel, and yet. . . .

"Something — ah — something — ah —" There was a feverish glint in his eye, and suddenly I knew what I was going to have to say.

"It looks like Petronius, only far, far *better,* of course!"

I knew at once that I had said the right thing, for the Emperor beamed and threw me a bag of money. The old fox had written the thing himself — was doubtless disseminating it as a test of loyalty! Well, that certainly put paid to Eros's contention that he had hired me at Cæsar's behest.

"Far from being displeased at him," said Nero with his mouth full of peacocks' brains, "I am thinking of giving Drusianus some kind of political appointment . . . a consulship perhaps, or even a procuratorial position . . . I've even assigned a high-level member of my staff to . . . ah . . . act as his financial advisor. . . ." He indicated the eunuch.

It dawned on me that Eros's financial advice was probably the last thing Q. Drusianus Otho needed. It was the eunuch's greed that had led him to try to pay me into effecting the man's downfall, that much was certain. I had taken Eros's money and owed him some kind of investigation; I had also taken the money — not to mention the lubricious fluids — of the Lady Volumnia, and I owed her something too. And who had turned Chrysolithos in? Surely not the very Lady who relied on him for all her banking needs at odd hours of the night.

The God of State lost interest in me, since I wasn't talking about the arts. He called Petronius over for a chat about Homer. I had to admire the poet's sangfroid; he gave absolutely no indication that he was planning to commit suicide, and I was sure that it would come as a complete shock to Nero, who hated surprises.

Idly I watched the next number, a small group of Andabatæ. These are the lowliest criminals, who are given helmets without eyeholes and unwieldy weapons, and swing blindly at each other until all are slain — an incorrigibly tasteless entertainment, and fit only for the vulgar element.

The fight was drawing to a close, and slaves were removing the helmets of the slain and fastening hooks to their feet so they could be dragged out through the Gates of Death. Now the sun was low on the horizon, and the few remaining wretches, staggering about, cast huge shadows against the sea of togas in the patricians' balconies. One could not see too clearly what was going on, but it chanced that a ray of flickering, sooty light, cast upon the arena by a Christianos who was being burned alive on a lofty display cross, fell upon the face of one of the dead Andabatæ just as he was being hauled away.

It was the face of Chrysolithos the banker.

Surely I am imagining this! I thought to myself. I squinted; the red sunlight made my eyes water; yet still I could have sworn, by Jupiter and all the Immortals, that that face was none other's. There was even a great red smudge on his temple whence, earlier that afternoon, his brains had been spurting forth upon my virginal garments.

119

Chrysolithos had died twice in the same day.

Somehow — my detective's intuition assured me — the resurrection of the old Judæan banker was the key to the whole affair.

For was not resurrection also the crux (no pun intended) of the Christianoi religion? Did these people not believe so strongly in a physical afterlife that they had not hesitated to set fire to Rome itself, the quicker to bring about their prophesied apocalypse? Were they not so confident of this resurrection that they did not even mind being killed in the circus? Why, instead of showing the proper terror when being eaten by lions, they would stand around singing their catchy hymn tunes, completely undermining the public service aspect of their deaths. These people really believed in resurrection all right.

Well, what if they'd actually found a way to do it?

There was only one way to find out, and to do that I would have to slip around to the Gates of Death as soon as the games were done for the day.

Sunset over the amphitheatron: I was just in time to catch the imposing figure of Babalavus climbing out of a litter and speaking to the guards at one of the back entrances. I was in costume once more, impersonating Ioannes of Damascus. As soon as Babalavus was admitted, I crept up behind the two guards and, placing my hands about their necks, put them both to sleep with a certain nerve pinch that induces a temporary state of narcosis. I followed Babalavus down the dank staircase. He was too intent on his business to notice me.

There is no sight more depressing than the bowels of a circus. The stench of animal dung was everywhere; in the half dark one could make out the cages of exotic beasts. Cramped though the bestiaries were, the human prisoners fared even worse, for they were a far less valuable commodity. One could hear, from behind dungeon doors, the screams of the panicstricken and the frenzied copulations of those who knew this lovemaking would be their last. From some torture-chamber lower down came the crack of the flagellum, the squeak of the rack, the hiss of the red-hot iron on human flesh, and, of course, the ever noisome screaming.

Babalavus strode through labyrinthine corridors, turning this way and that with the confidence of one who had come here often. I followed. After a while he ascended some steps, and we were in a chamber with an egress into a back alley.

We had arrived at the hall of the butchers, where the criminals killed that day were being methodically quartered and shoved into large baskets by slaves. Arms, legs, heads, and buttocks protruded from enormous containers which were even now being loaded onto carts; the meat would be sold to various menageries around the city, for the wild animals at the circus itself had to be kept hungry.

The butchers worked quickly, but there was still a heap of some two or three hundred corpses, their feet still pierced from the hooks that had been used to haul them off the sand. Little boys were engaged in divesting these corpses of clothing, jewelry, hairpins, anything that could be recycled. Indeed, I thought, the entertainment industry has been hard hit by the Emperor's financial cutbacks!

Concealing myself behind the pile of dead bodies, I watched Babalavus bargaining with one of the overseers. There were a few relatives hanging around, hoping to bribe one of the slaves into releasing their lamented for a decent burial; a sobbing couple rooted through the piles of body parts, looking for their son.

Babalavus took out a bag of gold and presented it to the overseer. Greed gleamed in the man's eyes; he turned, barked out an order, and presently a wagon pulled up to the entrance, and — as Babalavus pointed to one corpse after another — they were loaded onto the cart. I recognized Chrysolithos amongst the fallen. I thought I saw a few other Christianoi too.

This was no time for reflection. I had to find out what was going on.

Quickly, under cover of the wall of dead bodies, I disrobed, smeared myself with dead men's blood, plunged my arms into an open abdomen and pulled out a piece of intestine with which to drape myself . . . then, when no one was looking, I sneaked behind the busy butchers and managed to clamber onto the cart while Babalavus's back was turned.

As chance would have it, I had landed right on top of Chrysolithos. He was dead all right. They were all dead. It was a necrophiliac's dream come true; alas, this had never been one of my favorite perversions. More bodies were being shoveled on top of me. A woman's half amputated breast rammed into my mouth, almost suffocating me; blood oozed into my nostrils and slicked my limbs so that I slid back and forth like a fish at the market. The stench was unendurable.

When the cart began to move, things got even worse. Even now it irks me to recall the discomfort of our journey. Every rut, every cobble made the bodies slip and slither and marinated me in their bodily effluvia. I could see nothing, for there were at least three layers of dead people crammed on top of me. I could hear the voice of Babalavus urging the horses on and singing snatches of barbarian music.

At length we stopped. The bodies — myself among them — were unloaded one at a time. I concentrated on acting out my most demanding rôle, that of a corpse. I felt myself being lifted by the arms and legs. I made myself limp. They laid me down on a rocky surface. When I finally permitted myself to peek, I saw that I was lying in an immense morgue. The bodies of Christianoi lay in neat rows on the stone floor of what seemed to be a vast cave; it was one of the natural chambers into which the catacombs led, though I could not remember which one. To my surprise, Chrysolithos the banker lay not two paces from me, to my left; eviscerated as he was, he was not a pretty sight.

Suddenly, I heard a familiar voice shriek out: "By the Sacred Paraclete! It's Ioannes of Damascus! Oh, how could they have killed such a holy man?" The Lady Volumnia ran out from the shadows and knelt by my side, covering my face and chest with so many kisses that I feared that, in my nakedness, I would accidentally reveal my lust.

"Do not worry, my Lady." It was Babalavus, standing beside her. He was clad only in a loincloth. His face was hideously painted in whiteface with streaks of black and red. "If Shangó wills it, he will not be dead for long."

There were others like Babalavus in the background, some with drums and marimbas. Other Negroes clutched chickens and turtles in their arms.

From somewhere far away, I heard Christianoi psalms being sung. One of their love-feasts was taking place. It was cold, and it was hard to keep my teeth from chattering.

At last, the love-feast seemed to end, and Christianoi crowded into the chamber. Volumnia and Babalavus were handing out phials of some potion. At length, Babalavus addressed the throng: "O Christianoi," he said, "it has become necessary, for political reasons, for the Lady Volumnia to denounce some of you to the secret police in order to save her husband's career. You will probably be arrested before dawn, so that you can be ready in time for the morning tableaux."

His announcement caused a sensation

as some wailed, others complained, and others still cried out their jubilation at the propinquity of their redemption.

"Doubtless a number of you are afraid that the resurrection of the body will not occur as promised. That is why I have been invited to join you, and why I have prepared this potion. Do not forget, in your hour of martyrdom, to swallow the pufferfish elixir before going onstage! Otherwise the magic will not work. . . ."

Several of the crowd began to voice their objections. Some complained that the blessed apostle Simon Cephas had made no mention of any pufferfish elixir. Others shouted that Babalavus was no Christianos and had no right to order them around. Like every other Judæan sect, the Christianoi love to quarrel over the minutiæ of dogma, and do so even when death is imminent. At length, the Lady Volumnia appealed for silence.

"Please, my brothers and sisters —" she said. "Just do what he says. The police are even now making their way toward this catacomb. You're all going to die anyway, so you might as well be decent about it."

A chorus of *amens* and *hallelujahs* echoed around the cave. Then, at a signal from Lady Volumnia, there began an ominous music, all drums and high-pitched keening and grunts and babblings. Above it all I could hear the phrase "Oba kosó!" repeated over and over. I knew it must be a ritual formula of these Iorubæ.

At that moment Babalavus went into a trance.

He fell to his knees and began to heave and buck like an angry minotaur. His pupils vanished into their sockets, and animal cries emanated from his throat. Sweat poured down his face and torso.

"Behold! He is speaking in tongues!" Lady Volumnia shouted, though I knew very well that this was nothing of the kind.

Babalavus began to do a jerky sort of dance. He leapt over corpses. He made clawing gestures in the air, as though he were possessed by some jungle creature. The pounding went on. It was hypnotic. Suddenly he was holding the skull-amphora in his hands, and asperging us corpses with its contents — a foul-smelling concoction of herbs and blood.

Then he was joined by his tribesmen, whooping wildly as they sliced the heads off turtles and chickens and began to slop their blood liberally over us. It was becoming harder and harder to play dead. Soon I was going to have to sneeze, or cough, or —

Chrysolithos began to twitch! As the chanting rose to a deafening pitch, as the black mages pranced about and sprinkled us with foul fluids, all the corpses fibrillated wildly. I soon realized that I had better start wiggling myself, or I would look out of place. I started to jerk about with a vengeance, and when the corpses began to stand up, each with a glazed look in its eye, I too scrambled to my feet and attempted to mimic their rhythmic swaying. Soon the corpses were all lumbering this way and that, each one with a look of profound bewilderment, as though awakening from a drunken stupor. Chrysolithos was going round and round in circles, as one who has been struck in the head with a poker.

I heard Lady Volumnia cry out above the uproar: "Behold the resurrection promised to you by the Christianoi prophets! Death is an illusion! You will not die in the arena tomorrow; as long as your body can be recovered in one piece, you will be brought back to life as good as new! Zombificati sunt!"

What kind of a word was *zombificatus*? It must mean that we had been made into *nzambi*, the Living Dead of which Babalavus had spoken to the Emperor. But as I looked around me I could see that this resurrection was a far cry from that promised in the utterances of the Christianoi. These *nzambi* were hardly human. They gibbered. Intestines dangled from their ripped abdomens. Arms and legs were missing. Heads lolled. Sputum and vomitus dribbled from their lips, and brain tissue trickled from their cracked skulls. It was hard for me to appear as disgusting as they, for I had no wounds; but I shambled and gibbered and swung my arms aimlessly along with them, while trying to work my way up to where Lady Volumnia and Babalavus were standing so as to be able to hear what they were saying.

"You have done well, O Babalavus!" she was telling him. "I shall not forget how you allowed me to betray the Christianoi, thus salving my husband's reputation, while at the same time providing this supernatural means of assuaging my betrayal of the religion I hold so dear. . . ."

A piercing shriek issued from Babalavus' throat. All at once the music stopped. We *nzambi* stood, waiting, a little threatening. The unzombified Christianoi backed away, terrified — who would not be? — and I do not doubt that many were reconsidering the most cherished tenets of their faith.

At that moment, bucinæ blared. We heard the tramp-tramp-tramp of Roman soldiers. It was the Prætorians. They burst into the chamber so quickly that there was no time for a stampede. The crowd were too stunned to scream. With professional speed and detachment, the secret police clapped everyone in chains — living and dead — and marched us all back to the amphitheatron, flogging us for good measure as we staggered along the dim streets.

I was thrown into a cramped prison cell along with my *nzambi* companions. There were also Christianoi who were not yet zombificati. Most sat around praying to their God, but one or two were heard bitterly complaining that this death and rebirth was somehow not quite as advertised. One was even suggesting that, if they should survive their martyrdom, they should bring suit in the tribunes' court against the cult for making these false claims. I had no time for specious arguments or theological speculation. I had to get out of there before the morning spectacle, for I did not possess a phial of the pufferfish elixir which had, it seemed, to be imbibed shortly before death for the Ioruban ritual to work.

In the flickering torchlight, I could see that some of the *nzambi* were gnawing on each other's innards. It was entirely possible that I would not even survive until the show started. I stumbled forward to the portal, which had a tiny grille through which I could see one of the guards. I banged to get his attention.

"My good man! I," I said importantly, "am Publius Viridianus, private investigator. I was spying on the Christianoi on the Emperor's behalf; I have been apprehended in error. Release me at once!"

The guard peered at me. "Publius Viridianus, the most famous detective in Rome?" he said. "Try another one! You don't look a bit like him with your big nose and your scraggly beard!"

I plucked off my false nose and thrust it in his face. He raised an eyebrow. "False nose, eh?"

I started pulling my beard off. "This is false, too. Look, hurry up, I don't want my cover blown; luckily the Christianoi are too busy arguing about dogma to notice our conversation."

"By the pudenda of Venus!" said the decurion. He called for the keymaster and in a few moments I was free, and had a good woolen cloak to cover my nakedness. It turned out that the guard was quite an intellectual, for he would not let me depart until I had autographed a scroll of my memoirs which I had been vain enough to have published the previous year, and which he just happened to be reading.

"On no account," I said, "must you

reveal that I have been here tonight. I will ensure that you are amply rewarded — but if this gets out —" I made a throat slitting gesture.

"High political intrigue, is it, sir?" said the decurion. "I loves a good intrigue, by the Gods! Don't you worry about the reward; just you mention me in the next volume . . . it's Olus Dolabella, and you must remember to spell my prænomen the plebeian way: O-L-U-S, not A-U-L-U-S; it's a point of pride in my family you see, we've been spelling it that way since my great-uncle done divorced my patrician great-aunt, she was one of the Scipiones, you know —"

"Yes, yes," I mumbled, hoping my litterbearers would still be waiting at the other entrance of the amphitheatron.

"Treacherous lot, them Christianoi," he continued. "What a stroke of luck we had this tipoff from the Lady Volumnia. I wonder what's in it for her! I understand these people" — his voice dropped to a whisper — "eats human flesh, they does."

"They do indeed," I said, shuddering as I remembered the sight of one *nzambi* nibbling at another's loose body parts.

He wanted to know everything about their foul practices and orgies. I persuaded him to shut up only by letting him keep my nose as a souvenir, and giving him the slip while he gazed at it in adoration.

It surprised me a little to see Eros wandering through the corridors, scribbling feverishly on a wax tablet. He did not notice me, for I hid myself in the shadow of an archway. He met Babalavus; they had a brief conversation; he handed the magician a bag of money and they parted company. Why was he up so early, and what was he doing here, so far from the offices of the Imperial privy purse? Ah, but of course — the Emperor had appointed him Q. Drusianus Otho's

financial advisor. Naturally he would be at the games, checking the figures — how many Christianoi at so much overhead per victim, how many tons of hay for the elephants, that sort of thing. But why was Babalavus in his pay?

Interesting, I thought; very interesting.

The mosaic stones were finally beginning to fall into place. But I still had to figure out who was behind it all — who stood to benefit — who was manipulating whom, and why. I would have to go through another day of spectacle, disguised as the Lady Julilla once more, for only from the Vestals' box could I eavesdrop on everything that was going on in the Editor's Pavilion. Unfortunately, I wasn't slated to be her double that day; nevertheless, I figured that she would not mind, since there was nothing she despised more than carrying out the endless round of litanies and sacrifices that were her lot.

It was the tenth hour; in two short hours (and the night hours are shortest in summer) would come dawn. I urged my bearers to make haste.

It was simple enough to enter the Temple of Vesta and take the secret passageway that led from the main courtyard to the private vestiarium next to Lady Julilla's bedroom. A dozen sets of ceremonial robes hung from hooks. The Lady, with her back to me, was already up and seated on a sella, pinning her shawl in place with a silver fibula. She did not hear me enter, for I am nothing if not stealthy. I crept up behind her and tapped her on the shoulder.

She turned around and, seeing me, screamed.

I managed to cover her mouth just in time. Her scream became a gurgle.

"Just what in the name of all the Gods are you doing here?" I said.

"I might ask the same thing of you," said the Lady Volumnia, for that was who it was. "To tell you the truth, the

Lady Julilla asked me to — ah — impersonate her at a morning sacrifice, because she had another — ah — appointment."

So that was why Lady Volumnia had winked so knowingly at me the night our litters collided! Thinking that I was that wayward old Vestal Virgin, she had assumed I was returning from some tryst! I could not help laughing. "I was about to impersonate her myself!" I said. "I never realized that she had more than one — ah — accomplice."

As I said this, I was taking a robe off the wall and getting into it. I put on one of Lady Julilla's wigs and, sitting down in front of the mirror, started applying the whiteface and dabbing kohl on my eyelashes.

"You really seem quite professional at it," said Lady Volumnia. "Well, I'm pleased to learn that I'm off the hook today; I'm really too tired to pull off the charade."

"Up all night?" I said.

She clammed up.

"I know all about the zombifications," I said. She gasped. "Don't worry — I really see no harm in it — the Christianoi are criminals, and I really don't care whether they die once or a thousand times. And you know, it isn't really resurrection at all — the elixir seems to put them into a kind of catatonic state, and when they are awakened in the zombification rite they are not quite themselves anymore. But I'm not going to berate you for playing on the credulity of a bunch of losers."

"Thank you," she said. "I love my husband so much, O Viridianus! Even when I allowed you to possess this admittedly shopworn body of mine, it was because I love my husband and will stop at nothing to prevent him from coming to harm . . . you do understand, don't you?"

I murmured something appropriate about the power of conjugal love.

"I mean," she said, "I had a lot of fun at the Christianoi meetings, singing those tuneful hymns and chumming with slaves and riff-raff; there's something so *elemental* about the lower classes, you know. Of course, I had to betray them for the sake of my husband's reputation, but I was so plagued by guilt about it —"

"You're a very sensitive soul, Clarissima," I said.

"That's why when Eros introduced me to Babalavus —"

So the plot was thickening even in the moment of its unravelling! Somehow Eros had engineered the whole thing . . . but why?

I explained to Volumnia why I needed to go to the circus in the guise of the Vestal Virgin. "Why don't you stay here," I said, "while I go into Julilla's bedroom and tell her I'll take her place today? I'll only be a moment."

She nodded, then kissed me for luck. I placed the last layer of veils over my head and crept into Lady Julilla's cubiculum.

"Lady Julilla, it's me," I said. There was no answer, but I fancied I heard a faint scuffling noise somewhere in the chamber. Perhaps it was merely a mouse. A single lamp burned by the Vestal's bedside. She was not in bed. Nor did I see any telltale bulges behind the drapes. It was a sparsely furnished room, as befitted its occupant's otherworldly vocation; a few busts of Emperors stared at one from marble pediments of various heights; there was a couch and an altar for private devotions. Several fumigators spewed clouds of incense into the air, which added to the gloom. Near the window was Lady Julilla's capacious bed, wide enough for the entire Prætorian guard it seemed, canopied with veils of damascene.

I had no time to wonder about the Lady's whereabouts, for I heard someone scrambling at the open window, and I dived into the bed.

To my horror, a blubbery mound of

flesh, perfumed to the gills and attired in the height of nouveau-riche tastelessness, came tumbling through the window, rubbed its backside, stood up, began to shamble towards me, panting like a hippopotamos with sunstroke.

"My beloved," it squawked. "I simply had to come. I could stay away no longer!" It was all too apparent that the Lady Julilla's secret lover was none other than the emasculated Eros, and that if I did nothing I would soon become the receptacle of his sacrilegious lust!

It was too late. Eros bounced onto the bed, arms outstretched, and I had to duck to avoid his proffered lips. "I've pulled it off," he gloated, "the impudent get-rich-quick scheme I told you of . . . soon it will all pay off . . . and then I'll be able to take you away, far from here . . . far from the long arm of Cæsar . . . beyond the reach of Rome itself! Yes, my darling; you have but to say the word and I am yours forever!"

I am no fool. I realized that all I had to do was lie there, avoiding the eunuch's advances, and he would eventually cough up the solution to the entire puzzle. Once more I wriggled free of his grasp, making little whimpering noises such as I imagined the randy old hussy might make were she there to reciprocate the creature's passions.

"Oh, Julilla, you're such a tease," Eros said. He managed to get me in a kind of amorous wrestling lock, and his mouth descended on mine.

"You're so masterly," I said, "but I've got a headache."

"Headache — splendid!" he said. I know how you love it with a dollop of pain."

Pain! Clearly the Lady Julilla's appetites had been rendered decidedly deviant by her years of abstinence.

"I have my flagellum right under my tunic, my dear," said Eros.

"Er . . . it's that time of the month," I temporized in my best falsetto.

"You adorable old minx," he said, "you know it hasn't been that time of the month in fifteen years. . . ."

So much for that. I prepared to either give myself away or yield to his caresses. I allowed him to chase me around the bed for a while, and then said at last, in sudden inspiration, "Before we consummate our love, O Eros, tell me more of your brilliant machinations! You know how . . . aroused I get with talk of political intrigue. . . ."

Eros let go of me. I clasped my hands, fluttered my eyelids, and looked as adoring as I could. I had guessed, correctly, that political gossip was, for the aging Vestal, the most stimulating kind of foreplay.

"It's chicanery at its most devious!" he said. "Syrian political savvy, Judæan financial wizardry — combined with the secret black arts of unconquered lands! I've hired a Negro mage to reanimate corpses of hundreds of Christianoi, so they can be killed over and over again in the arena. And the Christianoi love it! They think it's their day of resurrection or something."

"But — what advantage can this bring you?"

"Women and mathematics simply don't mix, do they?" he said, and I did not remind him that his equipment was little different from a woman's. "Look, the Christianoi are reckoned into the expenses of the games at so much per head, based on the overhead amortization of previous games . . . do you follow?" I did not, but continued to listen raptly. "A certain sum is charged against the privy purse per Christianos for his execution; in other words, the execution, which would normally be carried out by the state, is franchised out to the editor of the games. Another sum is also charged against the editor's accounts to cover the actual cost of execution; this is a pro rata share of the total costs of the executions, as calculated from previous spectacles, with allowance for the debasement of the currency and so on and so forth. The upshot of all this is, a properly placed person — such as — ahem — the Imperially-appointed financial advisor to Q. Drusianus Otho — can, by recycling the Christianoi over and over, funnel money from both the privy purse *and* the editorial budget into his own — ah — slush fund, from which —"

"Surely you did not concoct so labyrinthine a scheme entirely by yourself, O Eros!" I said.

"Well, I did have help from a certain Judæan banker, one Chrysolithos — but luckily I was able to have him silenced — and to seize his estate besides," he said, grinning.

"Chrysolithos! Good heavens, my family banks with him."

"Oh, the bank will go on as usual," Eros said. "It will merely be serving other interests." He began stroking my neck. "But enough of this nonsense! Let us get down to the real business of the morning —"

"But wait! I am so worried for you . . . won't you get into trouble? What of Drusianus and the Lady Volumnia?"

"Oh, I've already taken care of *them*. Babalavus the mage has convinced that airhead that she's saving her Christianoi friends from death while simultaneously protecting her husband from scandal . . . I have that detective to thank for that, whatsisname —"

"Publius Viridianus."

"Yes — I have hired him to look for hanky-panky, and he will soon find that — because of the recycling of the Christianoi — that goody-goody prig's books will not be in order — he will be found to have been cheating the Imperial privy purse — at which point — zombificatus! And his vigilant denouncer will be in a fine position to — ah — take over the Villa Drusiana, which has the most splendid view of Vesuvius."

The jig was up. But just as I was about to whip off my disguise, the eunuch seized me in his surprisingly powerful embrace and planted his tongue firmly against my gritted teeth. If I attempted to speak, that tongue would surely gain admittance into that cavity whither no man — let alone a gelding — had ever gone before.

At that moment, however, Lady Volumnia rushed into the room and began pummeling the eunuch with her fists. I was so startled I almost bit off his tongue.

"Monster!" she screamed. "You told me that Viridian had been sent to discredit my husband — but you never told me *you* had hired him to do it!"

"Juli— J-J-Julilla!" he said, looking from me to Volumnia. "Volumnia!"

"You, my dear Eros, are ruined," I said, ripping off my veils and dropping my voice back to its commanding baritone. "You may as well commit suicide now, for the Prætorians will be knocking on your door by sunset."

"P. Viridianus!" he shrieked.

"Indeed," I said, as I wiped the kohl from my eyes.

The eunuch looked at his two accusers in some bewilderment for a moment. Then he said, "You'll never get away with this. I have the ear of Cæsar! He'll never take the word of a known Christianos and a two-sestertius detective over that of a trusted civil servant. I'll hire the best lawyers in Rome! By the time I'm through with you —"

At that moment there came a sound like the rumbling of an earthquake. We all stared at the bed. It was quaking. The bedposts were clattering against the marble floor. I heard the jangling of an untuned lyre.

And at length, an imposing figure emerged from under the bed, clutching his instrument, garbed in a cloak of Imperial purple spangled with stars and moons.

We all prostrated ourselves.

"Divinitas!" we said.

"The ear of Cæsar, eh?" said the God

of State, glaring at the gelatinous Eros.
"Guards! Arrest this thing!"

And so, at the last minute, an extra
number was inserted in that afternoon's
games, between the Rape of the Sabine
Women by trained jackasses and the
battle between Pigmies and Amazons.
The punishment would fit the crime —
Eros was to suffer an undignified end,
the application of a molten gold enema
— but would be one that would only be
appreciated by true aficionados, since it
was hard to see and lacked spectacle.

Lady Julilla had been invited to share
the editor's pavilion, as had the Divinity
himself, who sat upon a gilded cathedra
shaped like a rearing lion. I asked her
if she regretted seeing her erstwhile
lover's demise.

"Not at all," she said, biting delicately
into a snow cone flavored with crushed
berries. "He was a brute."

"But how did the Emperor come to be
hiding under your bed?"

"Oh, he always does that. You see, the
idea of a Vestal Virgin coupling with a
eunuch excites him greatly; it is the
closest he can come to being reunited
with his mother, whom, as you know, he
was forced to have murdered. So we
came to a little — agreement. Were the
God to couple with me himself, it would
be a dreadful impiety and bring about
the downfall of the Empire; but since
Eros was a eunuch, strict propriety was
observed."

Wonders would never cease. Despite
her licentious lifestyle, the old bag had
managed to remain entirely intacta and
true to her vocation! She was, I had to
admit, a Roman through and through,
able to answer the most bewildering
moral dilemmas with pragmatic solu-
tions.

They were hauling away the last of
the violated women, and Eros was now
being wheeled in on an ingenious con-
traption that would allow him to spin
slowly while he agonized, thus providing

even the plebeians with a decent view of his suffering face. There was desultory applause from the audience; most were bored, waiting for the Pigmies and Amazons.

Eros was brought over to our box so that he could pay the customary respects to the Emperor before being killed. He appeared to have gone quite bonkers. "Rejoice, Autokrator!" he cried, and waved merrily at us. "Don't you worry — I'll be back!"

Perhaps a last-minute conversion to Christianity?

"I'm thinking of giving Babalavus your old job," said the Emperor. Then he took out his lyre. "You have been a very fine civil servant, O Eros, and afforded me much amusement besides." He winked at the Lady Julilla. "I shall therefore pay you the supreme compliment — I shall accompany your death with a song of my own composition."

He began to sing. It was very modern.

Lady Volumnia came sidling up to me. "Oh, Viridian," she said, "we're having a big party at our house tonight to celebrate my induction into the mysteries of Astarte — do come; my husband owes you a debt of gratitude and I have pledged to — pay it myself." She smiled seductively.

"The cult of Astarte — that's the one where the women give themselves randomly to passersby, isn't it?" I said. It was really difficult to keep these Oriental cults straight, though it did not surprise me that Lady Volumnia had already found a new one to amuse herself with.

Eros screamed. Politely, I looked away.

"I really can't go," I said. "I've a dinner party at Petronius's. In fact" — I looked at the sun — "it's almost the eighth hour now, and cena is at nine."

So saying, I turned my back on the entrancing if not unblemished Volumnia, on honest Drusianus and careful Julilla, and on our magnificent and fun-loving Divinity, and furthermore on the entirely satisfying excruciation of the eunuch Eros and the marmoreal splendor of the Neronian amphitheatron. I left the spectacle behind in order to spend a last evening with C. Petronius Arbiter, a dinner of classical simplicity and artful conversation.

What happened at that dinner is, of course, known to all men; after reading us his letter to Nero in which he catalogued the Divinity's many infamies, he caused his physician to open his veins and died as elegantly as he had lived. So famous is that dinner party that it eclipsed all memory of my exploits; and while the name of Petronius will live on, the scandal of Eros the eunuch, the titillating amours of the Lady Julilla, and the multiple resurrections of Christianoi by the art of zombification, are all things that, I am sure, history will mercifully forget. Ω

Escape the awful emptiness of missing your Weird Tales®!

A few weeks before you pick up your mailbox and move, as soon as you have a new address, please send us that new address (including the new ZIP code {all 9 digits if you can}) along with your old address and old ZIP code.

We'll miss you *fright*fully unless you do!

Write us at:

Weird Tales®
P.O. Box 13418
Philadelphia PA 19101-3418

We also publish *Weird Tales®* in hard covers!

Issues 290 through 296: trade edition $20 each (four or more, $12 each).

Issues 291–296: limited to 100 copies, signed by the featured author and artist and the editors: $50 each(four or more, $40 each). (Issue 290 is now sold out in this limited edition.)

Issues 297 onwards: limited to 200 copies, signed by featured author, artist, and editors, $30 each (four or more, including prepaid subscriptions for forthcoming issues, $25 each).

We take MasterCard and Visa: we need your card number, expiration date, and your signature on your order. We also accept money orders and checks.

Order from us at:
Terminus Publishing Co., Inc., P.O. Box 13418, Philadelphia PA 19101-3418.

www.ingramcontent.com/pod-product-compliance
Lightning Source LLC
Chambersburg PA
CBHW070602180626
46817CB00005B/1950